Harlan Ellison, the most outrageous and exciting talent in sf today, has compiled this dazzling anthology of stories especially written for *Dangerous Visions*. Winner of two Nebula awards and two Hugo awards, it is a landmark in speculative fiction.

Dangerous Visions is 'destined to become a landmark, a classic in the realm of sf. . . . A word of caution: this book is dangerous to the vision—it is very hard to put down'
—*Science Fiction Tim*

D1583831

Also available from Sphere Books

Dangerous Visions 3

**Edited and with a new introduction
by Harlan Ellison**

Illustrations by Leo and Diane Dillon

SPHERE BOOKS LIMITED
30/32 Gray's Inn Road, London WC1X 8JL

First published in Great Britain (in two volumes) by
David, Bruce & Watson Ltd 1971
Copyright © Harlan Ellison 1967, 1969
Published by Sphere Books (in three volumes) 1974

TRADE
MARK

Set in Intertype Baskerville

Printed in Great Britain by
Cox & Wyman Ltd, London, Reading and Fakenham

ISBN 0 7221 3302 2

Men learn from other men what they know of themselves, of the world in which they *must* live, and of the world in which they would *like* to live.

This book is dedicated with love, respect and admiration
to Leo & Diane Dillon
who painstakingly, out of friendship,
showed the editor that black is black, white is white, and that goodness can come from either; but never from gray.
And to their son, Lionel III
with a silent prayer that *his*
world will not resemble *our* world.

CONTENTS

INTRODUCTION TO THIS EDITION

If you missed volumes 1 and 2, gentle reader, go out and buy them, get them read, then come back to here. If you pass Go, you collect two-thirds of a work of love and you can free yourself from the jail of moribund mainstream writing. (I'll assume you went, did, and are back.)

Hello.

It's May of 1969 as I write this. Don Bensen of Berkley tells me the first two volumes of this vivisected *Dangerous Visions* are selling nicely, thank you. Well no one doubted that they would. All you have to do to ensure success is get thirty-two of the finest writers who ever came down the pike, turn them loose, let the Dillons illustrate them, and wrap them adoringly in copious introductory and addenda matter, and wait for the good folk to discover the joys therein contained.

So well have these joys been discovered that there will be a companion volume of *Dangerous Visions*. I have been working on it for almost a year as I write this. Title will be *Again Dangerous Visions*.

More writers, and different writers. None of whom were represented in this first book. And a strange, wonderful thing, in the new book. New writers. People of whom you may never have heard. Names like Hank Davis, and Josephine Saxton, and Greg Senford, and Evelyn Lief, and Ed Bryant.

Oh, there'll be names you recognize, too. Names like Piers Anthony, and Ben Bova, and Terry Carr, and Kate Wilhelm and Bernard Wolfe. But there are stories being written for this new book that will make you think *Dangerous Visions* was merely warm-up time.

Thirty thousand words by Richard Lupoff titled "With the Bentfin Boomer Boys on Little Old New Alabama," absolutely fresh and different novelettes like Ray Nelson's

"Time Travel for Pedestrians", Kate Wilhelm's beautiful "The Funeral", Piers Anthony's gut-wrenching "In The Barn". And firm, original voices like Graham Hall, N. John Harrison, James Sallis.

Because *Dangerous Visions* did its work well, friends. It started a flood. Damn the "Waves" of old or new speculative fiction, this is the wave, babies, it's the flood. A tidal surge of young writers showing their old masters where it's at. For when *Dangerous Visions* was in its preparatory stages, too many writers didn't believe the ballyhoo. They didn't believe they could really pull out all the stops and *go*. But Fritz Leiber believed it, and so did Phil Farmer, and Phil Dick, and Sonya Dorman, and Carol Emshwiller, and Chip Delany. *They* could dig it, and they worked heavy. Now everyone believes it, and I urge you not to miss the companion volume some time next year. A bigger book, bigger than *Dangerous Visions*, with writers who are not represented here. For *Dangerous Visions* taught us all a great lesson.

Next time out, we're not going for merely revolution: we're going to change the entire face of the genre.

We're going to use the stars for stepping-stones!

HARLAN ELLISON
Los Angeles
May 13th 1969

IF ALL MEN WERE BROTHERS, WOULD YOU LET ONE MARRY YOUR SISTER?

Introduction to

IF ALL MEN WERE BROTHERS WOULD YOU LET ONE MARRY YOUR SISTER?:

This will be the shortest introduction in the book. Because, of all the writers in this anthology, the one who *truly* needs no introduction is Theodore Sturgeon? Well, there's that, certainly. Because nothing anyone could say would prepare the reader for what is to follow, the first Sturgeon story in over three years? It's a valid point. Because each Sturgeon story is a long-awaited experience, no two alike, so why bother gilding the caviar? Okay, I'll accept that.

But none of them happens to be the reason why I am unable to write as beefy an introduction as the others in this book. The reason is simply that Sturgeon saved my life recently. Literally.

In February of 1966 I committed one of those incredible life-blunders that defy explanation or analysis. I entered into a marriage with a woman . . . a person . . . a something whose mind was as alien to me as the mind of a Martian might be. The union was a disaster, a forty-five-day nightmare that left me closer to the edge of the cliff than I had ever been. At the precise moment I thought surely I couldn't retain my grip on the handle of—everything, I received a letter from Ted Sturgeon. It was part of the interchange of letters that resulted in obtaining this story for the anthology, but it was concerned entirely with what was happening to me. It pulled together the sprung wires of my life. It was one of those pieces of honest concern that (if lucky) everyone will clutch onto at a terrible time of helplessness and desperation. It demonstrates the most obvious characteristic of Sturgeon's work—love. (We once talked about that. It became clear to Sturgeon and myself that I knew virtually nothing about love but was totally familiar with hate, while Ted

13

knew almost nothing about hate, yet was completely conversant with love in almost all its manifestations.) I would like, with Ted's permission, to quote from that letter. It will say infinitely more about his work and what motivates him than anything I could attempt. From here down, Sturgeon speaking:

"Dear Harlan: For two days I have not been able to get my mind off your predicament. Perhaps it would be more accurate to say that your predicament is on my mind, a sharp-edged crumb of discomfort which won't whisk away or dissolve or fall off, and when I move or think or swallow, it gigs me.

"I suppose the aspect that gigs me the most is 'injustice.' Injustice is not an isolated homogeneous area any more than justice is. A law is a law and is either breached or not, but justice is reciprocal. That such a thing should have happened to you is a greater injustice than if it happened to most representatives of this exploding population.

"I know exactly why, too. It is an injustice because you are on the side of the angels (who, by the way, stand a little silent for you just now). You are in the small company of Good Guys. You are that, not by any process of intellectualization and decision, but reflexively, instantly, from the glands, whether it shows at the checkout in a supermarket where you confront the Birchers, or in a poolroom facing down a famous bully, or in pulling out gut by the hank and reeling it up on the platen of your typewriter.

"There is no lack of love in the world, but there is a profound shortage in places to put it. I don't know why it is, but most people who, like yourself, have an inherent ability to claw their way up the sheerest rock faces around, have little of it or have so equipped themselves with spikes and steel hooks that you can't see it. When it shows in such a man—like it does in you—when it lights him up, it should be revered and cared for. This is the very nub of the injustice done you. It should not happen at all, but if it must happen, it should not happen to you.

"You have cause for many feelings, Harlan: anger, indignation, regret, grief. Theodor Reik, who has done some brilliant anatomizations of love, declares that its ending is in none of these things: if it is, there is a good possibility that some or one or all of them were there all along. It is ended with *indifference*—really ended with a real indifference. This is one of the saddest things I know. And in all my life, I have found one writer, once, who was able to describe the exact moment when it came, and it is therefore the saddest writing I have ever read. I give it to you now in your sadness. The principle behind the gift is called 'counter-irritation.' Read it in good health—eventual. I would like you to know that if it helps and sustains you at all, have my respect and affection. Yours, T. H. Sturgeon."

Thus ended the letter that helped and sustained me. Enclosed with the letter was No. 20 of "Twenty Love Poems based on the Spanish of Pablo Neruda", by Christofer Logue. From *Songs*, Hutchinson & Co., London, 1959. It is this freedom of giving, this ability and anxiousness to meet love and give it freely in all its forms, that makes Sturgeon the mythical creature that he is. Complex, tormented, struggling, blessed by incredible gentleness and, above all, enormously talented, what you have just read is the soul of Theodore Sturgeon. I pray you, go on now to the very best thing to be found in all writers: a sample of the work that motivates the life that is led. And thank you.

IF ALL MEN WERE BROTHERS, WOULD YOU LET ONE MARRY YOUR SISTER?

by Theodore Sturgeon

The Sun went Nova in the Year 33 A.E. "A.E." means "After the Exodus". You might say the Exodus was a century and a half or so A.D. if "A.D." means "After the Drive." The Drive, to avoid technicalities, was a device somewhat simpler than Woman and considerably more complicated than sex, which caused its vessel to cease to exist *here* while simultaneously appearing *there*, by-passing the limitations imposed by the speed of light. One might compose a quite impressive account of astrogation involving the Drive, with all the details of orientation *here* and *there* and the somewhat philosophical difficulties of establishing the relationships between them, but this is not that kind of a science fiction story.

It suits our purposes rather to state that the Sun went Nova with plenty of warning, that the first fifty years A.D. were spent in improving the Drive and exploring with un-manned vehicles which located many planets suitable for human settlement, and that the next hundred years were spent in getting humanity ready to leave. Naturally there developed a number of ideological groups with a most interesting assortment of plans for one Perfect Culture or another, most of which were at bitter odds with all the rest. The Drive, however, had presented Earth with so copious a supply of new worlds, with insignificant subjective distances between them and the parent, that dissidents need not make much of their dissent, but need merely file for another world and they would get it. The comparisons between the various cultural theories are pretty fascinating, but this is not that kind of a science fiction story either. Not quite.

Anyway, what happened was that, with a margin of a little more than three decades, Terra depopulated itself by its many thousands of ships to its hundreds of worlds (leaving behind, of course, certain die-hards who died, of course, certainly) and the new worlds were established with varying degrees of bravery and a pretty wide representation across the success scale.

It happened, however (in ways much too recondite to be described in this kind of a science fiction story), that Drive Central on Earth, a computer central, was not only the sole means of keeping track of all the worlds; it was their only means of keeping track with one another; and when this installation added its bright brief speck to the ocean of Nova-glare, there simply was no way for all the worlds to find one another without the arduous process of unmanned

16

Drive-ships and search. It took a long while for any of the new worlds to develop the necessary technology, and an even longer while for it to be productively operational, but at length, on a planet which called itself Terratu (the suffix meaning both "too" and "2") because it happened to be the third planet of a GO-type sun, there appeared something called the Archives, a sort of index and clearinghouse for all known inhabited worlds, which made this planet the communications central and general dispatcher for trade with them all and their trade with one another—a great convenience for everyone. A side result, of course, was the conviction on Terratu that, being a communications central, it was also central to the universe and therefore should control it, but then, that is the occupational hazard of all conscious entities.

We are not in a position to determine just what sort of a science fiction story this really is.

"Charli Bux," snapped Charli Bux, "to see the Archive Master."

"Certainly," said the pretty girl at the desk, in the cool tones reserved by pretty girls for use on hurried and indignant visitors who are clearly unaware, or uncaring, that the girl is pretty. "Have you an appointment?"

He seemed like such a nice young man in spite of his hurry and his indignation. The way, however, in which he concealed all his niceness by bringing his narrowed eyes finally to rest on her upturned face, and still showed no signs of appreciating her pretty-girlhood, made her quite as not-pretty as he was not-nice.

"Have you," he asked coldly, "an appointment book?"

She had no response to that, because she had such a book; it lay open in front of her. She put a golden and escalloped fingernail on his name therein inscribed, compared it and his face with negative enthusiasm, and ran the fingernail across the time noted. She glanced at the clockface set into her desk, passed her hand over a stud, and said, "A Mr. Charli uh Bux to see you, Archive Master."

17

"Send him in," said the stud.

"You may go in now."

"I know," he said shortly.

"I don't like you."

"What?" he said; but he was thinking about something else, and before she could repeat the remark he had disappeared through the inner door.

The Archive Master had been around long enough to expect courtesy, respect, and submission, to get these things, and to like them. Charli Bux slammed into the room, banged a folio down on the desk, sat down uninvited, leaned forward and roared redly, "Goddamit—'

The Archive Master was not surprised because he had been warned. He had planned exactly what he would do to handle this brash young man, but faced with the size of the Bux temper, he found his plans somewhat less useful than worthless. Now he was surprised, because a single glance at his gaping mouth and feebly fluttering hands—a gesture he thought he had lost and forgotten long ago—accomplished what no amount of planning could have done.

"Oh-h-h ... bitchballs," growled Bux, his anger visibly deflating. "Buggerly bangin' bumpkin' *bitch*balls." He looked across at the old man's horrified eyebrows and grinned blindingly. "I guess it's not your fault." The grin disappeared. "But of all the hydrocephalous, drool-toothed, cretinoid runarounds I have ever seen, this was the stupidest. Do you know how many offices I've been into and out of with this"—he banged the heavy folio—"since I got back?"

The Archive Master did, but, "How many?" he asked.

"Too many, but only half as many as I went to before I went to Vexvelt." With which he shut his lips with a snap and leaned forward again, beginning his bright penetrating gaze at the old man like twin lasers. The Archive Master found himself striving not to be the first to turn away, but the effort made him lean slowly back and back, until he brought up against his chair cushions with his chin up a little high. He began to feel a little ridiculous, as if he had been

18

bamboozled into Indian wrestling with some stranger's valet.

It was Charli Bux who turned away first, but it was not the old man's victory, for the gaze came off his eyes as tangibly as a pressing palm might have come off his chest, and he literally slumped forward as the pressure came off. Yet if it was Charlie Bux's victory, he seemed utterly unaware of it. "I think," he said after his long, concentrated pause, "that I'm going to tell you about that—about how I happened to get to Vexvelt. I wasn't going to—or at least, I was ready to tell you only as much as I thought you needed to know. But I remember what I had to go through to get there, and I know what I've been going through since I got back, and it looks like the same thing. Well, it's not going to be the same thing. Here and now, the runaround stops. What takes its place I don't know, but by all the horns of all the owls in Hell's northeast, I have been pushed around my last push. All right?"

If this was a plea for agreement, the Archive Master did not know what he would be agreeing to. He said diplomatically, "I think you'd better begin *some*where." Then he added, not raising his voice, but with immense authority, "And quietly."

Charli Bux gave him a boom of laughter. "I never yet spent upwards of three minutes with anybody that they didn't shush me. Welcome to the Shush Charli Club, membership half the universe, potential membership, everybody else. And I'm sorry. I was born and brought up on Biluly where there's nothing but trade wind and split-rock ravines and surf, and the only way to whisper is to shout." He went on more quietly, "But what I'm talking about isn't that sort of shushing. I'm talking about a little thing here and a little thing there and adding them up and getting the idea that there's a planet nobody knows anything about."

"There are thousands—"

"I mean a planet nobody *wants* you to know anything about."

"I suppose you've heard of Magdilla."

19

"Yes, with fourteen kinds of hallucinogenic microspores spread through the atmosphere, and carcinogens in the water. Nobody wants to go there, nobody wants anybody to go—but nobody stops you from getting information about it. No, I mean a planet not 99 per cent Terran Optimum, or 99 point 99, but so many nines that you might just as well shift your base reference and call Terra about 97 per cent in comparison."

"That would be a little like saying '102 per cent normal'," said the Master smugly.

"If you like statistical scales better than the truth," Bux growled. "Air, water, climate, indigenous flora and fauna, and natural resources six nines or better, just as easy to get to as any place else—and nobody knows anything about it. Or if they do, they pretend they don't. And if you pin them down, they send you to another department."

The Archive Master spread his hands. "I would say the circumstances prove themselves. If there is no trade with this, uh, remarkable place, it indicates that whatever it has is just as easily secured through established routes."

Bux shouted, "In a pig's bloody and protruding—" and then checked himself and wagged his head ruefully. "Sorry again, Archive Master, but I just been too mad about this for too long. What you just said is like a couple troglodytes sitting around saying there's no use building a house because everybody's living in caves." Seeing the closed eyes, the long white fingers tender on the white temples, Bux said, "I said I was sorry I yelled like that."

"In every city," said the Archive Master patiently, "on every settled human planet in all the known universe, there is a free public clinic where stress reactions of any sort may be diagnosed, treated or prescribed for, speedily, effectively, and with dignity. I trust you will not regard it as an intrusion on your privacy if I make the admittedly non-professional observation (you see, I do not pretend to be a therapist) that there are times when a citizen is not himself aware that he is under stress, even though it may be clearly, perhaps painfully obvious to others. It would not be a discourtesy, would it, or an unkindness, for some under-standing stranger to suggest to such a citizen that—"

"What you're saying, all wrapped up in words, is I ought to have my head candled."

"By no means. I am not qualified. I did, however, think that a visit to a clinic—there's one just a step away from here—might make—ah—communications between us more possible. I would be glad to arrange another appointment for you, when you're feeling better. That is to say, when you are . . . ah . . ." He finished with a bleak smile and reached toward the calling stud.

Moving almost like a Drive-ship, Bux seemed to cease to exist on the visitor's chair and reappeared instantaneously at the side of the desk, a long thick arm extended and a meaty hand blocking the way to the stud. "Hear me out first," he said, softly. Really softly. It was a much more astonishing thing than if the Archive Master had trumpeted like an elephant. "Hear me out. Please."

The old man withdrew his hand, but folded it with the other and set the neat stack of fingers on the edge of the desk. It looked like stubbornness. "I have a limited amount of time, and your folio is very large."

"It's large because I'm a bird dog for detail—that's not a brag, it's a defect: sometimes I just don't know when to quit. I can make the point quick enough—all that material just supports it. Maybe a tenth as much would do, but you see, I—well, I give a damn. I really give a high, wide, heavy damn about this. Anyway—you just pushed the right button in Charlie Bux. 'Make communication between us more possible.' Well, all right. I won't cuss, I won't holler, and I won't take long."

"Can you do all these things?"

"You're goddam—whoa, Charli." He flashed the thirty-thousand-candlepower smile and then hung his head and took a deep breath. He looked up again and said quietly, "I certainly can, sir."

"Well, then." The Archive Master waved him back to the visitor's chair: Charli Bux, even a contrite Charli Bux, stood just too tall and too wide. But once seated, he sat silent for so long that the old man shifted impatiently. Charli Bux looked up alertly, and said, "Just getting it sorted out, sir. A good deal of it's going to sound as if you could diagnose me for a stun-shot and a good long stay at the funny farm, yeah, and that without being modest about your professional knowledge. I read a story once about a little girl was afraid of the dark because there was little hairy purple man with poison fangs in the closet, and everybody kept telling her no, no, there's no such thing, be sensible, be brave. So they found her dead with like snakebite and her dog killed a little hairy purple and so on. Now if I told you there was sort of a conspiracy to keep me from getting information about a planet, and I finally got mad enough to go there and see for myself, and 'They' did their best to stop me; 'They' won me a sweepstake prize trip to somewhere else that would use up my vacation time; when I turned that down 'They' told me there was no Drive Guide orbiting the place, and it was too far to reach in real space (and that's a God, uh, doggone *lie*, sir!) and when I found a way to get there by hops, 'They' tangled up my credit records so I couldn't buy passage; why, then I can't say I'd blame you for peggin' me paranoid and doing me the kindness of getting me cured. Only thing was, these things did happen and they were not delusions, no matter what everybody plus two thirds of Charli Bux (by the time 'They' were done with me) believed. I had an ounce of evidence and I believed it. I had a ton of opinion saying otherwise. I tell you, sir, I *had* to go. I had to stand knee-deep in Vexvelt sweet grass with the cedar smell of a camp-fire and a warm wind in my face," *and my hands in the hands of a girl called Tyng, along with my heart and my hope and a dazzling wonder colored like sunrise and tasting like tears,* "before I finally let myself believe I'd been right all along, and there is a planet called Vexvelt and it does have all the things I knew it had," *and more, more, oh, more than I'll ever tell you about, old man.* He fell silent, his gaze averted and luminous.

"What started you on this—this quest?"

Charli Bux threw up his big head and looked far away and back at some all-but-forgotten detail. "Huh! 'd almost lost that in the clutter. Workin' for Interworld Bank & Trust, feeding a computer in the clearin'house. Not as dull as you might think. Happens I was a mineralogist for a spell, and the cargoes meant something to me besides a name, a quantity and a price. Huh!" came the surprised I've-found-it! little explosion. "I can tell you the very item. Feldspar. It's used in porcelain and glass, antique style. I got a sticky mind, I guess. Long as I'd been there, feldspar ground and bagged went for about twenty-five credits a ton at the docks. But here was one of our customers bringing it in for eight and a half F.O.B. I called the firm just to check; mind, I didn't care much, but a figure like that could color a statistical summary of imports and exports for years. The bookkeeper there ran a check and found it was so: eight and a half a ton, high-grade feldspar, ground and bagged. Some broker on Lethe: they hadn't been able to contact him again.

"It wasn't worth remembering until I bumped into another one. Niobium this time. Some call it columbium. Helps make steel stainless, among other things. I'd never seen a quotation for rod stock at less than a hundred and thirty-seven, but here was some—not much, mind you—at ninety credits *delivered*. And some sheets too, about 30 per cent less than I'd ever seen it before, freight paid. I checked that one out too. It was correct. Well smelted and pure, the man said. I forgot that one too, or I thought I had. Then there was that space-hand." *Moxie Magiddle—honest! that was his name. Squint-eyed little fellow with a great big laugh bulging the walls of the honky-tonk out at the spaceport. Drank only alcohol and never touched a needle. Told me the one about the fellow had a big golden screwhead in his belly button. Told me about times and places all over—full of yarns, a wonderful gift for yarning.* "Just mentioned in passing that Lethe was one place where the law was 'Have Fun' and nobody ever broke it. The whole place just one big transfer point and rest-and-rehab. A water world with only one speck of land in the tropics. Always warm, always easy. No

23

industry, no agriculture, just—well, services. Thousands of men spent hundreds of thousands of credits, a few dozen pocketed millions. Everybody happy. I mentioned the feldspar, I guess just so I would sound as if I knew something about Lethe too." *And laid a big fat egg, too. Moxie looked at me as if he hadn't seen me before and didn't like what he saw. If it was a lie I was telling it was a stupid one. "Y'don't dig feldspar out of a swamp, fella. You puttin' me on, or you kiddin' y'rself?" And a perfectly good evening dried up and blew away.* "He said it couldn't possibly have come from Lethe—it's a water world. I guess I could have forgotten that too but for the coffee beans. Blue Mountain Coffee, it was called; the label claimed it descended in an unbroken line from Old Earth, on an island called Jamaica. It went on to say that it could be grown only in high cool land in the tropics—a real mountain plant. I liked it better than any coffee I ever tasted but when I went back for more they were sold out. I got the manager to look in the records and traced it back to through the Terratu wholesaler to the broker and then to the importer— I mean, I *liked* that coffee!

"And according to him, it came from Lethe. High cool mountain land and all. The port at Lethe was tropical all right, but to be cool it would have to have mountains that were really mountains.

"The feldspar that did, but couldn't have, come from Lethe—and at those prices!—reminded me of the niobium, so I checked on that one too. Sure enough—Lethe again. You don't—you just do *not* get pure niobium rod and sheet without mines and smelters and mills.

"Next off-day I spent here at Archives and got the history of Lethe halfway back, I'll swear, to Ylem and the Big Bang. It was a swamp, it practically always has been a swamp, and something was wrong.

"Mind you, it was only a little something, and probably there was a good simple explanation. But little or not, it bothered me." *And besides, it had made me look like a horse's ass in front of a damn good man. Old man, if I told you how much time I hung around the spaceport looking for*

24

*that bandy-legged little space-gnome, you'd stop me now
and send for the stun-guns. Because I was obsessed—not a
driving addiction kind of thing, but a very small deep splin-
ter-in-the-toe kind of thing, that didn't hurt much but never
failed to gig me every single step I took. And then one
day—oh, months later—there was old Moxie Magiddle, and
he took the splinter out. Hyuh! Ol.' Moxie . . . he didn't
know me at first, he really didn't. Funny little guy, he has his
brains rigged to forget anything he doesn't like—honestly
forget it. That feldspar thing, when a fella he liked to drink
with and yarn to showed up to be a know-it-all kind of liar,
and to boot, too dumb to know he couldn't get away with
it—well, that qualified Charli for zero minus the price of
five man-hours of drinking. Then when I got him cornered—I all but wrestled him—and told about the feldspar
and the niobium and now the mountain-grown coffee, all of
it checked and cross-checked, billed, laded, shipped, in-
sured—all of it absolutely Lethe and here's the goddam
proof, why, he began to laugh till he cried, a little at himself,
a little at the situation, and a whole lot at me. Then we had a
long night of it and I drank alcohol and you know what? I'll
never in life find out how Moxie Magiddle can hold so much
liquor. But he told me where those shipments came from, and
gave me a vague idea why nobody wanted much to admit it.
And the name they call all male Vexveltians.* "I mentioned
it one day to a cargo handler," Bux told the Archive Master,
"and he solved the mystery—the feldspar and niobium and
coffee came from Vexvelt and had been transshipped at
Lethe by local brokers, who, more often than not, get hold
of some goods and turn them over to make a credit or so and
dive back into the local forgetteries.

"But any planet which could make a profit on goods of
this quality at such prices—transshipped, yet!—certainly
could do much better direct. Also, niobium is Element 41,
and Elkhart's Hypothesis has it that, on any planet where
you find elements in Periods Three to Five, chances are
you'll find 'em all. And that coffee! I used to lie awake at
night wondering what they had on Vexvelt that they liked

too much to ship, if they thought so little of their coffee that they'd let it out.

"Well, it was only natural that I came here to look up Vexvelt. Oh, it was listed at the bank, all right, but if there ever had been trade, it had been cleared out of the records long ago—we wipe the memory cells every fifty years on inactive items. I know at least that it's been wiped four times, but it could have been blank the last three.

"What do you think Archives has on Vexvelt?"

The Archive Master did not answer. He *knew* what Archives had on the subject of Vexvelt. He knew where it was, and where it was not. He knew how many times this stubborn young man had been back worrying at the mystery, how many ingenious approaches he had made to the problem, how little he had gotten, how much less he or anyone would get if they tried it today. He said nothing.

Charli Bux held up fingers to count. "Astronomical: no observations past two light-years. Nothing but sister planets (all dead) and satellites within two light-years. Cosmological: camera scan, if ever performed (but it must have been performed, or the damn thing wouldn't even be listed at all!), missing and never replaced. So there's no way of finding out where in real space it is, even. Geological: unreported. Anthropological: unreported. Then there's some stuff about local hydrogen tension and emission of the parent star, but they're not much help. And the summation in Trade Extrapolation: untraded. Reported undesirable. Not a word as to who reported it or why he said it.

"I tried to sidle into it by looking up manned exploration, but I could find only three astronauts' names in connection with Vexvelt. Troshan. He got into some sort of trouble when he came back and was executed—we used to kill certain criminals six, seven hundred years ago, did you know that?—but I don't know what for. Anyway, they apparently did it before he filed his report. Then Balrou. Oh—Balrou—he did report. I can tell you his whole report word for word: 'In view of conditions on Vexvelt contact is not recommended,' period. By the word, that must be the most expensive report ever filed."

It was, said the Archive Master, but he did not say it aloud.

"And then somebody called Allman explored Vexvelt but—how did the report put it—'it was found on his return that Allman was suffering from confinement fatigue and his judgment was so severely impaired that his report is discounted'. Does that mean it was destroyed, Archive Master?"

Yes, thought the old man, but he said, "I can't say."

"So there you are," said Charli Bux. "If I wanted to present a classic case of what the old books called persecution mania, I'd just have to report things exactly as they happened. Did I have a right to suspect, even, that 'They' had picked me as the perfect target and set up those hints—low-cost feldspar, high-quality coffee—bait I couldn't miss and couldn't resist. Did I have the right to wonder if a living caricature with a comedy name—Moxie for-god's-sake Magiddle—was working for Them? Then, what happened next, when I honestly and openly filed for Vexvelt as my next vacation destination? I was told there was no Drive Guide orbiting Vexvelt—it could only be reached through normal space. That happens to be a lie, but there's no way of checking on it here, or even on Lethe—Moxie never knew. Then I filed for Vexvelt via Lethe and a real-space transport, and was told that Lethe was not recommended as a tourist stop and there was no real-space service from there anyhow. So I filed for Botil, which I *know* is a tourist stop, and which I know has real-space shuttles and charter boats, and which the star charts call Kricker III while Lethe is Kricker V, and that's when I won the God—uh, the sweepstakes and a free trip to beautiful, beautiful Zeenip, paradise of paradises with two indoor 36-hole golf courses and free milk baths. I gave it to some charity or other, I said to save on taxes, and went for my tickets to Botil, the way I'd planned. I had it all to do over because they'd wiped the whole transaction when they learned about the sweepstakes. It seemed reasonable but it took so long to set it all up again

27

that I missed the scheduled transport and lost a week of my vacation. Then when I went to pay for the trip my credit showed up zero, and it took another week to straighten out that regrettable error. By that time the tour service had only one full passage open, and in view of the fact that the entire tour would outlast my vacation by two weeks, they wiped the whole deal again—they were quite sure I wouldn't want it."

Charli Bux looked down at his hands and squeezed them. The Archives Office was filled with a crunching sound. Bux did not seem to notice it. "I guess anybody in his right mind would have got the message by then, but 'They' had underestimated me. Let me tell you exactly what I mean by that. I *don't* mean that I am a man of steel and by the Lord when my mind is made up it stays made. And I'm not making brags about the courage of my convictions. I had very little to be convinced about, except that there was a whole chain of coincidences which nobody wanted to explain even though the explanation was probably foolishly simple. And I never thought I was specially courageous.

"I was just—scared. Oh, I was frustrated and I was mad, but mostly I was scared. If somebody had come along with a reasonable explanation I'd've forgotten the whole thing. If someone had come back from Vexvelt and it was a poison planet (with a pocket of good feldspar and one clean mountainside) I'd have laughed it off. But the whole sequence—especially the last part, trying to book passage—really scared me. I reached the point where the only thing that would satisfy me as to my own sanity was to stand and walk on Vexvelt and *know* what it was. And that was the one thing I wasn't being allowed to do. So I couldn't get my solid proof and who's to say I wouldn't spend the next couple hundred years wondering when I'd get the next little splinter down deep in my toe? A man can suffer from a thing, Master, but then he can also suffer for fear of suffering from a thing. No, I was scared and I was going to stay scared until I cleared it up."

"My." The old man had been silent, listening, for so long that his voice was new and arresting. "It seems to me that

28

there was a much simpler way out. Every city on every human world has free clinics where—"

"That's twice you've said that," crackled Charli Bux. "I have something to say about that, but not now. As to my going to a patch-up parlor, you know as well as I do that they don't change a thing. They just make you feel good about being the way you are."

"I fail to see the distinction, or what is wrong if there is one."

"I had a friend come up to me and tell me he was going to die of cancer in the next eight weeks, 'just in time,' he says, and whacks me so hard I see red spots, 'just in time for my funeral,' and off he goes down the street whooping like a loon."

"Would it be better if he huddled in his bed terrified and in pain?"

"I can't answer that kind of a question, but I do know what I saw is just as wrong. Anyway—there was something out there called Vexvelt, and it wouldn't make me feel any better to get rolled through a machine and come out thinking there isn't something called Vexvelt, and don't tell me that's not what those friendly helpful spot removers would do to me."

"But don't you see, you'd no longer be—"

"Call me throwback. Call me radical if you want to, or ignorant." Charli Bux's big voice was up again and he seemed angry enough not to care. "Ever hear that old line about 'in every fat man there's a thin man screaming to get out'? I just can't shake the idea that if something is *so*, you can prick, poke and process me till I laugh and scratch and giggle and admit it ain't so after all, and even go out and make speeches and persuade other people, but away down deep there'll be a me with its mouth taped shut and its hands tied, bashing up against my guts trying to get out and say it is so after all. But what are we talking about me for? I came here to talk about Vexvelt."

"First tell me something—do you really think there was a 'They' who wanted to stop you?"

"*Hell* no. I think I'm up against some old-time stupidity that got itself established and habitual, and that's how come there's no information in the files. I don't think anybody today is all that stupid. I like to think people on this planet can look at the truth and not let it scare them. Even if it scares them they can think it through. As to that rat race with the vacation bookings, there seemed to be a good reason for each single thing that happened. Science and math have done a pretty good job of explaining the mechanics of 'the bad break' and 'a lucky run', but neither of them ever got repealed."

"So." The Master tented his fingers and looked down at the ridgepole. "And just how did you manage to get to Vexvelt after all?"

Bux flicked on his big bright grin. "I hear a lot about this free society, and how there's always someone out to trim an edge off here and a corner there. Maybe there's something in it, but so far they haven't got around to taking away a man's freedom to be a damn fool. Like, for example, his freedom to quit his job. I've said it was just a gruesome series of bad breaks, but bad breaks can be outwitted just as easily as a superpowerful masterminding 'They'. Seems to me most bad breaks happen inside a man's pattern. He gets out of phase with it and every step he takes is between the steppin' stones. If he can't phase in, and if he tries to maintain his pace, why there's a whole row of stones ahead of him laid just exactly where each and every one of them will crack his shins. What he should do is head upstream. It might be unknown territory, and there might be dangers, but one thing for sure, there's a whole row of absolutely certain, absolutely planned agonies he is just not going to have to suffer."

"How did you get to Vexvelt?"

"I told you." He waited, then smiled. "I'll tell you again. I quit my job. 'They', or the 'losing streak', or the stinking lousy Fates, or whatever had a bead on me—they could do it to me because they always knew where I was, when I'd be the next place, and what I wanted. So they were always waiting for me. So I headed upstream. I waited till my vacation was over and left the house without any luggage and went to my local bank and had all my credits before I could have any tough breaks. Then I took a Drive jumper to Lunatu, booked passage on a semi-freight to Lethe."

"You booked passage, but you never boarded the ship."

"You know?"

"I was asking."

"Oh," said Charli Bux. "Yeah, I never set foot in that cozy little cabin. What I did, I slid down the cargo chute and got buried in Hold No. 2 with a ton of oats. I was in an interesting position, Archive Master. In a way I'm sorry nobody dug me out to ask questions. You're not supposed to stow away but the law says—and I know exactly what it says—that a stowaway is someone who rides a vessel without booking passage. But I did book passage, and paid in full, and all my papers were in order for where I was going. What made things a lot easier, too, was that where I was going nobody gives much of a damn about papers."

"And you felt you could get to Vexvelt through Lethe."

"I felt I had a chance, and I knew of no others. Cargoes from Vexvelt *had* been put down on Lethe, or I wouldn't have been sucked into this thing in the first place. I didn't know if the carrier was Vexveltian or a tramp (if it was a liner I'd have known it) or when one might come or if it would be headed for Vexvelt when it departed. All I knew was that Vexvelt had shipped here for sure, and this was the only place where maybe they might be back. Do you know what goes on at Lethe?"

"It has a reputation."

"Do you *know*?"

The old man showed a twinge of irritation. Along with respect and obedience, he had become accustomed to catechizing and not to being catechized. "Everyone knows about Lethe."

Bux shook his head. "They don't, Master."

The old man lifted his hands and put them down. "That kind of thing has its function. Humanity will always—"

"You approve of Lethe and what goes on there."

"One neither approves nor disapproves," said the Archive Master stiffly. "One knows about it, recognizes that for some segments of the species such an outlet is necessary, realizes that Lethe makes no pretensions to being anything but what it is, and then—one accepts, one goes on to other things. How did you get to Vexvelt?"

"On Lethe," said Charli Bux implacably, "you can do anything you want to or with any kind of human being, or any number of combination of them, as long as you can pay for it."

"I wouldn't doubt it. Now, the next leg of your trip—"

"There are men," said Charli Bux, suddenly and shockingly quiet, "who can be attracted by disease—by sores, Archive Master, by the stumps of amputated limbs. There are people on Lethe who cultivate diseases to attract such men. Crones, Master, with dirty leather skin, and boys and little—"

"You will cease this nauseating—"

"In just a minute. One of the unwritten and unbreakable traditions of Lethe is that, what anyone pays to do, anyone else may pay to watch."

"*Are you finished?*" It was not Bux who shouted now.

"You accept Lethe. You condone Lethe."

"I have not said I approve."

"You trade with Lethe."

"Well, of course we do. That doesn't mean we—"

"The third day—night, rather, that I was there," said Bux, overriding what was surely about to turn into a helpless sputter, "I turned off one of the main streets and into an alley. I knew this might be less than wise, but at the moment there was an ugly fight going on between me and the corner, and some wild gunning. I was going to turn right and go to the other avenue anyway, and I could see it clearly through the alley.

"I couldn't describe to you how fast this happened, or explain where they came from—eight of them, I think, in an alley, not quite dark and very narrow, when only a minute before I had been able to see it from end to end.

32

"I was grabbed from all sides all over my body, lifted, slammed down flat on my back and a bright light jammed in my face.

"A woman said, 'Aw shoot, 'tain't him.' A man's voice said to let me up. They picked me up. Somebody even started dusting me off. The woman who had held the light began to apologize. She did it quite nicely. She said they had heard that there was a—Master, I wonder if I should use the word."

"How necessary do you feel—"

"Oh, I guess I don't have to; you know it. On any ship, any construction gang, in any farm community—anywhere where men work or gather, it's the one verbal bullet which will and must start a fight. If it doesn't, the victim will never regain face. The woman used it as casually as she would have said Terran or Lethean. She said there was one right here in town and they meant to get him. I said, 'Well, how about that.' It's the one phrase I know that can be said any time about anything. Another woman said I was a good big one and how would I like to tromp him. One of the men said all right, but he called for the head. Another began to fight him about it, and a third woman took off her shoe and slapped both their faces with one swing of the muddy sole. She said for them to button it up or next time she'd use the heel. The other woman, with the light, giggled and said Helen was Veddy Good Indeed that way. She spoke in a beautifully cultivated accent. She said Helen could hook out an eye neat as a croupier. The third woman suddenly cried out, 'Dog turds!' She asked for some light. The dog turds were very dry. One of the men offered to wet them down. The women said no—they were her dog turds and she would do it herself. Then and there she squatted. She called for a light, said she couldn't see to aim. They turned the light on her. She was one of the most beautiful women I have ever seen. Is there something wrong, Master?"

"I would like you to tell me how you made contact with Vexvelt," said the old man a little breathlessly.

"But I am!" said Charli Bux. "One of the men pressed

through, all grunting with eagerness, and began to mix the filth with his hands. And then, by a sort of sixth sense, the light was out and they were simply—*gone!* Disappeared. A hand came out of nowhere and pulled me back against a house wall. There wasn't a sound—not even breathing. And only then did the Vexveltian turn into the alley. How they knew he was coming is beyond me.

"The hand that had pulled me back belonged to the woman with the light, as I found out in a matter of seconds. I really didn't believe her hand meant to be where I found it. I took hold of it and held it, but she snatched it away and put it back. Then I felt the light bump my leg. And the man came along toward us. He was a big man, held himself straight, wore light-colored clothes, which I thought was more foolhardy than brave. He walked lightly and seemed to be looking everywhere—and still could not see us.

"If this all happened right this minute, after what I've learned about Vexvelt—about Lethe too—I wouldn't hesitate, I'd know exactly what to do. What you have to understand is that I didn't know anything at all at the time. Maybe it was the eight against one that annoyed me." He paused thoughtfully. "Maybe that coffee. What I'm trying to say is that I did the same thing then, in my ignorance, that I'd do now, knowing what I do.

"I snapped the flashlight out of the woman's hand and got about twenty feet away in two big bounds. I turned the light on and played it back where I'd come from. Two of the men had crawled up the sheer building face like insects and were ready to drop on the victim. The beautiful one was crouched on her toes and one hand; the other, full of filth, was ready to throw. She made an absolutely animal sound and slung her handful, quite uselessly. The others were flattened back against wall and fence, and in the light, for a long second, they flattened all the more, blinking. I said over my shoulder, 'Watch yourself, friend. You're the guest of honor, I think.'

"You know what he did? He laughed. I said. 'They won't get by me for a while. Take off.' 'What for?' says he, squeezing past me. 'There's only eight of them.' And he marches straight down on them.

"Something rolled under my foot and I picked it up—half a brick. What must have been the other half of it hit me right on the breastbone. It made me yelp, I couldn't help it. The tall man said to douse the light, I was a target. I did, and saw one of them in silhouette against the street at the far end, standing up from behind a big garbage can. He was holding a knive half as long as his forearm, and he rose up as the big man passed him. I let fly with the brick and got him right back of the head. The tall man never so much as turned when he heard him fall and the knife go skittering. He passed one of the human flies as if he had forgotten he was there, but he hadn't forgotten. He reached up and got both the ankles and swung the whole man screaming off the wall like a flail, wiping the second one off and tumbling the both of them on top of the rest of the gang.

"He stood there with the back of his hands on his hips for a bit, not even breathing hard, watching the crying, cursing mix-up all over the alley pavement. I came up beside him. One, two got to their feet and ran limping. One of the women began to scream—curses, I suppose, but you couldn't hear the words. I turned the light on her face and she shut right up.

" 'You all right?' says the tall man.

"I told him, 'Caved in my chest is all, but that's all right, I can use it for a fruit bowl lying in bed.' He laughed and turned his back on the enemy and led me the way he had come. He said he was Vorhidin from Vexvelt. I told him who I was. I said I'd been looking for a Vexveltian, but before we could go on with that a black hole opened up to the left and somebody whispered, 'Quick, quick.' Vorhidin clapped a hand on my back and gave me a little shove. 'In you go, Charli Bux of Terratu.' And in we went, me stumbling all over my feet down some steps I didn't know were there, and then again because they weren't there. A big door boomed closed behind us. Dim yellow light came on. There was a little man with olive skin and shiny, oily mustachios.

'Vorhidin, for the love of God, I told you not to come into town, they'll kill you.' Vorhidin only said, 'This is Charli Bux, a friend.' The little man came forward anxiously and began to pat Vorhidin on the arms and ribs to see if he was all right.

"Vorhidin laughed and brushed him off. 'Poor Tretti! He's always afraid something is going to happen! Never mind me, you fusspot. See to Charli here. He took a shot in the bows that was meant for me.' The little one, Tretti, sort of squeaked and before I could stop him he had my shirt open and the light out of my hand switched on and trained on the bruise. 'Your next woman can admire a sunset,' says Vorhidin. Tretti's away and back before you can blink and sprays on something cool and good and most of the pain vanished.

" 'What do you have for us?' and Tretti carries the light into another room. There's stacks of stuff, mostly manufactured goods, tools and instruments. There was a big pile of trideo cartridges, mostly music and new plays, but a novel or so too. Most of the other stuff was one of a kind. Vorhidin picked up a forty-pound crate and spun it twice by diagonal corners till it stopped where he could read the label. 'Molar spectroscope. Most of this stuff we don't really need but we like to see what's being done, how it's designed. Sometimes ours are better, sometimes not. We like to see, that's all.' He set it down gently and reached into his pocket and palmed out a dozen or more stones that flashed till it hurt. One of them, a blue one, made its own light. He took Tretti's hand and pulled it to him and poured it full of stones. 'That enough for this load?' I couldn't help it—I glanced around the place and totted it up and made a stab estimate—a hundred each of everything in the place wouldn't be worth that one blue stone. Tretti was goggle-eyed. He couldn't speak. Vorhidin wagged his head and laughed and said, 'All right, then,' and reached into his pants pocket again and ladled out four or five more. I thought Tretti was going to cry. I was right. He cried.

"We had something to eat and I told Vorhidin how I

36

happened to be here. He said he'd better take me along. I said where to? and he said Vexvelt. I began to laugh. I told him I was busting my brains trying to figure some way to make him say that, and he laughed too and said I'd found it, all right, twice over. 'Owe you a favor for that,' he says, dipping his head at the alley side of the room. 'Reason two, you wouldn't live out the night on Lethe if you stayed here.' I wanted to know why not, because from what I'd seen there were fights all the time, then you'd see the fighters an hour later drinking out of the same bowl. He says it's not the same thing. Nobody helps a Vexveltian but a Vexveltian. Help one, you are one, far as Lethe was concerned. So I wanted to know what Lethe had against Vexvelt, and he stopped chewing and looked at me a long time as if he didn't understand me. Then he said, 'You really don't know anything about us, do you?' I said, not much. 'Well,' he says, 'now there's three good reasons to bring you.'

"Tretti opened the double doors at the far end of the storeroom. There was a ground van in there, with another set of doors into the street. We loaded the crates into it and got in, Vorhidin at the tiller. Tretti climbed a ladder and put his eyes to something and spun a wheel. 'Periscope,' Vorhidin told me. 'Looks like a flagpole from outside.' Tretti waved his hand at us. He had tears running down his cheeks again. He hit a switch and the doors banged out of the way. The van screeched out of there as the doors bounced and started back. After that Vorhidin drove like a little old lady. One-way glass. Sometimes I wondered what those crowds of drunks and queers would do if they could see in. I asked him, 'What are they afraid of?' He didn't seem to understand the question. I said, 'Mostly when people gang up on somebody, it's because one way or another they're afraid. What do they think you're going to take away from them?'

"He laughed and said, 'Their decency.' And that's all the talk I got out of him all the way out to the spaceport.

"The Vexveltian ship was parked miles away from the terminal, way the hell and gone at the far end of the pavement near some trees. There was a fire going near it. As we

37

got closer I saw it wasn't near it, it was spang under it. There was a big crowd, maybe half a hundred, mostly women, mostly drunk. They were dancing and staggering around and dragging wood up under the ship. The ship stood up on its tail like the old chemical rockets in the fairy stories. Vorhidin grunted, 'Idiots,' and moved something on his wrist. The rocket began to rumble and everybody ran screaming. Then there was a big explosion of steam and the wood went every which way, and for a while the pavement was full of people running and falling and screaming, and cycles and ground cars milling around and bumping each other. After a while it was quiet and we pulled up close. The high hatch opened on the ship and a boom and frame came out and lowered. Vorhidin hooked on, threw the latches on the van bed, beckoned me back there with him, reached forward and set the controls of the van, and touched the thing on his wrist. The whole van cargo section started up complete with us, and the van started up and began to roll home by itself.

"The only crew he carried," said Charli Bux carefully, "was a young radio officer." *With long shining black wings for hair and bits of sky in her tilted eyes, and a full and asking kind of mouth. She held Vorhidin very close, very long, laughing the message that there could be no words for this: he was safe.* "Tamba, this is Charli. He's from Terratu and he fought for me." *Then she came and held him too, and she kissed him; that incredible mouth, that warm strong soft mouth, why, he and she shared it for an hour; for an hour he felt her lips on his, even though she had kissed him for only a second. For an hour her lips could hardly be closer to her than they were to his own astonished flesh.* "The ship blasted off and headed sunward and to the celestial north. It held this course for two days. Lethe has two moons, the smaller one just a rock, an asteroid. Vorhidin matched velocities with it and hung half a kilo away, drifting in."

And the first night he had swung his bunk to the after bulkhead and had lain there heavily against the thrust of the jets, and against the thrust of his heart and his loins. Never had he seen such a woman—only just become woman, at

38

that. So joyful, so utterly and so rightly herself. Half an hour after blastoff: "Clothes are in the way on ship, don't you think? But Vorhidin says I should ask you, because customs are different from one world to another, isn't that so?"

"Here we live by your customs, not mine," Charli had been able to say, and she had thanked him, thanked him! and touched the bit of glitter at her throat, and her garment fell away. "There's much more privacy this way," she said, leaving him. "A closed door means more to the naked; it's closed for a real reason and not because one might be seen in one's petticoat." She took her garment into one of the staterooms. Vorhidin's. Charli leaned weakly against the bulkhead and shut his eyes. Her nipples were like her mouth, full and asking. Vorhidin was casually naked but Charli kept his clothes on, and the Vexveltians made no comment. The night was very long. For a while part of the weight on Charli turned to anger, which helped. Old bastard, silver-temples. Old enough to be her father. But that could not last, and he smiled at himself. He remembered the first time he had gone to a ski resort. There were all kinds of people there, young, old, wealthy, working, professionals; but there was a difference. The resort, because it was what it was, screened out the pasty-faced, the round-shouldered lungless sedentaries, the plumping sybarites. All about him had been clear eyes, straight backs, and skin with the cosmetics of frost and fun. Who walked idled not, but went somewhere. Who sat lay back joyfully in well-earned weariness. And this was the aura of Vorhidin—not a matter of carriage and clean color and clear eyes, though he certainly had all these, but the same qualities down to the bone and radiating from the mind. A difficult thing to express and a pleasure to be with. Early on the second day Vorhidin had leaned close when they were alone in the control room and asked him if he would like to sleep with Tamba tonight. Charli gasped as if he had been clapped on the navel with a handful of crushed ice. He also blushed, saying, "If she, if she—" wildly wondering how to ask her. He need not have wondered, for "He'd love to, honey," Vorhidin bellowed. Tamba popped her face

into the corridor and smiled at Charli. "Thank you so much," she said. And then (after the long night) it was going to be the longest day he had ever lived through, but she let it happen within the hour instead, sweetly, strongly, unhurried. Afterward he lay looking at her with such total and long-lasting astonishment that she laughed at him. She flooded his face with her black hair and then with her kisses and then all of him with her supple strength; this time she was fierce and most demanding until with a shout he toppled from the very peak of joy straight and instantly down into the most total slumber he had ever known. In perhaps twenty minutes he opened his eyes and found his gaze plunged deep in a blue glory, her eyes so close their lashes meshed. Later, talking to her in the wardroom, holding both her hands, he turned to find Vorhidin standing in the doorway. He was on them in one long stride, and flung an arm around each. Nothing was said. What could be said?

"I talked a lot with Vorhidin," Charli Bux said to the Archive Master. "I never met a man more sure of himself, what he wanted, what he liked, what he believed. The very first thing he said when I brought up the matter of trade was 'Why?' In all my waking life I never thought to ask that about trade. All I ever did, all anyone does, is to trade where he can and try to make it more. 'Why?' he wanted to know. I thought of the gemstones going for that production-line junk in the hold, and pure niobium at manganese prices. One trader would call that ignorance, another would call it good business and get all he could—glass beads for ivory. But cultures have been known to trade like that for religious or ethical reaons—always give more than you get in the other fellow's coin. Or maybe they were just—*rich.* Maybe there was so much Vexvelt that the only thing they could use was—well, like he said: manufactures, so they could look at the design 'sometimes better than ours, sometimes not.' So I asked him.

"He gave me a long look that was, at four feet, exactly like" *drowning in the impossibly blue lakes of Tamba's eyes, but watch yourself, don't think about that when you talk to this old man* "holding still for an X-ray continuity. Finally he said, 'Yes, I suppose we're rich. There's not much we need.'

"I told him, all the same, he could get a lot higher prices for the little he did trade. He just laughed a little and shook his head. 'You have to pay for what you get or it's no good. If you "Trade well," as you call it, you finish with more than you started with; you didn't pay. That's as unnatural as energy levels going from lesser to greater, it's contrary to ecology and entropy.' Then he said, 'You don't understand that.' I didn't and I don't."

"Go on."

"They have their own Drive cradle back of Lethe's moon, and their own Guide orbiting Vexvelt. I told you—all the while I thought the planet was near Lethe; well, it isn't."

"Now, that I do *not* understand. Cradles and guides are public utilities. Two days, you say it took. Why didn't he use the one at the Lethe port?"

"I can't say, sir. Uh—"

"Well?"

"I was just thinking about that drunken mob building a fire under the ship."

"Ah yes. Perhaps the moon cradle is a wise precaution after all. I have always known, and you make it eminently clear, that these people are not popular. All right—you made a Drive jump."

"We made a Drive jump." Charli fell silent for a moment, reliving that breathless second of revelation as black, talc-dusted space and a lump moonlet winked away to be replaced by the great arch of a purple-haloed horizon, marbled green and gold and silver and polished blue, with a chromium glare coming from the sea on the planet's shoulder. "A tug was standing by and we got down without trouble." The spaceport was tiny compared even with Lethe—eight or ten docks, with the warehouse area under them and passenger and staff areas surrounding them under a deck. "There were no formalities—I suppose there's not enough space travel to merit them."

"Certainly no strangers, at any rate," said the old man smugly.

"We disembarked right on the deck and walked away." *Tamba had gone out first. It was sunny, with a warm wind, and if there was any significant difference between this gravity and that of Terratu, Charli's legs could not detect it. In the air, however, the difference was profound. Never before had he known air so clear, so winy, so clean—not unless it was bitter cold, and this was warm. Tamba stood by the silent, swiftly moving "up" ramp, looking out across the foothills to the most magnificent mountain range he had ever seen, for they had everything a picture-book mountain should have—smooth vivid high-range, shaggy forest, dramatic gray, brown, and ocher rock cliff, and a starched white cloth of snowcap tumbled on the peaks to dry in the sun. Behind them was a wide plain with a river for one margin and foothills for the other, and then the sea, with a wide golden beach curving a loving arm around the ocean's green shoulder. As he approached the pensive girl the warm wind curled and laughed down on them, and her short robe streamed from her shoulders like smoke, and fell about her again. It stopped his pace and his breath and his heart for a beat, it was so lovely a sight. And coming up beside her, watching the people below, the people rising on one ramp and sliding down the other, he realized that in this place clothing had but two conventions—ease and beauty. Man, woman and child, they wore what they chose, ribbon or robe, clogs, coronets, cummerbunds or kilts, or a ring, or a snood, or nothing at all. He remembered a wonderful line he had read by a pre-Nova sage called Rudofsky, and murmured it:* Modesty is not so simple a virtue as honesty. *She turned and smiled at him; she thought it was his line. He smiled back and let her think so.* "You don't mind waiting a bit? My father will be along in a moment and then we'll go. You're to stay with us. Is that all right?"

Did he mind. Would he wait, bracketed by the thundering colors of that mountain, the adagio of the sea. Is that all right. There was nothing, no way, no word to express his re-

sponse but to raise his tense fists as high as he could and shout as loud as he could and then turn it into laughter and to tears.

Vorhidin, having checked out his manifests, joined them before Charli was finished. He had locked gazes with the girl, who smiled up at him and held his forearm in both her hands, stroking and he laughed and laughed. "He drank too much Vexvelt all at once," she said to Vorhidin. Vorhidin put a big warm hand on Charli's shoulder and laughed with him until he was done. When he had his breath again, and the water-lenses out of his eyes, Tamba said, "That's where we're going."

"Where?"

She pointed, very carefully. Three slender dark trees like poplars came beseeching out of a glad tumble of luminous light willow-green. "Those three trees."

"I can't see a house ..."

Vorhidin and Tamba laughed together: this pleased them. "Come."

"We were going to wait for—"

"No need to wait any longer. Come."

Charli said, "The house was only a short walk from the port, but you couldn't see the one from the other. A big house, too, trees all around it and even growing up through it. I stayed with the family and worked." He slapped the heavy folio. "All this. I got all the help I needed."

"*Did* you indeed." The Archive Master seemed more interested in this than in anything else he had heard so far. Or perhaps it was a different kind of interest. "Helped you, did they? Would you say they're anxious to trade?"

The answer to this was clearly an important one. "All I can say," Charli Bux responded carefully, "is that I asked for this information—a catalogue of the trade resources of Vexvelt, and estimates of F.O.B. prices. None of them are very far off a practical, workable arrangement, and every single one undercuts the competition. There are a number of reasons. First of all, of course, is the resources themselves—almost right across the board, unbelievably rich.

43

Then they have mining methods like nothing you've ever dreamed of, and harvesting, and preserving—there's no end to it. At first blush it looks like a pastoral planet—well, it's not. It's a natural treasure house that has been organized and worked and planned and understood like no other planet in the known universe. Those people have never had a war, they've never had to change their original cultural plan; it works, Master, it *works*. And it has produced a sane healthy people which, when it goes about a job, goes about it single-mindedly and with . . . well, it might sound like an odd term to use, but it's the only one that fits: with joy. . . . I can see you don't want to hear this."

The old man opened his eyes and looked directly at the visitor. At Bux's cascade of language he had averted his face, closed his eyes, curled his lip, let his hands stray over his temples and near his ears, as if it was taking a supreme effort to keep from clapping the palms over them.

"All I can hear is that a world which has been set aside by the whole species, and which has kept itself aloof, is using you to promote a contact which nobody wants. Do they want it? They won't get it, of course, but have they any idea of what their world would be like if this"—he waved at the folio—"is all true? How do they think they could control the exploiters? Have they got something special in defenses as well as all this other?"

"I really don't know."

"I know!" The old man was angrier than Bux had yet seen him. "What they are is their defense! No one will *ever* go near them, not *ever*. Not if they strip their whole planet of everything it has, and refine and process the lot, and haul it to their spaceport at their own expense, and give it away free."

"Not even if they can cure cancer?"

"Almost all cancer is curable."

"They can cure *all* cancer."

"New methods are discovered every—"

"They've had the methods for I don't know how many years. Centuries. *They have no cancer.*"

44

"Do you know what this cure is?"

"No, I don't. But it wouldn't take a clinical team a week to find out."

"The incurable cancers are not subject to clinical analysis. They are all deemed psychosomatic."

"I know. That is exactly what the clinical team would find out."

There was a long, pulsing silence. "You have not been completely frank with me, young man."

"That's right, sir."

Another silence. "The implication is that they are sane and cancer-free because of the kind of culture they have set up."

This time Bux did not respond, but let the old man's words hang there to be reheard, reread. At last the Archive Master spoke again in a near whisper, shaking and furious. "Abomination! Abomination!" Spittle appeared on his chin: he seemed not to know. "I would—rather—die——eaten alive —with cancer—and raving *mad* than live with such sanity as that."

"Perhaps others would disagree."

"No one would disagree! Try it? Try it! They'll tear you to pieces! That's what they did to Allman. That's what they did to Balrou! We killed Troshan ourselves—he was the first and we didn't know then that the mob would do it for us. That was a thousand years ago, you understand that? And a thousand years from now the mob will still do it for us! And that—that *filth* will go to the locked files with the others, and someday another fool with too much curiosity and not enough decency and his mind rotten with perversion will sit here with another Archive Master, who will send him out as I'm sending you out, to shut his mouth and save his life or open it and be torn to pieces. Get *out!* Get *out!* Get *out!*" His voice had risen to a shriek and then a sort of keening, and had rasped itself against itself until it was a painful forced whisper and then nothing at all: the old eyes glared and the chin was wet.

Charli Bux rose slowly. He was white with shock. He said

quietly, "Vorhidin tried to tell me, and I wouldn't believe it. I couldn't believe it. I said to him, 'I know more about greed that you do; they will not be able to resist those prices.' I said, 'I know more about fear than you do; they will not be able to stand against the final cancer cure.' Vorhidin laughed at me and gave me all the help I needed.

"I started to tell him once that I knew more about the sanity that lives in all of us, and very much in some of us, and that it could prevail. But I knew while I was talking that I was wrong about that. Now I know that I was wrong in everything, even the greed, even the fear, and he was right. And he said Vexvelt has the most powerful and the least expensive defense ever devised—sanity. He was right."

Charli Bux realized then that the old man, madly locking gazes with him as he spoke, had in some way, inside his head, turned off his ears. He sat there with his old head cocked to one side, panting like a foundered dog in a dust bowl, until at last he thought he could shout again. He could not. He could only rasp, he could only whisper-squeak, "Get out! Get out!"

Charli Bux got out. He left the folio where it was; it, like Vexvelt, defended itself by being immiscible—in the language of chemistry, by being noble.

It was not Tamba after all, but Tyng who captured Charli's heart.

When they got to the beautiful house, so close to everything and yet so private, so secluded, he met the family. Breerho's radiant—almost heat-radiant—shining red hair, and Tyng's, showed them to be mother and daughter. Vorhid and Stren were the sons, one a child, the other in his mid-teens, were straight-backed, wide-shouldered like their father, and by the wonderful cut and tilt of their architectured eyes, were brothers to Tyng, and to Tamba.

There were two other youngsters, a lovely twelve-year-old girl called Fleet, who was singing when they came in, and for whose song they stopped and postponed the introductions, and a sturdy tumblebug of a boy they called Handr, possibly the happiest human being any of them would ever see. In time Charli met the parents of these two, and black-haired Tamba seemed much more kin to the mother than to flame-haired Breerho.

It was at first a cascade of names and faces, captured only partially, kaleidoscoping about in his head as they all did in the room, and making a shyness in him. But there was more love in the room than ever the peaks of his mind and heart had known before, and more care and caring.

Before the afternoon and evening were over, he was familiar and accepted and enchanted. And because Tamba had touched his heart and astonished his body, all his feelings rose within him and narrowed and aimed themselves on her, hot and breathless, and indeed she seemed to delight in him and kept close to him the whole of the time. But when the little ones went off yawning, and then others, and they were almost alone, he asked her, he begged her to come to his bed. She was kind as could be, and loving, but also completely firm in her refusal. "But, darling, I just can't now. I can't. I've been away to Lethe and now I'm back and I *promised*."

"Promised who?"

"Stren."

"But I thought . . ." He thought far too many things to sort out or even to isolate one from another. Well, maybe he hadn't understood the relationships here—after all, there were four adults and six children and he'd get it straight by tomorrow who was who, because otherwise she—oh. "You mean you promised Stren you wouldn't sleep with me."

"No, my silly old dear. I'll sleep with Stren tonight. Please, darling, don't be upset. There'll be other times. Tomorrow. Tomorrow morning?' She laughed and took his cheeks in her two hands and shook his whole head as if she could make the frown drop off. "Tomorrow morning *very* early?"

"I don't mean to be like this my very first night here, I'm sorry, I guess there's a lot I don't understand," he mumbled in his misery. And then anguish skyrocketed within him and he no longer cared about host and guest and new customs

47

and all the rest of it. "I love you," he cried, "don't you know that?"

"Of course, of course I do. And I love you, and we will love one another for a long, long time. Didn't you think I knew that?" Her puzzlement was so genuine that even through pain-haze he could see it. He said, as close to tears as he felt a grown man should ever get, that he just guessed he didn't understand.

"You will, beloved, you will. We'll talk about it until you do, no matter how long it takes." Then she added, with absolutely guileless cruelty, "Starting tomorrow. But now I have to go, Stren's waiting. Good night, true love," and she kissed the top of his averted head and sprinted away lightly on bare tiptoe.

She had reached something in him that made it impossible for him to be angry at her. He could only hurt. He had not known until these past two days that he could feel so much or bear so much pain. He buried his face in the cushions of the long couch in the—living room?—anyway, the place where indoors and outdoors were as tangled as his heart, but more harmoniously—and gave himself up to sodden hurt.

In time, someone knelt beside him and touched him lightly on the neck. He twisted his head enough to be able to see. It was Tyng, her hair all but luminous in the dimness, and her face, what he could see of it, nothing but compassion. She said, "Would you like me to stay with you instead?" and with the absolute honesty of the stricken, he cried, "There couldn't be anyone else instead!"

Her sorrow, its genuineness, was unmistakable. She told him of it, touched him once more, and slipped away. Sometime during the night he twisted himself awake enough to find the room they had given him, and found surcease in utter black exhaustion.

Awake in daylight, he sought his other surcease, which was work, and began his catalogue of resources. Everyone tried at one time or another to communicate with him, but unless it was work he shut it off (except, of course, for the irresistible Handr, who became his fast and lifelong friend). He found Tyng near him more and more frequently, and usefully so; he had not become so surly that he would refuse a stylus or reference book (opened at the right place) when it was placed in his hand exactly at the moment he needed it. Tyng was with him for many hours, alert but absolutely silent, before he unbent enough to ask her for this or that bit of information, or wondered about weights and measures and man-hour calculations done in the Vexveltian way. If she did not know, she found out with a minimum of delay and absolute clarity. She knew, however, a very great deal more than he had suspected. So the time came when he was chattering like a macaw, eagerly planning the next day's work with her.

He never spoke to Tamba. He did not mean to hurt her, but he could sense her eagerness to respond to him and he could not bear it. She, out of consideration, just stopped trying.

One particularly knotty statistical sequence kept him going for two days and two nights without stopping. Tyng kept up with him all the way without complaint until, in the wee small hours of the third morning, she rolled up her eyes and collapsed. He staggered up on legs gone asleep with too much sitting, and shook the statistics out of his eyes to settle her on the thick fur rug, straighten the twisted knee. In what little light spilled from his abandoned hooded lamp, she was exquisite, especially because of his previous knowledge that she was exquisite in the most brilliant of glares. The shadows added something to the alabaster, and her unconscious pale lips were no longer darker than her face, and she seemed strangely statuesque and non-living. She was wearing a Cretan sort of dress, a tight stomacher holding the bare breasts cupped and supporting a diaphanous skirt. Troubled that the stomacher might impede her breathing, he unhooked it and put it back. The flesh of her midriff where it had been was, to the finger if not to the eye, pinched and ridged. He kneaded it gently and pursued indefinable thoughts through the haze of fatigue: pyrophyllite, Lethe, brother, recoverable vanadium salts, Vorhidin, precipitate, Tyng's watching me. Tyng in the almost dark was watching him. He took his eyes from her and looked down her body to his hand. It had stopped moving some vague time ago, slipped into slumber of its own accord. Were her eyes open now or closed? He leaned forward to see and over-balanced. They fell asleep with their lips touching, not yet having kissed at all.

The pre-Nova ancient Plato tells of the earliest human, a quadruped with two sexes. And one terrible night in a storm engendered by the forces of evil, all the humans were torn in two; and ever since, each has sought the other half of itself. Any two of opposite sexes can make something, but it is usually incomplete in some way. But when one part finds its true other half, no power on earth can keep them apart, nor drive them apart once they join. This happened that night, beginning at some moment so deep in sleep that neither could ever remember it. What happened to each was all the way into new places where nothing had ever been before, and it was forever. The essence of such a thing is acceptance, and lest he be judged, Charli Bux ceased to judge quite so much and began to learn something of the ways of life around him. Life around him certainly concealed very little. The children slept where they chose. Their sexual play was certainly no more enthusiastic or more frequent than any other kind of play—and no more concealed. There was very much less talk about sex than he had ever encountered in any group of any age. He kept on working hard, but no longer to conceal facts from himself. He saw a good many things he had not permitted himself to see before, and found to his surprise that they were not, after all, the end of the world.

He had one more very, very bad time coming to him. He sometimes slept in Tyng's room, she sometimes in his. Early one morning he awoke alone, recalling some elusive part of the work, and got up and paddled down to her room. He realized when it was too late to ignore it what the soft singing sound meant; it was very much later that he was able to realize his fury at the discovery that this special song was not his alone to evoke. He was in her room before he could stop himself, and out again, shaking and blind.

He was sitting on the wet earth in the green hollow under a willow when Vorhidin found him. (He never knew how Vorhidin had accomplished this, nor for that matter how he had come there himself.) He was staring straight ahead and had been doing so for so long that his eyeballs were dry and the agony was enjoyable. He had forced his fingers so hard down into the ground that they were buried to the wrists. Three nails were bent and broken over backwards and he was still pushing.

Vorhidin did not speak at all at first, but merely sat down beside him. He waited what he felt was long enough and then softly called the young man's name. Charli did not move. Vorhidin then put a hand on his shoulder and the result was extraordinary. Charli Bux moved nothing visibly but the cords of his throat and his jaw, but at the first touch of the Vexveltian's hand he threw up. It was what is called clinically "projectile" vomiting. Soaked and spattered from hips to feet, dry-eyed and staring, Charli sat still. Vorhidin, who understood what had happened and may even have expected it, also remained just as he was, a hand on the young man's shoulder. "Say the words!" he snapped.

Charli Bux swiveled his head to look at the big man. He screwed up his eyes and blinked them, and blinked again. He spat sour out of his mouth, and his lips twisted and trembled. "Say the words," said Vorhidin quietly but forcefully, because he knew Charli could not contain them but had vomited rather than enunciate them. "Say the words."

"Y-y—" Charli had to spit again. "You," he croaked. "You—her *father*!" he screamed, and in a split second he became a dervish, a windmill, a double flail, a howling wolverine. The loamy hands, blood-muddy, so lacked control from the excess of fury that they never became fists. Vorhidin crouched where he was and took it all. He did not attempt to defend himself beyond an occasional small accurate movement of the head, to protect his eyes. He could heal from almost anything the blows might do, but unless

51

the blows were spent, Charli Bux might never heal at all. It went on for a long time because something in Charli would not show, probably would not even feel, fatigue. When the last of the resources was gone, the collapse was sudden and total. Vorhidin knelt grunting, got painfully to his feet, bent dripping blood over the unconscious Terran, lifted him in his arms, and carried him gently into the house.

Vorhidin explained it all, in time. It took a great deal of time, because Charli could accept nothing at all from any-one at first, and then nothing from Vorhidin, and after that, only small doses. Summarized from half a hundred con-versations, this is the gist:

"Some unknown ancient once wrote," said Vorhidin, " 'Tain't what you don't know that hurts you; it's what you do know that ain't so.' Answer me some questions. Don't stop to think. (Now that's silly. Nobody off Vexvelt ever stops to think about incest. They'll say a lot, mind you, and fast, but they don't think.) I'll ask, you answer. How many bisexual species—birds, beasts, fish and insects in-cluded—how many show any sign of the incest taboo?"

"I really couldn't say. I don't recall reading about it, but then, who'd write such a thing? I'd say—quite a few. It would be only natural."

"Wrong. Wrong twice, as a matter of fact. *Homo sapiens* has the patent, Charli—all over the wall-to-wall universe, only mankind. Wrong the second: it would *not* be natural. It never was, it isn't, and it never will be natural."

"Matter of terms, isn't it? I'd call it natural. I mean, it comes naturally. It doesn't have to be learned."

"Wrong. It does have to be learned. I can document that, but that'll wait—you can go through the library later. Ac-cept the point for the argument."

"For the argument, then."

"Thanks. What percentage of people do you think have sexual feelings about their siblings—brothers and sisters?"

"What age are you talking about?"

"Doesn't matter."

"Sexual feelings don't begin until a certain age, do they?"

52

"Don't they? What would you say the age is, on the average?"

"Oh—depends on the indi—but you did say 'average', didn't you? Let's put it around eight. Nine maybe."

"Wrong. Wait till you have some of your own, you'll find out. I'd put it at two or three minutes. I'd be willing to bet it existed a whole lot before that, too. By some weeks."

"I don't believe it!"

"I know you don't," said Vorhidin. " 'Strue all the same. What about the parent of the opposite sex?"

"Now, that would have to wait for a stage of consciousness capable of knowing the difference."

"Wel-l-l—you're not as wrong as usual," he said, but he said it kindly. "But you'd be amazed at how early that can be. They can smell the difference long before they can see it. A few days, a week."

"I never knew."

"I don't doubt that a bit. Now, let's forget everything you've seen here. Let's pretend you're back on Lethe and I ask you, what would be the effects on a culture if each individual had immediate and welcome access to all the others?"

"*Sexual* access?" Charlie made a laugh, a nervous sort of sound. "Sexual excess, I'd call it."

"There's no such thing," said the big man flatly. "Depending on who you are and what sex, you can do it only until you can't do it any more, or you can keep on until finally nothing happens. One man might get along beautifully with some mild kind of sexual relief twice a month or less. Another might normally look for it eight, nine times a day."

"I'd hardly call that normal."

"I would. Unusual it might be, but it's 100 per cent normal for the guy who has it, long as it isn't pathological. By which I mean, capacity is capacity, by the cupful, by the horsepower, by the flight ceiling. Man or machine, you do no harm by operating within the parameters of design. What does do harm—lots of it, and some of the worst kind—is guilt

53

and a sense of sin, where the sin turns out to be some sort of natural appetite. I've read case histories of boys who have suicided because of a nocturnal emission, or because they yielded to the temptation to masturbate after five, six weeks of self-denial—a denial, of course, that all by itself makes them preoccupied, absolutely obsessed by something that should have no more importance than clearing the throat. (I wish I could say that this kind of horror story lives only in the ancient scripts, but on many a world right this minute, it still goes on.)

"This guilt and sin thing is easier for some people to understand if you take it outside the area of sex. There are some religious orthodoxies which require a very specific diet, and the absolute exclusion of certain items. Given enough indoctrination for long enough, you can keep a man eating only (we'll say) 'flim' while 'flam' is forbidden. He'll get along on thin moldy flim and live half starved in a whole ware-house full of nice fresh flam. You can make him ill—even kill him, if you have the knack—just by convincing him that the flim he just ate was really flam in disguise. Or you can drive him psychotic by slipping him suggestions until he acquires a real taste for flam and gets a supply and hides it and nibbles at it secretly every time he fights temptation and loses.

"So imagine the power of guilt when it isn't a flim-and-flam kind of manufactured orthodoxy you're violating, but a deep pressure down in the cells somewhere. It's as mad, and as dangerous, as grafting in an ethical-guilt structure which forbids or inhibits yielding to the need for the B-vitamin complex or potassium."

"Oh, but," Charli interrupted, "now you're talking about vital necessities—survival factors."

"I sure as hell am," said Vorhidin in Charli's own idiom, and grinned a swift and hilarious—and very accu-rate—imitation of Charli's flash-beacon smile. "Now it's time to trot out some of the things I mentioned before, things that can hurt you much more than ignorance—the things you know that ain't so." He laughed suddenly. "This is kind of fun, you know? I've been to a lot of worlds, and some are

54

miles and years different from others in a thousand ways: but this thing I'm about to demonstrate, this particular shut-the-eyes, shut-the-brains conversation you can get anywhere you go. Are you ready? Tell me, then: what's wrong with incest? I take it back—you know me. Don't tell me. Tell some stranger, some fume-sniffer or alcohol addict in a spaceport bar." He put out both hands, the fingers so shaped that one could all but see light glisten from the imaginary glass he held. He said in a slurred voice, "Shay, shtranger, whut's a-wrong wit' in-shest, hm?" He closed one eye and rolled the other toward Charli.

Charli stopped to think. "You mean, morally, or what?"

"Let's skip that whole segment. Right and wrong depend on too many things from one place to another, although I have some theories of my own. No—let's be sitting in this bar and agree that incest is just awful, and go on from there. What's really wrong with it?"

"You breed too close, you get faulty offspring. Idiots and dead babies without heads and all that."

"I knew it! I knew it!" crowed the big Vexveltian. "Isn't it wonderful? From the rocky depths of a Stone Age culture through the brocades and knee-breeches sort of grand opera civilizations all the way out to the computer technocracies, where they graft electrodes into their heads and shunt their thinking into a box—you ask that question and you get that answer. It's something everybody just *knows*. You don't have to look at the evidence."

"Where do you go for evidence?"

"To dinner, for one place, where you'll eat idiot pig or feeble-minded cow. Any livestock breeder will tell you that, once you have a strain you want to keep and develop, you breed father to daughter and to granddaughter, and then brother to sister. You keep that up indefinitely until the desirable trait shows up recessive, and you stop it there. But it might never show up recessive. In any case, it's rare indeed when anything goes wrong in the very first generation; but you in the bar, there, you're totally convinced that it will. And are you prepared to say that every mental retard is the

55

product of an incestuous union? You'd better not, or you'll hurt the feelings of some pretty nice people. That's a tragedy that can happen to anybody, and I doubt there's any more chance of it between related parents than there is with anyone else.

"But you still don't see the funniest ... or maybe it's just the oddest part of that thing you know that just ain't so. Sex is a pretty popular topic on most worlds. Almost every aspect of it that is ever mentioned has nothing to do with procreation. For every mention of pregnancy or childbirth, I'd say there are hundreds which deal only with the sex act itself. But mention incest, and the response always deals with offspring. Always! To consider and discuss a pleasure or love relationship between blood relatives, you've apparently got to make some sort of special mental effort that nobody, anywhere, seems able to do easily—some not at all."

"I have to admit I never made it. But then—what *is* wrong with incest, with or without pregnancy?"

"Aside from moral considerations, you mean. The moral consideration is that it's a horrifying thought, and it's a horrifying thought because it always has been. Biologically speaking, I'd say there's nothing wrong with it. Nothing. I'd go even further, with Dr. Phelvelt—ever hear of him?"

"I don't think so."

"He was a biological theorist who could get one of his books banned on worlds that had never censored anything before—even on worlds which had science and freedom of research and freedom of speech as the absolute keystones of their whole structure. Anyway, Phelvelt had a very special kind of mind, always ready to take the next step no matter where it is, without insisting that it's somewhere where it isn't. He thought well, he wrote well, and he had a vast amount of knowledge outside his speciality and a real knack for unearthing what he happened not to know. And he called that sexual tension between blood relatives a survival factor."

"How did he come to that?"

"By a lot of separate paths which came together in the same place. Everybody knows (this one *is* so!) that there are evolutionary pressures which make for changes in a species. Not much (before Phelvelt) had been written about stabilizing forces. But don't you see, inbreeding is one of them?"

"Not offhand, I don't."

"Well, look at it, man! Take a herd animal as a good example. The bull covers his cows, and when they deliver heifers and the heifers grow up, he covers them too. Sometimes there's a third and even fourth generation of them before he gets displaced by a younger bull. And all that while, the herd characteristics are purified and reinforced. You don't easily get animals with slightly different metabolisms which might tend to wander away from the feeding ground the others were using. You won't get high-bottom cows which would necessitate Himself bringing something to stand on when he came courting." Through Charli's shout of laughter he continued, "So there you have it—stabilization, purification, greater survival value—all resulting from the pressure to breed in."

"I see, I see. And the same thing would be true of lions or fish or tree toads, or—"

"Or any animal. A lot of things have been said about Nature, that she's implacable, cruel, wasteful and so on. I like to think she's—reasonable. I concede that she reaches that state cruelly, at times, and wastefully and all the rest. But she has a way of coming up with the pragmatic solution, the one that works. To build in a pressure which tends to standardize and purify a successful stage, and to call in the exogene, the infusion of fresh blood, only once in several generations—that seems to me most reasonable."

"More so," Charlie said, "than what we've always done, when you look at it that way. Every generation a new exogene, the blood kept churned up, each new organism full of pressures which haven't had a chance with the environment."

"I suppose," said Vorhidin, "you could argue that the incest taboo is responsible for the restlessness that pulled mankind out of the caves, but that's a little too simplistic for me. I'd have preferred a mankind that moved a little more slowly, a little more certainly, and never fell back. I think the ritual exogamy that made inbreeding a crime and 'deceased wife's sister' a law against incest is responsible for another kind of restlessness."

He grew very serious. "There's a theory that certain normal habit patterns should be allowed to run their course. Take the sucking reflex, for example. It has been said that infants who have been weaned too early plague themselves all their lives with oral activity—chewing on straws, smoking intoxicants in pipes, drinking out of bottle by preference, nervously manipulating the lips, and so on. With that as an analogy, you may look again at the restlessness of mankind all through his history. Who but a gaggle of frustrates, never in their lives permitted all the ways of love within the family, could coin such a concept as 'motherland' and give their lives to it and for it? There's a great urge to love Father, and another to topple him. Hasn't humanity set up its beloved Fathers, its Big Brothers, loved and worshiped and given and died for them, rebelled and killed and replaced them? A lot of them richly deserved it, I concede, but it would have been better to have done it on its own merits and not because they were nudged by a deep-down, absolutely sexual tide of which they could not speak because they had learned that it was unspeakable.

"The same sort of currents flow within the family unit. So-called 'sibling rivalry' is too well known to be described, and the frequency of bitter quarreling between siblings is, in most cultures and their literature, a sort of cliché. Only a very few psychologists have dared to put forward the obvious explanation that, more often than not, these frictions are inverted love feelings, well salted with horror and guilt. It's a pattern that makes conflict between siblings all but a certainty, and it's a problem which, once stated, describes its own solution. . . . Have you ever read Vexworth? No? You should—I think you'd find him fascinating. Ecologist; in his way quite as much of a giant as Phelvelt."

"Ecologist—that has something to do with life and environment, right?"

"Ecology has *everything to* do with life and environment; it studies them as reciprocals, as interacting and mutually controlling forces. It goes without saying that the main aim and purpose of any life form is optimum survival; but 'optimum survival' is a meaningless term without considering the environment in which it has to happen. As the environment changes, the organism has to change its ways and means, even its basic design. Human beings are notorious for changing their environment, and in most of our history in most places, we have made these changes without ecological considerations. This is disaster, every time. This is overpopulation, past the capabilities of producing food and shelter enough. This is the rape of irreplaceable natural resources. This is the contamination of water supplies. And it is also the twisting and thwarting of psychosexual needs in the emotional environment.

"Vexvelt was founded by those two, Charli—Phelvelt and Vexworth—and is named for them. As far as I know it is the only culture ever devised on ecological lines. Our sexual patterns derive from the ecological base and are really only a very small part of our structure. Yet for that one aspect of our lives, we are avoided and shunned and pretty much unmentionable."

It took a long time for Charli to be able to let these ideas in, and longer for him to winnow and absorb them. But all the while he lived surrounded by beauty and fulfillment, by people, young and old, who were capable of total concentration on art and learning and building and processing, people who gave to each other and to their land and air and water just a little more than they took. He finished his survey largely because he had started it; for a while he was uncertain of what he would do with it.

When at length he came to Vorhidin and said he wanted to stay on Vexvelt, the big man smiled, but he shook his head. "I know you want to, Charli—but do you?"

59

"I don't know what you mean." He looked out at the dark bole of one of the Vexveltian poplars; Tyng was there, like a flower, an orchid. "It's more than that," said Charli, "more than my wanting to be a Vexveltian. You need me."

"We love you," Vorhidin said simply. "But—need?"

"If I went back," said Charli Bux, "and Terratu got its hands on my survey, what do you think would become of Vexvelt?"

"You tell me."

"First Terratu would come to trade, and then others, and then others; and then they would fight each other, and fight you . . . you need someone here who knows this, really knows it, and who can deal with it when it starts. It will start, you know, even without my survey; sooner or later someone will be able to do what I did—a shipment of feldspar, a sheet of pure metal. They will destroy you."

"They will never come near us."

"You think not. Listen: no matter how the other worlds disapprove, there is one force greater: greed."

"Not in this case, Charli. And this is what I want you to be able to understand, all the way down to your cells. Unless you do, you can never live here. We are shunned, Charli. If you had been born here, that would not matter so much to you. If you throw in your lot with us, it would have to be a total commitment. But you should not make such a decision without understanding how completely you will be excluded from everything else you have ever known."

"What makes you think I don't know it now?"

"You say we need defending. You say other-world traders will exploit us. That only means you don't understand. Charli: listen to me. Go back to Terratu. Make the strongest presentation you can for trade with Vexvelt. See how they react. Then you'll know—then you can decide."

"And aren't you afraid I might be right, and because of me, Vexvelt will be robbed and murdered?"

And Vorhidin shook his big head, smiling, and said, "Not one bit, Charli Bux. Not one little bit."

So Charli went back, and saw (after a due delay) the Archive Master, and learned what he learned, and came out and looked about him at his home world and, through that, at all the worlds like it; and then he went to the secret place where the Velveltian ship was moored, and it opened to him. Tyng was there, Tamba, and Vorhidin. Charli said, "Take me home."

In the last seconds before they took the Drive jump, and he could look through the port at the shining face of Terratu for the last time in his life, Charli said, "Why? Why? How did Human beings come to hate this one thing so much that they would rather die insane and in agony than accept it? How did it happen, Vorhidin"

"I don't know," said the Vexveltian.

Afterword:

And now you know what sort of a science fiction story this is, and perhaps something about science fiction stories that you didn't know before.

I have always been fascinated by the human mind's ability to think itself to a truth, and then to take that one step more (truly the basic secret of all human progress) and the inability of so many people to learn the trick. Case in point: "We mean to get that filth off the newsstands and out of the bookstores." Ask why, and most such crusaders will simply point at the "filth" and wonder that you asked. But a few will take one step more: "Because youngsters might get their hands on it." That satisfies most, but ask: "And suppose they do?" a still smaller minority will think it through to: "Because it's bad for them." Ask again: "In what way is it bad for them?" and a handful can reach this: "It will arouse them." By now you've probably run out of crusaders, but if there are a couple left, ask them, "How does being aroused harm a child?" and if you can get them to take that one more step, they will have to take it out of the area of emotional conviction and into the area of scientific research. Such studies are avilable, and invariably they show that such arousement is quite harmless—indeed, there is something abnormal about anyone who is not or cannot be so roused. The only possible harm that can result comes not from the sexual response itself but from the guilt-making and punitive attitude of the social environment—most of all that part of it which is doing the crusading.

Casting about for some more or less untouched area in which to exercise this one-step-more technique, I hit on this one. That was at least twenty years ago, and I have had to wait until now to find a welcome for anything so unsettling. I am, of course, very grateful. I hope the yarn starts some fruitful argument.

What a torturous and plotful genesis! I think, over all, the haunt was my desperate desire to give you the very best I could, as close as possible to your purpose in the anthology, a feeling inflamed by the news I got from Mills at one point that you had been bitterly disappointed by some of the submissions you had received, hence my desire to make up to you other people's defalcations. All this overlaid on a series of shattering personal experiences which included a pretty complete breakdown on September 4th and a very difficult (though highly successful) rebuilding process afterward. Your story is the first in a long, long time, and as such is especially meaningful to me; I hope it is to you too.

Let's see, that Saturday, the twelfth, was the third day of three days and nights I had been slogging away at it, and at last I had it going the way I wanted to. And it seems I have these good kind friends whom we will call Joe and Selma (because I have the feeling—very strong— that you will meet them one day). And they are close and helpful and admiring (and admired) friends and they were with me all the way in my struggle, and they live in Kingston. When noon (Saturday) came and went they were here running coffee and more or less shouting encouragement, and they said never mind missing the last mail at Woodstock, they'd stick around until it was finished and run it into the central post office in Kingston where it would get off even late Saturday night. Betimes Selma had to leave but Joe stuck around. 'Long about six Selma called to find out how it was going because now their

own affairs were pressing: Joe had to take a bus to Stroudsburg where he would spend a week. He said for her to pack
for him, he'd be in in plenty of time. Finally I was done and
he grabbed the envelopes (one to Ashmead and one to you)
and jumped in his car and beat it. I was so bushed I couldn't
sleep and spent almost the whole night glassy-eyed; when
you called the next day I was something like delirious.

Comes—what was it, Thursday? I was more normal and
biting nails over how much you might have liked or hated
the story so called you, to find to my very real horror that
you didn't have it. Events here had been sort of complex as
well: my wife has gone to Mexico and I have the four kids to
ride herd on. So anyway when I hung up on you I called
Ashmead and found he hadn't gotten the ms. either, and sat
there trying to find an alternative to going right out of my
mind. I felt a little like the guy in the story talking about
what "They" were doing to him. Then I called Selma and
told her and she just didn't believe it. She said she'd call
back. She phoned Stroudsburg and asked Joe and Joe was
just as horrified. Seems he'd arrived home that Saturday just
in time to throw on his traveling suit and be driven to the
bus. He thought she mailed it and she thought he mailed it.
So *where was it?*

I got into my car and drove to their house and she was in
what I can euphemistically call a State. And thank the Lord
for that because taking care of her State kept me from going
into one of my own. It must have hit us both in the same
instant because we practically cracked our heads together
jumping up to look in their car, and there were the effing
envelopes, with all the red and white hurry-up stickers all
over them, slid down between the right front seat back and
thence under the seat. I can even reconstruct their exact
trajectory. Joe's big and long-legged and Selma's a little bit
of a thing, and that Saturday night he ran out of my house
with the envelopes and put them on the seat beside him and
they slid back. Then when she drove him to the bus she slid
the seat forward and down they went underneath. Anyway I
made her promise not to commit suicide until after she

63

talked to me again and then maybe we'd do it together, and scooted back to Woodstock where I knew I'd catch an out-going mail.

All of which, being the truth, is too incredible for anyone's fiction book, and is not intended for the uses you said you wanted to put some material to in the book. I'm a little hazy about what exactly it was you did say but it was something to the effect that you wanted a bio (oh yes, I recall saying that the very idea gives me amnesia) and some words about the circumstances that produced the story. All right, I'll try to do both: see attached.

Anyway, Harlan, whether or not you like the story I'm glad you asked me and I'm glad I did it. It broke a lot of kinds of ice. I'm back at my *Playboy* story and will at long last be firing yarns at them regularly. I've reread the story twice and once thought it was dreadful and once thought it was wonderful. It has a kind of structure I've never used before; usually I employ one "angle" character who alone thinks and feels and remembers, and with whom the reader identifies, while everyone else *acts* angry or *says* sorrowful things or has no memories unless he says them aloud. But in this one I (more or less) stayed in the minds of minor charac-ters and watched the protagonist through their eyes. Also that trick of self-interruption in italics is one I shall polish and perfect and use again. . . . What I'm trying to say is that you put the tools back in my hands they feel very good. So thanks. Even if you don't like it. If that's the case I'll give you back your advance. I'm working again and can say that and mean it.

WHAT HAPPENED TO AUGUSTE CLAROT?

Introduction to

WHAT HAPPENED TO AUGUSTE CLAROT?

I have nothing to say about Larry Eisenberg. Except that he
ought to be put away. I have nothing to say about this *thing*
that follows except for buying it *I* ought to be put away. And
if you break up at it as much as I did when I read it, then
you ought to be put away, because the damned thing makes
no sense, and I don't care if I *did* try to reject it seventeen
times, and I don't care if Larry Ashmead at Doubleday got
the same reaction and said go ahead and buy it, because
everyone knows Ashmead should have been put away years
ago!

Of himself, Eisenberg has this to say: "I've been selling
since 1958, first humor, then science fiction, then humorous
science fiction. My 'Dr. Belzov's Kasha Oil Diet' (a guide for
the fat) appeared in *Harper's*. 'The Pirokin Effect' (in which
I prove there are Jews on Mars) is in Judith Merril's tenth
annual of *The Year's Best SF*. Around July 1966, *Limericks
for the Loo,* a collection of original bawdy limericks (co-
authored by George Gordon), was published in England.
Games People Shouldn't Play (same co-author) was published in America in November 1966. To support my wife
and two children, I do research in bio-medical electro-
nics."

A likely story, indeed! And for those who may ask why
such a piece of *dreck* as what follows should get into a book
of "dangerous visions", let me assure you that its convincing
everyone who's read it that it *should* be here makes it the
most dangerous thing since Typhoid Mary. You hold him
down— I'll call the fuzz.

WHAT HAPPENED TO AUGUSTE CLAROT?

By Larry Eisenberg

(Who among us has not speculated on the whereabouts of Judge Crater? In Paris, the disappearance of Auguste Clarot caused an equally large splash.)

When I was summoned posthaste to the topsy turvy office of Emile Becque, savage editor of *L'Expresse*, I knew in my bones that an assignment of extraordinary dimensions awaited me. Becque glared at me as I entered, his green-tinted eyeshade slanted forward like an enormous bill.

We sat there, neither of us saying a word, for Becque is a strong believer in mental telepathy. After several moments I had gathered nothing but waves of hatred for a padded expense account and then, all at once, I knew. It was *l'affaire Clarot*. I leaped to my feet crying out, "I will not let you down, Emile," and stumbled (almost blinded by tears) out of his office.

It was an intriguing assignement and I could hardly believe it had fallen to me. The disappearance of Auguste Clarot, Nobel-prizewinning chemist, some fifteen years earlier, had thrown all of Paris into a turmoil. Even my mother, a self-centered bourgeoise given to surreptitious squeezing of tomatoes to reduce their price, had remarked to me that the Earth could hardly have swallowed up so eminent a scientist.

On a hunch, I went to see his wife, Madame Ernestine Clarot, a formidable woman with a black mustache and pre-eminent bosom. She received me with dignity, camomile tea, and a crepe-fringed portrait of her husband. I tried to trick her into spilling the beans by alluding to rumors that Clarot had gone to Buenos Aires with a *poulet* from Montmartre. Although her eyes filled with tears at this egregious insult, Madame Ernestine quietly defended her husband's honor. I

68

flushed to the roots, apologized a thousand times, and even offered to fight a duel with anyone she might choose, but she would not spare me the pain of my humiliation.

Later, at the Café Pere-Mere, I discussed the matter with Marnay, charming, insouciant, but completely unreliable. He told me, on his honor, that he could find out for me (at a price) where Clarot was. I knew he was lying and he knew that I knew he was lying, but on sadistic impulse I accepted his offer. He blanched, drained his pernod at a gulp, and began to drum with furious fingers on the table top. It was evident that he now felt honor bound to find Clarot but did not know how to do it.

I bade Marnay a courteous adieu and left the Café Pere-Mere. So distracted was Marnay that he did not notice that the check was unpaid until I was almost out of sight. I ignored his frenzied semaphoring and struck up a temporary acquaintance with a lovely young maiden who was patrolling the Boulevard Sans Honneur.

In the morning, when I awoke, she had fled with my wallet containing, among other things, five hundred new francs and a list of aphrodisiacs which I had purchased from a gypsy. I had the very devil of a time with the concierge, who did not entertain the truth of my story for a single moment. He broke into violent abuse as I delineated what had occurred and began to belabor me about the neck and arms with a chianti bottle from which, *hélas*, he had removed the straw covering.

I sat on the curb, black and blue, penniless and at my wit's end as to how I might proceed. I could not go back to Emile Becque and tell him how I had been duped. Honor forbade so humiliating a course. But Fate in the guise of an American tourist's lost credit card intervened. Within hours I had wined and dined sumptuously, having outfitted myself to the nines at Manchoulette's exclusive haberdashery.

I inhaled the bracing winelike air of Paris at twilight and stood there, surveying the twinkling buttocks of energetic women hastening to affairs of the heart. All at once I saw an enormous Chinese staggering under a terrible burden of laundry. He winked at me and thrust the bundle into my unsuspecting hands, toppling me to the ground. When I had arisen, kicking and struggling to free myself of the cloying cloth, he had vanished into a nearby kiosk.

I stared at the bundle, terrified at the prospect of what it might contain, but at last I summoned up my nerve and loosened the double knots. There was nothing within but four undershorts and eleven dirty shirts with two collars that needed turning. A written note within, almost painful in its intensity, implored the avoidance of starch in the under-shorts.

As I mulled over the secret meaning of this event, Marnay appeared before me like a wraith materializing out of smoke. He glared at me, his eyes laced with the most curious red lines, held up a white embossed card and then fell forward, a victim (as I later learned) of an exploded bladder, a medical event last recorded over a century earlier.

I picked up the card and waved its dull white edge under my nose. There was at once a heady and yet repellent fragrance wafted toward me. The card itself bore the name A. Systole, 23 Rue de Daie. Easing the corpse under a bush of eglantine where some venturesome dog would surely discover it before morning, I made my way to the residence of Monsieur Systole. It was, I found, a dark structure of brownstone, no more than forty feet in height but still kept spick and span by a thorough and constant owner.

I stepped up to the gargoyle knocker just as a small poodle passing along the sidewalk turned and snarled at me in the most unfriendly manner. I have always prided myself on an uncanny rapport with poodles and I was quite taken aback by the sheer nastiness of this neurotic creature. I rapped the knocker once, twice, ever so gently but nonetheless firmly because the poodle's leash was frayed and might give way under his insistent tugging.

A florid face appeared behind a sliding mahogany panel, a face too well fed and too well lived. One of the enormous eyes winked at me and then the door swung wide and I was assisted in by means of strong fingers tugging at my elbow.

Later, over a flaming anisette, Clarot, for it was indeed he, told me everything.

"You have seen my wife?" he said, nodding encouragingly at me.

"I certainly have," I said apologetically.

"Then you can see why I skipped the roost," said Clarot. "But how was I to live? To deliver myself to a chemist's shop would have meant certain exposure. I decided to turn my efforts toward a venture at once creative and lucrative, yet something not requiring an outlay of too many francs."

"You succeeded, of course," I cried, unable to contain myself.

"Handsomely," said Clarot. He rose to his feet and stretched his bloated frame like a monstrous cat. "Come after me and you shall see," he said boastfully.

I followed his limping form through room after room of Chinese modern, averting my eyes from some of the more extreme examples. Below, in the basement, was the most ramshackle of all laboratories with broken retorts strewn about, an idle Bunsen burner lying on its side, and a mortar of solidified chemicals with a pestle imbedded in the mass.

"It was within this hallowed dungeon that I discovered the aromatic which incenses all canines," said Clarot. "One whiff and the mildest of lap dogs becomes a raging monster, determined to attack me and tear me to bits."

"Of what earthly use could such an aromatic be?" I cried.

Clarot placed his finger to one side of his nose, sagely.

"It gets me bitten over and over again," he said, smiling crookedly.

"Bitten? Merciful God!"

"You forget the law, my good fellow. I am judicious, of course, and permit my permeated trouser leg within range of only the tiniest of dogs. Nevertheless, some of the little beggars bite like the very devil."

He leaned over and massaged a shinbone thoughtfully.

"But the owners," he resumed, "settle generously at the

71

threat of a lawsuit. At least most of them do. I live quite handsomely on the proceeds as you can see."

"Then the odor on your card?"

"Was *aromatique Clarot*."

"You won't mind if all this appears in *L'Expresse*?" I said, for every good reporter worth his salt wishes to protect his sources.

"Mind?" said Clarot airily. "Why on earth should I? As we chatted here, I liberally doused your trouser legs with my aromatic. When I press the chartreuse button on this wall, it will release my hypertensive bloodhounds, who will proceed to tear you into very tiny bits."

It was a gross blunder on Clarot's part. Soft living had put him terribly out of condition and it took me but a short moment of struggling and kicking to divest him of his trousers and place my own pair on his naked legs. I then pressed the chartreuse button and stepped out of the room, ignoring Clarot's cries for mercy.

As I left the brownstone house I was struck at the base of the skull by a nearsighted *cocotte*, betrayed by Clarot and mistaking me for him because I wore his fawn-colored trousers. Her blow sent me to the curb where I narrowly averted being run over by a blue Funke, a British sports car.

I lay in the charity ward at L'Hôpital des Trois Balles, amnesiac for over three months. My memory restored, I tottered over to the office of *L'Expresse* and discovered that Emile Becque had been garroted by the huge Chinese, who had misread his telepathic silence in the face of demands that he pay his delinquent laundry bill.

The new editor, a sullen Breton, listened to my halting explanation with unflagging attention. When I had finished, he escorted me to the door and placed his iron-tipped toe to my rump, enabling me to leave at an extraordinary burst of speed.

I had no choice but to seek out Madame Clarot once more. After a short but impassioned courtship, she joined me at my apartment over the Tavern of the Four Griffins. She no longer sips camomile tea and it is with considerable nostalgia that I look back upon the day when she greeted me with cold sobriety. But then, I owe *that* much to Clarot.

Afterword:

It may be that, unknown to myself, "Auguste Clarot" is riddled with displaced symbolism. Perhaps I can't cope with escalated brotherhood in Vietnam, equal but separate mistreatment for men of color, and bulging clichés mouthed in high and low places. "Auguste Clarot" was a joyful catharsis for me and, I hope, for the reader.

ERSATZ

Introduction to
ERSATZ:

The act of collaboration, between writers as very definitely
opposed to the act of collaboration between lovers, is only
satisfying when it is ended, never while it is being performed. It has been my annoyance and pleasure to have
collaborated with perhaps half a dozen writers in the eleven
years I've been a professional. (I have never been a lover of
any of them.) With Avram Davidson I wrote a Ring Lard-
neresque bit of tomfoolery so fraught with personal jokes
and literary references that I was compelled to write a
10,000-word article explaining the story, to accompany the
7,000-word fiction before it could be sold. Not unexpectedly,
the story was called "Up Christopher to Madness" and the
article was titled "Scherzo for Schizoids". With Huckleberry
Barkin I wrote a *Playboy* story of humorous seduction
(which I contend is a contradiction in terms) called "Would
You Do It for A Penny?" and with Robert Silverberg a
crime story called "Ship-Shape Pay-Off". I even wrote a
story with Budrys once.

But collaborating is generally a dismal chore, fraught with
such traps as conceptual disagreement, clash of styles, incipi-
ent laziness, verbosity, confusion and simple bad writing.
How Pratt & De Camp or Nordhoff & Hall did it, I will
never fully understand. Yet with two writers I have been
able to collaborate easily, and the products have been something more than either of us might have attained singly. The
first is Joe L. Hensley, who appears elsewhere in this book,
and of whom there is much to say; but in another place. The
second is Henry Slesar, of whom there is much to say here. I
am delighted at the opportunity to say these things, for they
have been in my mind many years, and since they verge on
being a poem of love, they are obviously not the kind of
thing one can say to a man's face.

(The concept of affection between men has been so emasculated—literally—that to display any sign of joy at the presence or companionship or understanding of another man is taken, by the yahoos, as a sure sign of faggotry. I choose not to dignify the implication, yet will state bluntly that I do not subscribe to the snide theory there is anything between Batman and Robin but big-brotherliness. Some folks just have a one-track gutter.)

I think the operable element in any successful collaboration is friendship. Based on respect and admiration and trust in the other man's morality, sense of craft and sense of fairness. To accept another writer's judgment on the form and direction of a story, one must first respect and admire what the other has done on his own. He must have paid his dues. Then, it must be unconsciously safe for one to go with the other man's instincts as to what the story is saying in larger terms, in terms of ethic and morality. Only then does one feel safe in allowing the unformed creation to be molded by other hands. And finally, by the extensions and implications of friendship, one knows the other man wants a unified whole, a product of *two* minds and individual talents, rather than one story that has been stolen from another man's store of minutiae. Yes, I think friendship must be present if the collaboration is to succeed. Henry Slesar and I have been friends for over ten years.

I first met Henry after a lecture I delivered at New York University in 1956. The presumption of me telling a class on creative writing how to function in the commercial arena, after only one year of professional work, was staggering. But apparently (Henry has told me many times) up till that time the class had been fed gross amounts of the usual literary horse manure, a great deal of theory culled from inept texts, but very little practical advice on how to sell what the class had written. Since I was a selling writer—for however short a time, at that time—I felt justified only in telling them where to get the best buck, and how to keep from being shafted, rather than how to pick up the mantle of Chekhov. (Comment: as demonstrated by the preponderance of writers in this volume *alone*, memorable writers are born, not trained. I believe this firmly. Oh, it's possible to learn how to handle the English language in a competent manner, it is even possible to learn how to plot like a computer. But that is something else: it is the difference between being an author and being a writer. The former get their names on books, the latter write. Of all the writing courses I have known—as class member, guest lecturer, auditor or interested listener—I have encountered only one that seemed to know where it was at. That was the series of classes given by Robert Kirsch at UCLA. He laid it on the line in the first ten minutes that, if they couldn't write already, they'd better sign up for another subject, because he was ready and able to teach them the superficialities, but the spark of creativity had to be there or they'd wind up merely masturbating. Born, not made, despite what the reading-fee agencies tell their poor befuddled victims.)

After the class, Henry and I got together many times. He was at that time creative director for the Robert W. Orr advertising agency. (Henry is the man who created the Life Saver advertisement that was merely a page of candies laid out in rows, with the inked-in words, "Don't lick this page." It was an award winner, and so is Henry.) But aside from Bix Beiderbecke records, Henry's driving urgency was for writing. I have never met a man who so wanted to set words on paper and who, from the very first, had such a sure, talented manner of so doing. Within the first year of his career he sold to *Ellery Queen's Mystery Magazine*, *Playboy* and over a dozen other top markets. We would get together of an evening, either in my tiny apartment on West Eighty-second Street off Amsterdam, or his sprawling residence overlooking West End Avenue, and after a few hours of chitchat between us and our wives (I was, at that juncture, married to Disaster Area No. 1), we would vanish into Henry's office and do a short story. Complete in one evening. Usually science fiction or detective stories: "The Kissing Dead", "Sob Story", "Mad Dog", "RFD No. 2", "The Man with the Green Nose". We worked well together, though not entirely rationally. Sometimes I would start with a title and a first paragraph, writing something so off-beat and peculiar that there was no place to go plot-wise. Or Henry would open the story and write a thousand words of devious plot threads, leaving off in mid-speech. Once in a while we plotted the whole thing out in advance. But whichever form or direction was used, we always got a salable story from the collaboration. We sold everything we ever wrote together. It was a parlor trick, a party game, a hobby that paid for itself in enjoyment and cigarette money.

Henry Slesar was born in 1927 in Brooklyn. He is the personification of quality and tact and honor in a field singularly spare in such qualities: he is an advertising man. He has been vice-president and creative director of three top New York agencies and is now president and CD of his own: Slesar & Kanzer, Inc., founded 1965. As a writer he has published over 600 stories, novels, etc., to such markets as *Playboy, Cosmopolitan, Diners Club Magazine,* all of the men's magazines, mystery magazines and most of the science fiction magazines. He has been anthologized fifty-five times, has written three novels including *The Gray Flannel Shroud* (Random House), which won the 1959 Mystery Writers of America Edgar as Best First Mystery Novel. He has had two short-story collections published, both introduced by Alfred Hitchcock, who looks with great favor on our Henry, who has written over sixty television scripts, many of which were for the Hitchcock half-hour and hour series. He has also written for *77 Sunset Strip, The Man from UNCLE, Run for Your Life* and half a dozen of the coveted high-paying pilot film assignments. He has written four motion pictures for Warner Bros.

Henry is married to one of the loveliest women any writer possesses—the O. in his pen name O. H. Leslie—and has one daughter—the Leslie of the pseudonym. They all live together in New York City, which is a pleasant arrangement.

The Henry Slesar story in this anthology is only 1100 words long. About half the length of this introduction, I now realize. There are two comments to be made on this bizarre fact. First, my admiration and friendship for Slesar know no bounds—not even the simple bounds of conversation of verbiage. The second is more important. Henry Slesar is a master of the short-story story. He can kill you with a line. He takes 1100 words to do what lesser writers would milk for 10,000 words. If there is a better short-story writer working in America today, I can't think of his name, and I've got a helluva memory.

ERSATZ

by Henry Slesar

There were sixteen hundred Peace Stations erected in the eighth year of the conflict, the contribution of the few remaining civilians on the American continent; sixteen hundred atomproofed shelters where the itinerant fighting man could find food, drink and rest. Yet Sergeant Tod Halstead, in five dreary months of wandering across the wastelands of Utah, Colorado, and New Mexico, had relinquished hope of finding even one. In his lead-lined aluminum armor he appeared to be a perfectly packaged war machine, but the flesh within the gleaming housing was weak and unwashed and weary of the lonely, monotonous task of seeking a friend to join or an enemy to kill.

He was a Rocket Carrier, Third Class, the rank signifying that it was his duty to be a human launching pad for the four hydrogen-headed rockets strapped to his back, their fuses to be ignited by a Rocket Carrier, Second Class, upon command and countdown by a Rocket Carrier, First Class. Tod had lost the other two thirds of his unit months before; one of them had giggled and slipped a bayonet in his throat; the other had been shot and killed by a sixty-year-old farm wife who was resisting his desperate, amorous advances.

Then early one morning, after he was certain that the

burst of light in the east was the sun and not the enemy's atomic fire, he trudged along a dusty road and saw beyond the shimmering waves of heat a square white building set amid a grove of naked gray trees. He stumbled towards it, and knew it was no mirage of the man-created desert, but a Peace Station. In its doorway a white-haired man with a Father Christmas face beckoned and smiled and helped him inside.

"Thank God," Tod said, falling into a chair. "Thank God. I'd almost given up . . ."

The jolly old man clapped his hands, and two young boys with hair like eagles' nests came running into the room. Like service station attendants, they set about him busily, removing his helmet, his boots, unhooking his weapons. They fanned him, chafed his wrists, put cool lotion on his forehead; a few minutes later, his eyes closed, and with sleep approaching, he was conscious of a gentle hand on his cheek, and woke to find his months-old beard gone.

"There now," the station manager said, rubbing his hands in satisfaction. "Feel better, soldier?"

"Much better," Tod said, looking about at the bare but comfortable room. "How does the war go with you, civilian?"

'Hard," the man said, no longer jolly. "But we do our best, serving the fighting men as we can. But relax, soldier; food and drink will be here soon. It won't be anything special; our ersatz supply is low. There's a new chemical beef we've been saving, you can have that. I believe it's made of wood bark, but it's not at all bad on the tongue."

"Do you have a cigarette?" Tod said.

He proffered a brown cylinder. "Ersatz, too, I'm afraid; treated wool fibers. But it burns, anyway."

Tod lit it. The acrid smoke seared his throat and lungs; he coughed, and put it out.

"I'm sorry," the station manager said sadly. "It's the best we have. Everything, everything is ersatz; our cigarettes, our food, our drink . . . the war goes hard with us all."

Tod sighed and leaned back. When the woman came out

of the doorway, bearing a tray, he sat up and his eyes were first for the food. He didn't even notice how lovely she was, how her ragged, near-transparent gown hugged her rounded breasts and hips. When she bent towards him, handing him a steaming bowl of strange-smelling broth, her blonde hair tumbled forward and brushed his cheek. He looked up and caught her eyes; they dropped shyly.

"You'll feel better after this," she said huskily, and made a movement with her body that dulled his appetite for food, created a different kind of hunger. It was four years since he had seen a woman like this. The war had taken them first, with bombs and radioactive dust, all the young women who remained behind while the men escaped to the comparative safety of battle. He dipped into the broth and found it vile, but he downed every drop. The wood-based beef was tough and chewy, but it was better than the canned rations he had grown accustomed to. The bread tasted of seaweed, but he slathered it with an oily rancid oleo and chewed great mouthfuls.

"I'm tired," he said at last. "I'd like to sleep."

"Yes, of course," the Peace Station manager said. "This way, soldier, come this way."

He followed him into a small windowless room, its only furniture a rusty metal cot. The sergeant dropped across its canvas mattress wearily, and the station manager closed the door quietly behind him. But Tod knew he wouldn't sleep, despite his sated stomach. His mind was too full, and his blood was streaming too fast through his veins, and the ache for the woman was strong in his body.

The door opened and she came in.

She said nothing. She came to the bed and sat beside him. She leaned over and kissed his mouth. "My name is Eleanora," she whispered, and he seized her roughly. "No, wait," she said, wriggling coyly out of his grasp. She got off the cot and went to the corner of the room.

He watched her slither out of her clothing. The blonde hair slipped as she pulled the dress over her head, and the curls hung at a crazy angle over her brow. She giggled, and put the wig back into position. Then she reached behind her and unhooked the brassiere; it dropped to the floor, revealing the flat slope of the hairy chest. She was about to remove the rest of her undergarments when the sergeant started to scream and run for the door; she reached out and held his arm and crooned words of love and pleading. He struck the creature with all the strength in his fist, and it fell to the floor, weeping bitterly, its skirt hoisted high on the muscular, hairy legs. The sergeant didn't pause to retrieve his armor or his weapons; he went out of the Peace Station into the smoky wasteland, where death awaited the unarmed and despairing.

Afterword:

"Ersatz" is a rejected story. It was returned to me by an editor who simply said, "Don't like the future-war stuff." He isn't the only one with the attitude. Several editors feel that future wars don't really constitute a "dangerous vision", and prefer their authors to steer clear of the subject. Atomic conflicts are "trite". Postatomic holocausts are "cliché". Armageddon is "overdone". In the world of fiction, at least, there is some opinion that our case of atomic jitters has been cured, and that readers would rather do without reminders of ruin and radiation. But the playing field of science fiction is the future, and the future has to be extrapolated from the ingredients of the present. And if you don't think that those ingredients of doom are still with us, your radio needs tubes, your prescription needs changing, and you have wax in your ears. Personally, I hope our authors, particularly the science fiction writers who have special privileges and talents, continue to barrage the world with fresh words on the subject, to make us continually afraid of what might be, and continually concerned with prevention and cure. To me, the most dangerous vision of all is the one that's rose-colored, and I'm grateful that the editor of this volume has spectacles of clear glass.

GO, GO, GO, SAID THE BIRD

Introduction to

GO, GO, GO, SAID THE BIRD:

To know Sonya Dorman is to love her, if you'll pardon the mickey-mouse on my part. Also, it might bug her husband Jerry, who has very powerful forearms, and with whom Sonya Dorman raises and shows Akitas (a kind of Japanese baby pony of a dog that looks as if it should want to tear out your jugular but generally only wants to slobber drool all over you in slaphappy friendliness) at their Parnassus Kennels in Stony Point, New York, which has got to be the most strictured syntax since Victor Hugo did a twenty-two-page sentence in *The Hunchback of Notre Dame,* which is the shape this sentence is in.

She writes, in reply to a request for autobiographical goodies: "My auto. story is so preposterous I hardly know what to tell you. I did not have a classical education. I went to private schools (progressive) in New England, with the result that I have very little education but am just crummy with culture. I grew up around horses but can't afford them now, which is why I raise and show Akitas— the perceptive dog for sensitive people—in between writing poems and stories. Have been a cook, receptionist, riding instructor, flamenco dancer and married. I like speculative fiction because I believe art and science should be lovers, not enemies or adversaries.

None of the foregoing, of course, will prepare you for the genuine horror and immediacy of the story kindly little Sonya has written. A story that can only be compared, and then only remotely, with the work of the late Shirley Jackson. It also says nothing about the substantial reputation she has acquired in the last few years as a contributor to magazines as various as *Cavalier, Galaxy, Redbook,* Damon Knight's excellent *Orbit I* anthology of originals, *The Satur-*

day Evening Whateveritis and *The Magazine of Fantasy &*
Science Fiction.

You can read Leight Brackett or Vin Packer or
C. L. Moore and think jeezus, the muscularity of the writing, and when you find out they are women, you say, jeezus,
they write like men, with strength. Or you read Zenna Hen-
derson and think, jeezus, she writes just like a woman, all
pastels. Or you can read Ayn Rand and think jeezus!

But that's another line of criticism.

But when you read Sonya Dorman you don't think of the
muscularity of male writing. You read it as written by a
woman, but there is no pretense. There is no attempt to
emulate the particular strengths of male writing. It is purely
female reasoning and attack, but it is *strong*. A special kind
of tensile strength. It is what is meant by something turned
out by a potent woman. It is a kind of writing *only* a woman
can do. Carol Emshwiller, who is elsewhere in this book, has
something like this strength, but most perfectly germinated
is S. Dorman's development. It deals with reality in the
unflinching way women *will* deal with it, when they are no
longer shucking themselves or those watching. And I submit
it is all the more teeth-clenching for the relentless truth it
proffers.

This is a memorable story, and provides merely one more
facet of the talent that writes under the drab by-line S. Dorman. It's a by-line you might watch for.

GO, GO, GO, SAID THE BIRD

by Sonya Dorman

Go, go, go, said the bird: human kind
Cannot bear very much reality.

T. S. Eliot

Seizing the shriek in her stained teeth, she ran away, in spite
of the voices crying after her from every crevice and glitter-

88

ing façade. Faces at the broken windows became a college of grins as she ran, still holding the shriek between her teeth, determined not to let it escape. Her heels ached from pounding down the concrete highways, leaping over cracks and gaps in what used to be the most traveled road in the country.

"Oh no, no," she sobbed as she ran.

Bindweed grasped her ankes and she tore it loose with frantic fingers and ran on.

Choices appeared at the roadside, the entrances to burrows, underground shanties. Once some thing flew down and landed near her, beckoning, but she shut her teeth on the writhing shriek and looked straight ahead, down the length of the cracked roadbed with its overgrown promenades at each side. She would continue on the obvious path, for fear of being lost beyond help.

"Here, chickie, here, chickie," called an old woman, beckoning, grinning, offering her a hidey-hole, perhaps at the expense of her hide, for she was still young, and succulent.

"No, no, no," she panted as she ran. For she was only thirty, and was unique, and to be eaten was all right, for people must exist, but to die was terrible. Plain and simple, she did not want to die. Not now, running for her life, and not ever, when her inevitable time came, but she was immediately concerned with now, and later on would have to take care of itself. Even as she ran, she began to tremble for later on, as if now weren't severe enough.

Think of it, she conversed in great gasps with herself, leaping over a crevasse where a southbound lane had split off from the main runway. Think of it, she insisted, scarcely having breath left but unable to control her mind, which was galloping faster than her weary legs.

I'm only thirty, I'm unique, there's no one in this world, this universe, who is me, with my memories:

Snapshot No. 1

It had snowed. She stood in the sagging doorway, bundled up for winter in her fur leggings, and waited for Marn. They would hunt some animal for the stewpot. She saw things in negative, according to the moonlight: white trees, dark snow pockets. A feather seemed to breathe near her.

"Hey, come on," Marn said, taking her by the shoulder, and they drifted like two dark flakes on to the powdered grass, toward the woods. "We'll smoke it," Marn said confidently, and the water ran into her mouth. The smokehouse was hot and dark, a womb out of which the good things were trundled for distribution. It was her good luck to be headman's woman. Her children were less cold and hungry. Still, she had a greasy feeling, somewhere, when she heard the cries of other children. Marn said it was because she was young.

Her furs had lateral stripes like those of a tiger. She was a headman's daughter, and wife of a headman. She was tall, educated, privileged, and at length on the sleeping skins she would burn like fat in Marn's fire.

"Come on, rest a wee," a young girl called to her, but she put on a burst of speed, for the girl's teeth were shining like daggers, and as she went, she sobbed to herself (saving her real breath for the running), No, I can't die, I'm not ready to. Oh no, no, and it was the same sound she had made that winter when:

Snapshot No. 2

The orchards had borne no fruit and the deer were famished. Back into the mountains withdrew all animals except those that were slaughtered where open water ran. By solstice there was no open water left. The fish slept at the bottom of the lake. Smelts would not rise to the cold, blue holes cut by the fishers. The leathers cracked and split on their feet, the chimney of the smokehouse stopped breathing, most of the fires were silent.

Into this famine was born her third child, with a bad foot. Holding him up in the air, Marn said, "He is not good," and snapped his neck.

"Oh no," she cried, holding her swollen abdomen with both palms and feeling the blood run down her thighs. "No, no," she cried to the headman, her man, for nine months in the hot dark, waiting, only to come to this? We are all going to come to this?

Marn handed the dead baby to the old woman, who took him out to the smokehouse. She lay in her blood and tears, crying, for the sizzled fat on the baby. Then the eyes dried, hers, and the baby's, in the fire smoke, and she felt it was all more than could be asked of any woman.

When the broken concrete split into a fork, one side going south, one west, she would have paused, to determine her advantage, but at the crotch of the fork two youngsters arrived with knives.

She wanted more than anything to stop and rest. There was no alternatives offered her; either she must run and run, or she must stop and be killed. She couldn't prevent her mind from balancing one against the other, even while she knew it was no choice to make.

"Catch your breath," the youngsters jeered at her, and she chose the west road without thinking. One of them hurled a chancy knife after her, which split open the skin of her shoulder. Ignoring the pale blood which poured down, she went on. I can't die now, she thought. I'm not ever going to die. I am the only I in this world. She knew there was too much of her to be lost, much which could never be anyone else, and it was all precious and irreplaceable. Why didn't they realize how important it was for her to survive? She contained:

Snapshot No. 3

After the hard winter, the iron world split open and flowers came up. It was so astonishing. She passed the place where Marn's last bone was buried (only a headman would have his skull buried, intact, the jaws still hinged as if speaking to his community) and went down to the riverbank where the children were bathing. Her Neely stood tall this spring. In spite of food shortages over the winter, he had filled out. At least Daddyporridge had helped to nourish him, and give him this spring strength.

"Ah, spring," said a lazy voice. There was Tichy, under the willow. He might have been next headman, but was too lazy, and more likely destined for the smokehouse if he didn't mind himself. Yet several community members had discovered he was quicker and livelier than predicted, and Marn himself had died under Tichy's hammer.

"Oh yes, it certainly is spring," she said, walking very slowly, approaching him with great care. For if he had disposed so quickly of her man, and was idling here, watching her son, what next?

Tichy put out an unclenched hand toward her, and she was surprised to take it and find it so warm. Then another surprise followed, for he gave a quick, skillful pull, and she fell full length on his body.

"Oh, no," she said, half smothered in his chin whiskers. "No, Tichy," for his teeth were at her and she didn't know, caught in his arms and legs, whether she was going to be loved or eaten or one at a time, or why.

"Hell yes," Tichy said. "After all, why not?"

He was reasonable. He let her have the best blanket in his hardwood hut, and when she couldn't find enough flavoring for the stew in the pot, he ate it anyway, without beating her.

Desperately holding the shriek, that siren to call them all out after her, between her teeth, she went on and on, breath rasping in her worn throat.

She would get back to Tichy. She was not going to die. There couldn't be anything in the world that really demanded her death, could there? Neely had taken the daughter of Gancho, a dark, low-browed girl with a peculiar sense of rightness. Not bad, she thought. Very good for Neely. I must get back before she has the baby. Who else will help her? She mustn't have the first one alone, only I can help her. I am needed, really, truly, I am needed very much. She'll be all alone, because:

Snapshot No. 4

Toward fall, when not even the warmest rains brought up another spear of wild asparagus, Neely and Tichy had a fight on the north slope of the dead orchard. Tichy gave Neely a blow with his hammer which knocked the young one over and might have done for him. Yet Neely got up on his feet once more, with his lips writhen back from his dark gums, showing his five teeth. Watching from the roof of the hardhut, she saw Neely rise up on his toes and split open Tichy's skull.

"That's my son!" she cried at the top of her lungs.

Then Neely brought home the dark girl, who snorted when he made love to her, and never got tired, and kept the floor swept. It was all right to have another woman in the hut, and especially a woman who understood the right and traditional. She was, after all, a headman's daughter, and not to be displaced.

"Gotcha!" yelled a woman, almost falling on her, as she swerved along an embankment. She kicked the woman in the belly and heard the anguished groan as she ran on.

"No, you haven't," she gasped, not just to the groaning woman, but to all of them, to the world. What made her think she would get back to Tichy, who was dead, skull and all? The grandchildren would welcome her. They were good children, lean and hard as nuts, the likeness of Neely. They'd be glad to see her, who would dandle them, feed them special treats, stir the stewpot for the dark girl while she and Neely went hunting. If the deer ever came back she would make them a roast. The drought had been so bad all summer the snakes had come. First the copperheads, with their smell of garlic in the mating season, like brown worms on the stones of the old world. Then the rattlers, with their hysterical warning which came too late. Poisoned flesh was worse

93

than no flesh. Moreover, a snakebitten person was generally dismembered before the poison had a chance to spread.

Now as she ran she saw landmarks of home which echoed in her mind. The country became happily familiar, for she had hunted here, with Marn, and then with Tichy. She wasn't going to die, not this time, not now, she would of course continue, for she was she, unique, full, splendid!

"I gotcha!" someone screamed in her ear, and she felt the blow, shattering her, and lay stunned by the side of the road, her muscles still running. The snapshots began to flicker in her mind; seasons of the year, people she had known, her sons, her daughters, herself above all, the only one, the only I am I in all the world of stars.

"No, no," she moaned as the man raised the ax over her forehead.

"Oh yes, yes," he said grinning with pleasure. Behind him the rest of the hunting party appeared. It was Neely with the dark girl, and two lean children.

"Neely," she screamed. "Save me. I'm your mother."

Neely grinned too, and said, "We're all hungry."

The ax fell, breaking her pictures into pieces, and they fell like snowflakes to the ground, where a little dust rose up and began to slowly settle. The small children began to squabble over the thumb bones.

Afterword:

Perhaps I wrote the story because sometimes that's the way the world seems, or perhaps I hope that when my daughter's generation grows up it won't need or want to run for its life, or perhaps because in the seventeenth century, Jeremy Taylor wrote: ". . . when it is enquired whether such a person be a good man or no, the meaning is not what does he believe, or what does he hope, but what he loves." Amen.

THE HAPPY BREED

Introduction to

THE HAPPY BREED

This is the second of two stories I bought from writers whose work I did not know. It came in, one of a pair, from Robert Mills, my own agent. The note accompanying it said simply, "You'll like the way he thinks." That, in the trade, is called the undersell. When I was younger, when I worked in a bookstore on Times Square, an area where the hard sell was invented (or at least perfected), I used the undersell—or "mush" as it is called—with only two items. The first was with a book called *The Alcoholic Women*. It was ostensibly a volume of case histories intended for medical students, dealing with psychiatric aberrations attendant on female alcoholism. But there was one passage, on page 73, if I recall properly, that was extremely steamy. Something about lesbianism, rather graphically reported by the lushed female herself. When we would get in one of the moist-palmed salesmen from Mashed Potato Falls, Wyoming, in search of "lively reading" (because he couldn't pick up some bimbo in a bar for the evening's release), we would conduct him to the rear of the shop and hold up the book. It invariably fell open on Page 73. "Here, read anywhere," we would say, jamming his nose, like a lump of silly putty, right onto that paragraph. His eyes would water. A pair of poached eggs. He would always buy the book. We stiffed them fourteen bucks for the thing. (I think it's in paperback now, for about half a buck, but them was in the days before Fanny Hill.) Page 73 held the only really "lively" action in the book. The rest was a jungle of electroshock therapy and stomach pumping. But the mush worked marvelously.

The other item was a twelve-inch Italian stiletto in the knife case. When a customer asked for a blade, I would unlock the case and pull out all that steel. I would hold it up, closed, to show it had no switch button on it. Then I would carelessly flip my wrist in a hard, downward movement, and the blade would snap open, quivering. It would usually be about two inches under the customer's tie knot. Eyes bulge. Poached eggs. Et cetera. Seven-buck sale. Every time.

The only times you can use the mush with any degree of assurance are the times you know for damn dead certain you've got a winning item, something that won't let go of them. Bob Mills was smart to use the mush on me. He knew he had a winner. John T. Sladek's "The Happy Breed" is a helluva story.

Sladek was born in Iowa on 12/15/37, and attended the University of Minnesota 19 years later as student No. 449731. He studied mechanical engineering, then English literature. He left school to work (Social Security No. 475-38-5320) as a technical writer, bar waiter and for the Great Northern Railway as switchman No. 17728. He thumbed through Europe with passport No. D776097 until he found himself standing in a soup line at Saint-Severin in Paris. He worked as a draftsman in New York, then returned to Europe. He is now living in England, registered as Alien No. E538368. He has been published in *New Worlds, Escapade, Ellery Queen's Mystery Magazine* and elsewhere. He has just finished his first novel of speculative fiction, *The Reproductive System.*

The only mushy thing about Sladek or his story is his lousy head for figures. Carry on.

THE HAPPY BREED

by John T. Sladek

A.D. 1987

"I don't know," said James, lifting himself from the cushions scattered like bright leaves on the floor. "I can't say that I'm really, you know, *happy*. Gin or something phony?"

"Aw, man, don't give me decisions, give me drink," said Porter. He lay across the black, tufted chaise that he called James's "shrink couch."

"Gin it is, then." James thumbed a button, and a martini glass, frosty and edible-looking, slid into the wall niche and filled. Holding it by the stem, he passed it to Porter, then raised his shaggy brows at Marya.

"*Nada*," she said. She was sprawled in a "chair", really a piece of sculpture, and one of her bare feet had reached out to touch Porter's leg.

James made himself a martini and looked at it with distaste. If you broke this glass, he thought, it would not leave any sharp edges to, say, cut your wrists on.

"What was I saying? Oh—I can't say I'm really *happy*, but then I'm not—uh—"

"Sad?" volunteered Marya, peering from under the brim of her deerstalker.

"Depressed. I'm not depressed. So I must be happy," he finished, and hid his confusion behind the glass. As he sipped, he looked her over, from her shapely calves to her ugly brown deerstalker. Last year at this time she'd been wearing a baseball cap, blue with gold piping. It was easy to remember it, for this year all the girls in the Village were wearing baseball caps. Marya Katyovna was always ahead of the pack, in her dress as well as in her paintings.

"How do you know you're happy?" she said. "Last week I thought I was happy too. I'd just finished my best work, and I tried to drown myself. The Machine pulled the drain. Then I was sad."

"Why did you try to kill yourself?" James asked, trying to keep her in focus.

"I had this idea that after a perfect work the artist should be destoyed. Dürer used to destroy the plates of his engravings after a few impressions."

"He did it for money," muttered Porter.

"All right then, like that architect in Arabia. After he created his *magnum opus*, the Sultan had him blinded, so he couldn't do any cheap copies. See what I mean? An artist's

99

life is supposed to lead toward his masterpiece, not away from it."

Porter opened his eyes and said, "Exist! The end of life is life. Exist, man, that's all you gotta do."

"That sounds like cheap existentialism," she snarled, withdrawing her foot. "Porter, you are getting more and more like those damned Mussulmen."

Porter smiled angrily and closed his eyes.

It was time to change the subject.

"Have you heard the one about the Martian who thought he was an Earthman?" James said, using his pleasant-professional tone. "Well, he went to his psychiatrist—"

As he went on with the joke, he studied the two of them. Marya was no worry, even with her dramatic suicide attempts. But Porter was a mess.

O. Henry Porter was his full adopted name, after some minor earlier writer. Porter was a writer, too, or had been. Up to a few months ago, he'd been considered a genius—one of the few of the twentieth century.

Something had happened. Perhaps it was the general decline in reading. Perhaps there was an element of self-defeat in him. For whatever reason, Porter had become little more than a vegetable. Even when he spoke, it was in the cheapest clichés of the old "hip" of twenty years ago. And he spoke less and less.

Vaguely, James tied it in with the Machines. Porter had been exposed to the Therapeutic Environment Machines longer than most, and perhaps his genius was entangled with whatever they were curing. James had been too long away from his practice to guess how this was, but he recalled similar baby/bathwater cases.

" 'So that's why it glows in the dark,' " James finished. As he'd expected, Marya laughed, but Porter only forced a smile, over and above his usual smirk of mystical bliss.

"It's an old joke," James apologized.

"You are an old joke," Porter enunciated. "A head-shrinker without no heads to shrink. What the hell do you do all day?"

"What's eating you?" said Marya to the ex-writer. "What brought you up from the depths?"

James fetched another drink from the wall niche. Before bringing it to his lips, he said, "I think I need some new friends."

As soon as they were gone, he regretted his boorishness. Yet somehow there seemed to be no reason for acting human any more. He was no longer a psychiatrist, and they were not his patients. Any little trauma he might have wrecked would be quickly repaired by their Machines. Even so, he'd have made an extra effort to side-step the neuroses of his friends if he were not able to dial FRIENDS and get a new set.

Only a few years had passed since the Machines began seeing to the happiness, health and continuation of the human race, but he could barely remember life before Them. In the dusty mirror of his unused memory there remained but a few clear spots. He recalled his work as a psychiatrist on the Therapeutic Environment tests.

He recalled the argument with Brody.

"Sure, they work on a few test cases. But so far these gadgets haven't done anything a qualified psychiatrist couldn't do," said James.

"Agreed," said his superior. "But they haven't made any mistakes, either. Doctor, these people are cured. Moreover, they're happy!"

Frank envy was written all over Dr. Brody's heavy face. James knew his superior was having trouble with his wife again.

"But, Doctor," James began, "These people are *not* being taught to deal with their environment. Their environment is learning to deal with them. That isn't medicine, it's spoon-feeding!"

"When someone is depressed, he gets a dose of ritalin, bouncy tunes on the Muzik, and some dear friend drops in on him unexpectedly. If he is manic or violent, he gets thorazine, sweet music, melancholy stories on TV, and maybe a cool bath. If he's bored, he gets excitement; if he's frustrated, he gets something to break; if—"

Brody interrupted. "All right," he said. "Let me ask you the sixty-four-dollar question: could you do better?"

No one could do better. The vast complex of Therapeutic Environment Machines which grew up advanced medicine a millennium in a year. The government took control, to ensure that anyone of however modest means could have at his disposal the top specialists in the country, with all the latest data and techniques. In effect, these specialists were on duty round the clock in each patient's home, keeping him alive, healthy and reasonably happy.

Nor were they limited to treat. The Machines had extensions clawing through the jungles of the world, spying on witch doctors and learning new medicines. Drug and dietary research became their domain, as did scientific farming and birth control. By 1985, when it became manifest that Machines could and did run everything better, and that nearly everyone in the country wanted to be a patient, the U.S. Government capitulated. Other nations followed suit.

By now, no one worked at all, so far as James knew. They had one and only one duty—to be happy.

And happy they were. One's happiness was guaranteed, by every relay and transistor from those that ran one's air conditioner right up to those in the chief complex of computers called MEDCENTRAL in Washington—or was it The Hague now? James had not read a newspaper since people had stopped killing each other, since the news had dwindled to weather and sports. In fact, he'd stopped reading the newspaper when the M.D. Employment Wanted ads began to appear.

There were no jobs, only Happiness Jobs—make-work invented by the Machines. In such a job, one could never find an insoluble or even difficult problem. One finished one's daily quota without tiring one's mind or body. Work was no longer work, it was therapy, and as such it was constantly rewarding.

Happiness, normality. James saw the personalities of all people drifting downward, like so many different intricate snowflakes falling at last into the common, shapeless mound.

"I'm drunk, that's all," he said aloud. "Alcohol's a depressant. Need another drink."

He lurched slightly as he crossed the room to the niche. The floor must have detected it, for instead of a martini his pressing the button drew blood from his thumb. In a second the wall had analyzed his blood and presented him with a glass of liquid. A sign lit: "Drink this down at once. Replace glass on sink."

He drained the pleasant-tasting liquid and at once felt drowsy and warm. Somehow he found his way to the bedroom, the door moving to accommodate him, and he fell into bed.

As soon as James R. Fairchild, AAAAGTR-RHO1A, was asleep, mechanisms went into action to save his life. That is, he was in no immediate danger, but MED 8 reported his decrease in life expectancy by .0005 years as a result of overindulgence, and MED19 evaluated his behavior, recorded on magnetic tape, as increasing his suicide index by a dangerous fifteen points. A diagnostic unit detached itself from the bathroom wall and careened into the bedroom, halting silently and precisely by his side. It drew more blood, checked pulse, temp, resp, heart and brain-wave pattern, and X-rayed his abdomen. Not instructed to go on to patellar reflexes, it packed up and zoomed away.

In the living room, a housekeeper buzzed about its work, destroying the orange cushions, the sculpture, the couch and the carpet. The walls took on an almost imperceptibly warmer tone. The new carpet matched them.

The furniture—chosen and delivered without the sleeping man's knowledge was Queen Anne, enough to crowd the room. Its polyethylene wraps were left on while the room was disinfected.

In the kitchen, PHARMO 9 ordered and received a new supply of anti-depressants.

It was always the sound of a tractor that awoke Lloyd Young, and though he knew it was an artificial sound, it cheered him all the same. Almost made his day start right. He lay and listened to it awhile before opening his eyes.

Hell, the real tractors didn't make no sound at all. They worked in the night, burrowing along and plowing a field in one hour that would take a man twelve. Machines pumped strange new chemicals into the soil, and applied heat, to force two full crops of corn in one short Minnesota summer.

There wasn't much use being a farmer, but he'd always wanted to have a farm, and the Machines said you could have what you wanted. Lloyd was about the only man in these parts still living in the country by now, just him and twelve cows and a half-blind dog, Joe. There wasn't much to do, with Them running it all. He could go watch his cows being milked, or walk down with Joe to fetch the mail, or watch TV. But it was quiet and peaceful, the way he liked it.

Except for Them and Their pesky ways. They'd wanted to give Joe a new set of machine eyes, but Lloyd said no, if the good Lord wanted him to see, He'd never have blinded him. That was just the way he'd answered Them about the heart operation, too. Seemed almost like They didn't have enough to keep 'em busy or something. They was always worrying about him, him who took real good care of himself all through M.I.T. and twenty years of engineering.

When They'd automated, he'd been done out of a job, but he couldn't hold that against Them. If Machines was better engineers that him, well, shoot!

He opened his eyes and saw he'd be late for milking if he didn't look sharp. Without even thinking, he chose the baby-blue overalls with pink piping from his wardrobe, jammed a blue straw hat on his head, and loped out to the kitchen.

His pail was by the door. It was a silver one to-day—yesterday it had been gold. He decided he liked the silver better, for it made the milk look cool and white.

The kitchen door wouldn't budge, and Lloyd realized it meant for him to put on his shoes. Dammit, he'd of liked to go barefoot. Dammit, he would of.

He would of liked to do his own milking, too, but They had explained how dangerous it was. Why, you could get kicked in the head before you knew it! Reluctantly, the Machines allowed him to milk, each morning, one cow that had been tranquilized and had all its legs fastened to a steel frame.

He slipped on his comfortable blue brogans and picked up his pail again. This time the kitchen door opened easily, and as it did, a rooster crowed in the distance.

Yes, there had been a lot of doors closed in Lloyd's face. Enough to have made a bitter man of him, but for Them. He knew They could be trusted, even if They had done him out of his job in nineteen and seventy. For ten years he had just bummed around, trying to get factory work, anything. At the end of his rope, until They saved him.

In the barn, Betsy, his favorite Jersey, had been knocked out and shackled by the time he arrived. The Muzik played a bouncy, lighthearted tune, perfect for milking.

No, it wasn't Machines that did you dirt, he knew. It was people. People and animals, live things always trying to kick you in the head. As much as he liked Joe and Betsy, which was more than he liked people, he didn't really trust 'em.

You could trust Machines. They took good care of you. The only trouble with Them was—well, They *knew* so much. They were always so damned smart and busy, They made you feel kind of useless. Almost like you were standing in Their light.

It was altogether an enjoyable ten minutes, and when he stepped into the cool milkhouse to empty the pail into a receptacle that led God knew where, Lloyd had a strange impulse. He wanted to taste the warm milk, something he'd promised not to do. They had warned him about diseases, but he just felt too good to worry this morning. He tilted the silver pail to his lips—

And a bolt of lightning knocked it away, slamming him to the floor. At least it felt like a bolt of lightning. He tried to get up and found he couldn't move. A green mist began spraying from the ceiling. Now what the hell was that? he wondered, and drifted off to sleep in the puddle of spilled milk.

The first MED unit reported no superficial injuries. Lloyd C. Young, AAAAMTL-RHO1AB, was resting well, pulse high, resp normal. MED 8 disinfected the area thoroughly and destroyed all traces of the raw milk. While MED 1 pumped his stomach and swabbed nose, throat, esophagus and trachea, MED 8 cut away and destroyed all his clothing. An emergency heating unit warmed him until fresh clothing could be constructed. Despite the cushioned floor, the patient had broken a toe in falling. It was decided not to move him but to erect bed and traction on the spot. MED 19 recommended therapeutic punishment.

When Lloyd awoke, the television came to life, showing an amiable-looking man with white hair.

"You have my sympathy," the man said. "You have just survived what we call a 'Number One Killer Accident,' a bad fall in your home. Our Machines were in part responsible for this, in the course of saving your life from—" The man hesitated, while a sign flashed behind him: "BACTERIAL POISONING." Then he went on, "—by physically removing you from the danger. Since this was the only course open to us, your injury could not have been avoided.

"*Except by you*. Only you can save your life, finally." The man pointed at Lloyd. "Only *you* can make all of modern science worth while. And only *you* can help lower our shocking death toll. You will co-operate, won't you? Thank you." The screen went dark, and the set dispensed a pamphlet.

It was a complete account of his accident, and a warning about unpasteurized milk. He would be in bed for a week, it said, and urged him to make use of his telephone and FRIENDS.

Professor David Wattleigh sat in the tepid water of his swimming pool in Southern California and longed to swim. But it was forbidden. The gadgets had some way of knowing what he was doing, he supposed, for every time he immersed himself deeper than his chest, the motor of the resuscitator clattered a warning from poolside. It sounded like the snarl of a sheepdog. Or perhaps, he reflected, a Hound of Heaven, an anti-Mephistopheles, come to tempt him into virtue.

Wattleigh sat perfectly still for a moment, then reluctantly he heaved his plump pink body out of the water. Ah, it was no better than a bath. As he passed into the house, he cast a glance of contempt and loathing at the squat Machine.

It seemed as if anything he wished to do was forbidden. Since the day he'd been forced to abandon nineteenth-century English literature, the constraints of *mechanica* had tightened about Wattleigh, closing him off from his old pleasures one by one. Gone were his pipe and port, his lavish luncheons, his morning swim. In place of his library, there now existed a kind of vending machine that each day "vended" him two pages of thoroughly bowdlerized Dickens. Gay, colorful, witty passages they were, too, set in large Schoolbook type. They depressed him thoroughly.

Yet he had not given up entirely. He pronounced anathema upon the Machines in every letter he wrote to Delphinia, an imaginary lady of his acquaintance, and he feuded with the dining room about his luncheons.

If the dining room did not actually withhold food from him, it did its best to take away his appetite. At various times it had painted itself bilious yellow, played loud and raucous music, and flashed portraits of naked fat people upon its walls. Each day it had some new trick to play, and each day Wattleigh outwitted it.

Now he girded on his academic gown and entered the dining room, prepared for battle. Today, he saw, the room was upholstered in green velvet and lit by a gold chandelier. The dining table was heavy, solid oak, unfinished. There was not a particle of food upon it.

Instead there was a blonde, comely woman.

"Hello," she said, jumping down from the table. "Are you Professor David Wattleigh? I'm Helena Hershee, from New York. I got your name through FRIENDS, and I just had to look you up."

"I—how do you do?" he stammered. By way of answer, she unzipped her dress.

MED 19 approved what followed as tending to weaken that harmful delusion, "Delphinia". MED 8 projected a year of treatment, and found the resultant weight loss could add as much as .12 year to patient Wattleigh's life.

After Helena had gone to sleep the professor played a few games with the Ideal Chessplayer. Wattleigh had once belonged to a chess club, and he did not want to lose touch with the game entirely. And one did get rusty. He was amazed at how many times the Ideal Chessplayer had to actually cheat to let him win.

But win he did, game after game, and the Ideal Chessplayer each time would wag its plastic head from side to side and chuckle, "Well, you really got me that time, Wattleigh. Care for another?"

"No," said Wattleigh, finally disgusted. Obediently the Machine folded its board into its chest and rolled off somewhere.

Wattleigh sat at his desk and started a letter to Delphinia.

"My Darling Delphinia," scratched his old steel pen on the fine, laid paper. "Today a thought occurred to me while I was (*swimming*) bathing at Brighton. I have often told you, and as often complained of the behavior of my servant, M——. It, for I cannot bring myself to call it "he" or "she", has been most distressing about my writing to you, even to the point of blunting my pens and hiding my paper.

I have not discharged it for this disgraceful show, for I am bound to it—yes, *bound* to it by a strange (*and terrible secret*) fate that makes me doubt at times which is master and which man. It reminds one of several old comedies in which, man and master having changed roles, and maid and mistress likewise, they meet, I mean, of course, in the works of."

Here the letter proper ended, for the professor could think of no name to fit. After writing, and lining out, "Dickens, Dryden, Dostoyevsky, Racine, Rousseau, Camus," and a dozen more, his inkwell ran dry. He knew it would be no use to inquire after more ink, for the Machine was dead set against this letter—

Looking out the window, he saw a bright pink- and yellow-striped ambulance. So, the doctor next door was going off to a zombie-land, was he? Or, correctly, to the Hospital for the Asocial. In the East, they called them "Mussulmen"; here, "zombies," but it all came to the same thing: the living dead who needed no elaborate houses, games, ink. They needed only intravenous nourishment, and little of that. The drapes drew themselves, so Wattleigh knew the doctor was being carried out then. He finished his interrupted thought.

—and in any case he was wholly dissatisfied with this letter. He had not mentioned Helena, luncheon, his resuscitator which growled at him, and so much more. Volumes more, if only he had the ink to write, if only his memory would not fail him when he sat down to write, if only—

James stood with his elbow on the marble mantelpiece of Marya's apartment, surveying the other guests and sizing them up. There was a farmer from Minnesota, incredibly dull, who claimed to have once been an engineer, but who hardly knew what a slide rule was. There was Marya in the company of some muscular young man James disliked at sight, an ex-mathematician named Dewes or Clewes. Marya was about to play chess with a slightly plump Californian, while his girl, a pretty little blonde thing called Helena Hershee, stood by to kibitz.

"I'm practically a champion," explained Wattleigh, setting up the pieces. "So perhaps I ought to give you a rook or two."

"If you like," said Marya. "I haven't played in years. About all I remember is the Fool's Mate."

James drifted over to Helena's side and watched the game.

"I'm James Fairchild," he said, and added almost defiantly, "M.D."

Helena's lips, too bright with lipstick, parted. "I've heard of you," she murmured. "You're the aggressive Dr. Fairchild who runs through friends so fast, aren't you?"

Marya's eyes came up from the game. Seemingly her eyes had no pupils, and James guessed she was full of ritalin. "James is not in the least aggressive," she said. "But he gets mad when you won't let him psychoanalyze you."

"Don't disturb the game," said Wattleigh. He put both elbows on the table in an attitude of concentration.

Helena had not heard Marya's remark. She had turned to watch the muscular mathematician lecture Lloyd.

"Hell yes. The Machines got to do all the bearing and raising of children. Otherwise, we'd have a population explosion, you get me? I mean we'd run out of food—"

"You really pick 'em, Marya," said James. He gestured at the young man. "Whatever became of that 'writer'? Porter, was it? Christ, I can still hear him saying, 'Exit, man!'" James snorted.

Marya's head came up once more, and tears stood in her pupil-less eyes. "Porter went to the hospital. He's a Mussulman now," she said brightly. "I wish I could feel something for him, but They won't let me."

"—it's like Malthus' law, or somebody's law. Animals grow faster than vegetables," the mathematician went on, speaking to the farmer.

"Checkmate," said Marya, and bounced to her feet, "James, have you a Sugarsmoke? Chocolate?"

He produced a bright orange cigar. "Only bitter orange, I'm afraid. Ask the Machine."

"I'm afraid to ask it for anything, today," she said. "It keeps drugging me—James, Porter was put away a month ago, and I haven't been able to paint since. Do you think I'm crazy? The Machine thinks so."

"The Machine," he said, tearing off the end of the cigar with his teeth, "is always right."

Seeing Helena had wandered away to sit on Marya's Chinese sofa, he excused himself with a nod and followed.

Wattleigh still sat brooding over the Fool's Mate. "I don't understand. I just can't understand," he said.

"—it's like the hare and the tortoise," boomed the mathematician. Lloyd nodded solemnly. "The slow one can't ever catch up, see?"

Lloyd spoke. "Well, you got a point. You got a point. Only I thought the slow one was the winner."

"Oh." Dewes (or Clewes) lapsed into thoughtful silence.

Marya wandered about the room, touching faces as if she were a blind person looking for someone she knew.

"But I don't understand!" said Wattleigh.

"I do," James mumbled about the cigar. The bitter-sweet smoke was thick as liquid in his mouth. He understood, all right. He looked at them, one by one: an ex-mathematician now having trouble with the difference between arithmetic and geometry; an ex-engineer, ditto; a painter not allowed to paint, not even to feel; a former chess "champion" who could not play. And that left Helena Hershee, mistress to poor, dumb Wattleigh.

"Before the Machines—?" he began.

"—I was a judge," she said, running her fingertips over the back of his neck provocatively. "And you? What kind of doctor were you?"

A.D. 1988

"It was during the Second World War," Jim Fairchild said. He lay on his back on the long, tiger-striped sofa, with a copy of *Hot Rod Komiks* over his eyes.

"I thought it only started in the sixties," said Marya.

"Yeah, but the *name* 'Mussulman'—that started in the Nazi death camps. There were some people in them who couldn't—you know—get with it. They stopped eating and seeing and hearing. Everybody called them 'Mussulmen', because they seemed like Moslems, mystics . . ."

His voice trailed off, for he was thinking of the Second World War. The good old days, when a man made his own rules. No Machines to tell you what to do.

He had been living with Marya for several months now. She was his girl, just as the other Marya, in *Hot Rod Komiks,* was the girl of the other Him, Jim (Hell-on-Wheels) White. It was a funny thing about Komiks. They were real life, and at the same time they were better than life.

Marya—his Marya—was no intellectual. She didn't like to read and think, like Jim, but that was okay, because men were supposed to do all the reading and thinking and fighting and killing. Marya sat in a lavender bucket seat in the corner, drawing with her crayons. Easing his lanky, lean body up off the sofa, Jim walked around behind her and looked at the sketch.

"Her nose is crooked," he said.

"That doesn't matter, silly. This is a fashion design. It's only the dress that counts."

"Well, how come she's got yellow hair? People don't have yellow hair."

"Helena Hershee has."

"No, she hasn't!"

"She has so!"

"No, it ain't yellow, it's—it ain't yellow."

Then they both paused, because Muzik was playing their favorite song. Each had a favorite of his own—Jim's was "Blap", and Marya's was "Yes, I Know I Rilly Care for You"—but they had one favorite together. Called "Kustomized Tragedy", it was one of the songs in which the Muzik imitated their voices, singing close harmony:

Jim Gunn had a neat little kustom job,

And Marya was his girl.
They loved each other with a love so true,
The truest in the worl'.
But Jim weren't allowed to drive his kar,
And Marya could not see;
Kust'mized Traju-dee-ee-ee.

The song went on to articulate how Jim Gunn wanted
more than anything in the worl' to buy an eye operation for
his girl, who wished to admire his kustom kar. So he drove to
a store and held it up, but someone recognized his kar. The
police shot him, but:

He kissed his Marya one last time;
The policeman shot her too.
But she said, "I can see your kustom, Jim!
It's pretty gold and bloo!"
He smiled and died embracing her,
Happy that she could see.
Kust'mized Traju-dee.

Of course, in real life, Marya could see very well, Jim had
no kar, and there were no policemen. But it was true for
them, nevertheless. In some sense they could not express,
they felt their love was a tragedy.

Knowing Jim felt lonesome and bloo, Marya walked over
and kissed his ear. She lay down beside him, and at once they
were asleep.

MEDCENTRAL's audit showed a population of
250,000,000 in NORTHAMER, stabilized. Other than a
few incubator failures, and one vat of accidentally infected
embryos, progress was as predicted, with birth and death
rates equal. The norm had shifted once more toward the
asocial, and UTERINE CONTROL showed 90.2 per cent
adult admissions at both major hospitals.

Trenchant abnormals were being regressed through ado-
lescence, there being no other completely satisfactory

method of normalizing them without shock therapy, and its attendant contraindications.

Lloyd pulled his pocket watch from the bib of his plaid overalls. The hands of Chicken Licken pointed straight up, meaning there was just time to fetch the mail before Farm Kartoons on TV. On Impulse, Lloyd popped the watch into his mouth and chewed. It was delicious, but it gave him little pleasure. Everything was too easy, too soft. He wanted exciting things to happen to him, like the time on Farm Kartoons when Black Angus tried to kill the hero, Lloyd White, by breaking up his Machine, and Lloyd White had stabbed him with a pitchfork syringe and sent him off to the hospital.

Mechanical Joe, knowing it was time to fetch the mail, came running out of the house. He wagged his tail and whined impatiently. It didn't make any difference that he wasn't a real dog, Lloyd thought as they strolled toward the mailbox. Joe still liked it when you scratched his ears. You could tell, just by the look in his eyes. He was livelier and a lot more fun than the first Joe.

Lloyd paused a moment, remembering how sad he'd been when Joe died. It was a pleasantly melancholy thought, but now mechanical Joe was dancing around him and barking anxiously. They continued.

The mailbox was chock-full of mail. There was a new komik, called *Lloyd Farmer and Joe*, and a whole big box of new toys.

Yet later, when Lloyd had read the komik and watched Farm Kartoon and played awhile with his building set, he still felt somehow heavy, depressed. It was no good being alone all the time, he decided. Maybe he should go to New York and see Jim and Marya. Maybe the Machines there were different, not so bossy.

For the first time another, stranger thought came to him. Maybe he should go *live* in New York.

DEAR DELPHINIA, (Dave printed). THIS IS GOING TO BE MY LAST LETTER TO YOU,

AS I DONT LOVE YOU ANY MORE. I KNOW NOW
WHAT HAS BEEN MAKING ME FEEL BAD, AND
IT IS YOU. YOU ARE REALLY MY MASHINE,
AREN'T YOU HA HA I'LL BET YOU DIDN'T
THINK I NEW.

NOW I LOVE HELENA MORE THAN YOU AND
WE ARE GOING AWAY TO NEW YORK AND SEE
LOTS OF FRIENDS AND GO TO LOTS OF
PARTYS AND HAVE LOTS OF FUN AND I DONT
CARE IF I DONT SEE YOU NO MORE.

LOVE, AND BEST OF LUCK TO A SWELL
KID,

DAVE W.

After an earthquake destroyed seventeen million occupants of the Western hospital, MEDCENTRAL ordered the
rest moved at once to the East. All abnormals not living near
the East hospital were also persuaded to evacuate to New
York. Persuasion was as follows:

Gradually, humidity and pressure were increased to .9 discomfort while, subliminally, pictures of New York were
flashed on all surfaces around each patient.

Dave and Helena had come by subway from LA, and they
were tired and cross. The subway trip itself took only two or
three hours, but they had spent an additional hour in the
taxi to Jim's and Marya's.

"It's an electric taxi," Dave explained, "and it only goes
about a mile an hour. I'll sure never make that trip
again."

"I'm glad you came," said Marya. "We've been feeling
terrible lonesome and bloo."

"Yes," Jim added, "and I got an idea. We can form a club,
see, against the Machines. I got it all figured out. We—"

"Babay, tell them about the zombies—I mean, the Mussulmen,' said Helena.

Dave spoke with an excited, wild look about him. "Jeez,
yeah, they had about a million cars of them on the train, all
115

packed in glass bottles. I wasn't sure what the hell they were at first, see, so I went up and looked at one. It was a skinny, hairless man, all folded up in a bottle inside another bottle. Weird-looking."

In honor of their arrival, the Muzik played the favorite songs of all four: "Zonk," "Yes, I Know I Rilly Care for You," "Blap," and "That's My Babay," while the walls went transparent for a moment, showing a breath-taking view of the gold towers of New York. Lloyd, who spoke to no one, sat in the corner keeping time to the music. He had no favorite song.

"I want to call this the Jim Fairchild Club," said Jim. "The purpose of this here club is to get rid of the Machines. Kick 'em out!"

Marya and Dave sat down to a game of chess.

"I know how we can do it, too," Jim went on. "Here's my plan: Who put the Machines in, in the first place? The U.S. Government. Well, there ain't any U.S. Government any more. So the Machines are illegal. Right?"

"Right," said Helena. Lloyd continued to tap his foot, though no Muzik was playing.

"They're outlaws," said Jim. "We oughta kill them!"

"But how?" asked Helena.

"I ain't got all the details worked out yet. Give me time. Because, you know, the Machines done us wrong."

"How's that?" asked Lloyd, as if from far away.

"We all had good jobs, and we were smart. A long time ago. Now we're all getting dumb. You know?"

"That's right," Helena agreed. She opened a tiny bottle and began painting her toenails.

"I think," said Jim, glaring about him, "the Machines are trying to make us all into Mussulmen. Any of you want to get stuffed into a bottle? Huh?"

"A bottle inside a bottle," Dave corrected, without looking up from his game.

Jim continued, "I think the Machines are drugging us into Mussulmen. Or else they got some kind of ray, maybe, that makes us stupider. An X ray, maybe."

"We gotta do something," said Helena, admiring her foot.

Marya and Dave began to quarrel about how the pawn moves.

Lloyd continued to tap his foot, marking time.

A.D. 1989

Jimmy had a good idea, but nobody wanted to listen. He remembered, once when he was an itsy boy, a Egg Machine that tooked the eggs out of their shells and putted them into plastic—things. It was funny, the way the Machine did that. Jimmy didn't know why it was so funny, but he laughed and laughed, just thinking about it. Silly, silly, silly eggs.

Mary had a idea, a real good one. Only she didn't know how to say it so she got a crayon and drew a great Big! picture of the Machines: Mommy Machine and Daddy Machine and all the little Tiny Tot Machines.

Loy-Loy was talking. He was building a block house. "Now I'm putting the door," he said. "Now I'm putting the lit-tle window. Now the—why is the window littler than the house? I don't know. This is the chimney and this is the steeple and open the door and where's all the people? I don't know."

Helena had a wooden hammer, and she was driving all the pegs. Bang! Bang! Bang! "One, two, three!" she said. "Banga-banga-bang!"

Davie had the chessmen out, lined up in rows, two by two. He wanted to line them all up three by three, only somehow he couldn't. It made him mad and he began to cry.

Then one of the Machines came and stuck something in his mouth, and everybody else wanted one and somebody was screaming and more Machines came and . . .

The coded message came to MEDCENTRAL. The last five abnormals had been cured, and all physical and mental functions reduced to the norm. All pertinent data on them were switched over to UTERINE SUPPLY, which clocked them in at 400 hrs GMT, day 1, yr 1989. MEDCENTRAL agreed on the time check, then switched itself off.

Afterword:

"The Happy Breed" demonstrates one version of what I like to think of as the Horrible Utopia. Ionesco's play, *The Bald Soprano*, had already shown a world without evil. In a sense, this was my model; I tried to show a world without pain. In both instances, the same phenomena obtain: without evil or pain, preference and choice are meaningless; personality blurs; figures merge with their backgrounds, and thinking becomes superfluous and disappears. I believe these are the inevitable results of achieving Utopia, if we make the mistake of assuming that Utopia equals perfect happiness. There is, after all, a pleasure center in everyone's head. Plant an electrode there, and presumably we could be constantly, perfectly happy on a dime's worth of electricity a day.

If not of happiness, then, of what material do we construct our Utopia? The avoidance of pain, perhaps? Perfect security from disease, accident, natural disaster? We gain these only at the cost of contact with our environment—ultimately at the cost of our humanity. We become "etherized", in both of Eliot's senses of the word: numb and unreal.

To some, this story might seem itself unreal and hypothetical. I can only point out that dozens of electronic firms are now inventing and developing new diagnostic equipment; in a short time physicians will depend almost entirely upon machines for accurate diagnoses. There is no reason why it must stop there, or at any point short of mechanical doctors.

If we elect to build machines to heal us, we must be certain we know what power we are giving them and what it is we ask in return. In "The Happy Breed" the agency through which the anesthetic world comes to be is a kind of genie, the Slave of the Pushbutton. It is a peculiarly literal-minded genie, and it will give us *exactly* what we ask, no more and no less. Norbert Wiener noticed the similarity between the behavior of literal-minded machines and that of magical agents in fairy tales, myths, ghost stories and even modern jokes.

Semele thought she wanted Jove to make love to her exactly as he would to a goddess—but it turned out to be with lightning. The sorcerer's apprentice thought he'd give up his work to a magical helper. Wells wrote of a rather dull-witted clerk who stopped the rotation of the earth suddenly. At one end of the spectrum are horror stories like "The Dancing Partner" or "The Monkey's Paw", and at the other is Lennie Bruce's joke about the druggist who left a genie to mind his store. Said the genie's first customer, "Make me a chocolate malted."

If we decide we really want health, security, freedom from pain, we must be willing to exchange our individuality for it. The use of any tool implies a loss of freedom, as Freud pointed out in *Civilization and Its Discontents*. When man started using a hand ax he lost the freedom to climb or walk on four limbs, but more important, he lost the freedom not to use the hand ax. We have now lost the freedom to do without computers, and it is no longer a question of giving them power over us, but of how much power, of what kind, and of how fast we turn it over to them.

A professor at the University of Minnesota once told me of a term when he was late in making up grades. The department secretary kept calling him, asking if he were ready to turn in his grades yet. Finally a clerk from administration called him. On learning the grades were still not ready, the clerk said exasperatedly, "But, Professor, the machines are waiting!"

They are indeed.

ENCOUNTER WITH A HICK

Introduction to

ENCOUNTER WITH A HICK:

The first time I saw Jonathan Brand, he was lounging on a grassy knoll in Milford, Pennsylvania, wearing hiking boots on his feet, a knapsack on his back, a six-blade tracker's knife on his belt and a badge sewn on his blue shirt indicating he was a member of the American Forestry Association, or somesuch. He was lying there propped on his elbows, a blade of grass in his mouth, watching half a dozen of the older, more sophisticated giants of the science fiction field dousing each other with beer from quart bottles on The Lawn of Damon Knight's home. Jonathan Brand was amused.

Kindness forbids my explaining why Jim Blish, Ted Thomas, Damon and Gordy Dickson were cavorting in such an unseemly manner. Kindness and a suspicion that it is this innocence of childhood or nature that supplies the *èlan* for their excellent writings, God forbid.

Jon was in Milford for the 11th Annual Science Fiction Writers Conference, a week of discussions, seminars and workshops in which members of the craft exchanged ideas, market information and wet shirts in the pursuance of greater facility in their chosen profession.

He made quite an impression on attendees. His ready wit, his familiarity with the genre, and most of all the work he submitted for consideration in the workshops made him a new voice to be listened to. The story he had put in for comment—an act very close to hara-kiri—was read by all the writers present, and the criticism was stiff. It always is. The naked ids and exposed predilections of a blue-ribbon gathering of fantasists is not guaranteed to balm one's creative soul or convince him he should be anything other than a hod carrier. But Jon and his story came off rather well. The praise was honest and with very few reservations.

So well off did he appear that I asked Jon if I might buy the story for this anthology. He did a few minor editing flourishes, and the yarn appears here.

Jonathan Brand admits he has been a graduate student for altogether too long. Carnegie Tech. He lives alone, walks to school each weekday in semester, hibernates in the summer, has no telephone, cherishes trolley cars, hates to talk or listen, likes to read and write, refuses to state his age, condition of marital servitude, background or any other damned thing that would make this introduction something more meaningful than an announcement that Jonathan Brand has written a very funny, slightly whacky, irreverent and definitely dangerous story for this book.

ENCOUNTER WITH A HICK

by Jonathan Brand

How would I know what made the simple hayseed flip his lid? He was old. He was simple. He was the final in hayseeds. Wouldn't you flip your lid? But nevertheless I will support my local police, I will testify to the conversation which preceded the dissolution of the cuddly patriarch. Who knows, *post hoc, ergo propter hoc*?

All right, all right, I *am* being serious. You think I'm not serious, you can look at my credit cards and diplomas. I got a Bachelor's, I got a Master's, I got about ten Doctorates, my dad operates a lot of planets, they gotta lotta universities. Which is incidentally how I came to attend this distinctly hip conference taking place right here in your picturesque old planet, namely the Colloquium of the Universe Academy of Sciences, North-West-Up Octant.

Myself, I would not say I was strictly an academic. I am more in the improvisation and drugs experience, but I am warm toward the academic milieu. Those eggs speak, I tell you, Your Honor, Officer, Sire, etc., it is all one sentence, they do not let themselves be trammeled, no punctuation or meaning, but oh the rhythm and structure and balance. Now those things constitute also judo, not to mention improvisation, not to mention sex, which are all key items in the life stream.

What do you mean—"stick to the point"? I am striving to give you the conspectus or overview of this egghead scene in which the whole interpersonal encounter was embedded, I mean me and my girl Patsy and this aged hick with his beard which is 100 per cent human hair, I and she and he and it all having drinks in the Continuum Bar in the Trans-Port Hotel, which is where the above Colloquium is being held. Yes, I know you know, Your Reverence, Squire, and/or Justice of the Peace.

Now you have the need to know with respect to Patsy? The bit with Patsy is she has this father who is primarily a rich man, also he is in the construction business like my own dad, and two sires are anxious to unite the dynasties, they yearn to cuddle, dangle, and burp a curly-headed heir, so they sent Patsy and me on this cruise together, it is all a transparent plot, our acquaintance is to ripen and mellow into love. The chick comes before the egg, ha-ha. Do not sweat it, Sheriff, Lawman, Gunslinger, do not wave and shake the long arm of the law, I am coming to the point. I shall be considerably grateful if and when *you* do not flip your noodle, one per day is sufficiently superfluous for me.

Okay, if you are truly all right, stop now twitching and I will proceed to recall at length and depth the precise conversation subsequent to which the loony old hayseed went critical, namely lay down upon the rug and chewed it, simultaneously foaming and weeping. As a start, he comes up to me in the bar, he introduces himself, I have a friendly face, I do not rebuff the humble. How would I remember the old peasant's name? It was Doctor something. This old guy, it seems he's the intellectual flower of his planet, absolutely the topmost blossom, I mean the apex in theology, music, surgery, politics, maybe improvisation and sex as well, I forget. He gives me the picture his planet is strictly bluegrass, I mean a net exporter of glass beads and rush mats, but all the same they pool their credits, the women folk melt down their golden earrings, they mail this old guy to the Colloquium. Heed me, I do not dump upon this laudable desire, namely for Podunk University to send a professor to the Colloquium, I dare say it does a lot for Podunk U.

So we were tossing the ball, we were pretty friendly, I am paying, and seeing how he was partly in theology and I am not aloof from the folk scene I am saying, "Well, fill me in, move me with mingled pity and terror, recount to me one of your doubtless beautiful old myths." Now this is fine with the grizzled old musician/priest/surgeon, he launches into a Creation Myth, than which I may say (having taken not a few courses in the past, courses in "The Past," ha-ha), than which there is nothing finer. But he is halfway through the noble recital, hallowed by centuries, handed down orally by dynasties of blind bards, the whole bit, when I suddenly receive the distinct impression that his planet is one of those built by my father's firm!

So this is quite a coincidence, and not stopping to think in my youthful enthusiasm, I pull out a pamphlet advertising my daddy's company which pioneered the Accelerated Photo-Synthetic Evolution process. To be sufficiently brief, this is a process for creating habitable planets from anything which swings in that right temperature zone where anthropoid types can walk around without any clothes on, which is a key experience, as I see it, I mean like drugs and sex and improvisation even. The actual process of creation is basically geared to planetary rotation, you have to get it spinning first, you work always on the sunside, seeing as the process requires two or three billion billion billion ergs, which is a measure of energy. There's really six complete phases, so you get the whole thing finished in time for the weekend, going once around the planet on each rotation, it's quite accelerated. Are you still with me? Actually *I* am not altogether with me, I have to confess the details are hazy to me, but it's all in our brochure. The first day you bring in your equipment, the second day you fix the rotation, the third day you consolidate the foundation, the fourth day you truck in soil and water and germ plasm, here's the gimmick now, you operate this Accelerated Photo-Synthetic Evolution deal, you breed accelerated cycles of life forms, on the fourth day it's land plants, you stabilize the weather by the fifth day, on the sixth day you seed the oceans and fix up the animals.

No shit, it's an interesting routine, cheap and quick, here's the firm's card in case you ever want a job done, nothing to it, it leaves some pretty loamy foamy topsoil (which we throw in free), the only mess is from time to time you dig up by-products of this Accelerated Evolution, bits of petrified bone and stuff, but that's no sweat. Anyway, on the sixth day you're ready for colonization, you bring in a guy and a chick, there's a bit of a ceremony and they're on their own. And they get to work with the fecundity bit, I mean it springs eternal in the human breast.

Okay, okay, do not nag. Where was I? Yes, when I get through retailing this to the hoary old cracker-barrel philosopher/priest/surgeon he is conspicuously not so pleased as I hope. I suppose I had noticeably trampled on his priceless cultural heritage a bit, though I meant no harm, I trespassed anyways. To be frank, the salted old peanut is now definitely enraged, I mean much madder than you are now, he is purple in the face and quivering from top to bottom. Also, what with seven or eight steins of kumiss and V8 inside him which I have paid for, this pensive wrinkled doctor/philosopher/bard/okie is approximately as high as an elephant's eye. I seem to see on his forehead the blinking sign which says ON THE AIR, and he stands up and points a gnarled old calloused finger and he says—and I quote his noble old sincere approach:

"Gird up thy loins now like a man. I will demand of thee and declare thou unto me." (You see I aim to reproduce his colorful dead language right down to its woolen jerkin. I should have taken notes. What a thesis.) "By whom were all things created, that are in heaven? All the stars of light, the heavens of heavens, and the waters that be above the heavens—who commanded, and they were created? Who set the stars in the firmament of heaven, to give light over the earth? He that darkeneth counsel, let him answer it."

These words were inspiringly composed and declaimed (the old cornball lacked nothing in those departments, especially with that beard), but they were incidentally his last, for it was soon after this that the herbivore cuts his mustard.

Now relax, Gendarme, Polizei, Beefeater, do not fret, I am hiding not one jot and/or tittle, I truly do not know what precise thing bugged him, all I can do is relate what was the last thing I did before his spectacular and regrettable collapse.

"A very good and cogent question, Doc baby, which I am glad you raised," I say, and I turn away from the decrepit politician/priest/surgeon/subsistence-farmer and I begin to rummage in Patsy's little old bottomless purse which is lying on the bar.

"What are you seeking, you bustard?" whoops Patsy, successfully attempting to contuse my ankle with her left shoe.

Now I think I was already recounting how her daddy has money like other folk have troubles, namely in considerable amounts. My own dad is rich, he is in the sub-division business, he owns more than two hundred galaxies, he is chairman of the local Kiwanis, he is solid, but Patsy's dad, he is bigger than all of us, he operates this Continuous Creation process, which is his very own patented and money-spinning property, oh, a genuine something-for-nothing proposition. And now I am in a position to tell you word for word what all I said before the old wowser puts on his supreme performance, when he drums his heels, he topples from the bar stool, he immolates himself upon the floor in an armageddon of cocktail sticks.

I turn to Patsy, my hot cross bun, and I say: "Peace, eskimo pie. Let me look in your purse. Did you not hear our new friend ask to see a picture of your dad?"

Afterword:

I believe in Jesus, Thoreau, and Mao Tse-tung—and not in God. However, I try to give as much serious thought to the last as to the first three. My story deals with the obvious fallacy in the argument from first cause, which assumes a connection between the creator of the universe and the source of ethics and salvation. To think that the creator of the universe is necessarily the moral superior of man is as naïve as to think that the builder of skyscrapers is greater than the carpenter just because his product is larger.

Back to earth: I must thank the Milford Science Fiction Writers Conference of 1966, but for which this story would not be where it is or quite what it is.

FROM THE GOVERNMENT
PRINTING OFFICE

Introduction to

FROM THE GOVERNMENT PRINTING OFFICE:

No one who has encountered them will soon forget Kris Neville's marvelous stories, "Bettyann" or "Special Delivery". They were written over fifteen years ago, and even today continue to turn up in anthologies of the best-in-genre. Kris Neville is a hearty man with an unplaceable Southern accent. He says it's a Missouri accent, but damned if it don't sound Texas. Kris Neville is what the writers of book-jacket copy call a "hard-living man". That means he milks every minute. He talks endlessly on topics without number, can drink under the table any three science fiction writers going (with the possible exception of George O. Smith), and manages to come up with fresh angles on themes generally considered well plowed. One such is the story that follows, submitted upon this editor's comment that DANGEROUS VISIONS was lacking a good story on the theme of education.

Kris Neville (has there ever been a more perfect name for a writer? I mean, if you had your choice of being known as Bernard Malamud or Louis Auchincloss, wouldn't *you* pick Kris Neville?) was born in Carthage, Missouri, in 1925, served in the U.S. Army during World War II, and received his degree in English from UCLA in 1950. His first science fiction story was published in 1949 ("The Hand from the Stars" in *Super Science Stories*), and since then he has sold some fifty-odd others. Some were *very* odd indeed.

For eleven years Kris was involved with research and development of epoxy resins. This is what is known in the trade as stick-to-it-iveness. Sorry.

In collaboration with Henry Lee, he has published two books on the subject from McGraw-Hill, one of which (selling for $32.50 in case you are in need) is a massive volume intended to be the definitive treatment of the subject. Additionally, with Drs. Lee and Stauffey, he has written a volume on new thermoplastic high polymers, to be published this year. He has been contributor to a number of symposiums and encyclopedias, and holds "a patent which has covered business into seven figures." His last industrial job was as program manager on research and development contracts, one of the more interesting involving work for the National Institutes of Health in the use of plastic materials for dental applications.

Kris is the author of one science fiction novel, *The Unearth People*, and since early in 1966 he has been a full-time writer. He lives in Los Angeles with wife and children.

FROM THE GOVERNMENT PRINTING OFFICE

by Kris Neville

At three and a half, it's logical for adults to wear eyeglasses to keep their eyeballs warm. Cold eyeballs is an adult affliction no different from many other adult afflictions equally as incomprehensible.

Adults talk always too loudly. A sonic boom for a whisper. Little ears hear the movement of air molecules in the quiet night, when listening for something else to happen.

Adults live too fast. What passes for thinking is habit. Press a button. Listen. Press a button. Listen. Open a drawer. One of the big bastards does it without thinking, doesn't really care what's in there, is looking for a special thing, and he closes the drawer and hasn't seen anything in it. Tiny hands, eyes peering over the rim, sees a strange little world in the drawer. There isn't enough time made to know the contents. Stop the press. Here is a thing that looks like a key. See how big it is. Wow! What sort of wild surface bug goes with it? Enormous! Nobody has ever seen one that big. Where do they keep it?

Now here's something: a thing for which there is no conceivable use at all. It has moving parts but it doesn't do anything. There's no place to plug it in. I'll bet rabbits made it. Chickens make eggs.

"Get out of that drawer! Let that alone!"

There she is. I knew it. Too good to last. What was I hurting? Ask what that is, they just kiss the problem off. Push the button. Listen. Tell you nonsense. Maybe she'll go away. Now what's this thing? Looks interesting. What do you suppose—

"Get *out* of there!"

Aw, hell! I'll try to reason with her. Maybe get a conversation going.

"Candy in here."

"There's no candy in there."

How can she possibly know that? No candy in there, indeed! My God, look at all the things there are in there. How can she possibly tell there's no candy: she hasn't even looked. It's not even her drawer. It's Poppa's. "What's this for?"

"It's not candy. Put it down."

No luck. Sometimes, though, you can get to them by talking about candy. Most times, like now, they don't think at all. I'll cry. Start quiet: it may take a long time. First a little blob, blob, waa. Makes you feel bad, but don't get carried away, you burn out too soon. May have to keep it up for a long time, start slow and easy. She'll wait to see how serious I am. It's easy if you don't rush into it. Get going good, the body takes over: close your eyes and listen. Lovely sounds. Like singing. Good voice. Lots of variety, up and down. I could go on like this all day.

At three and a half, you've been here forever, and it all hasn't been good, not by a damn sight.

Everything has always been too big. Heavy, awkward to handle. How tired you get! All the wrong size. They get big and dumb and you can't talk to them about anything important. Who cares how they make babies? But you want to watch, and they won't let you. You lay awake and wait and wait and wait while they whisper, loud as sonic booms, "Is he asleep?" Close your eyes and wait some more. Maybe they're afraid I'll laugh at them: they must look silly.

Listen, though, you get smart. You just try not to. They have this special book. Sometimes, though, it's not the book: it's like at the drawer, just now. They're not malicious, just dumb, some of the time.

The damned awful things they do in this book conspiracy, though. The time I had with toilet training; they were going to flush me down the toilet. I thought they would. I really believe they would have. I was scared shitless. But something went wrong, lucky for me, and they didn't, after all. I ought to be grateful to them, I guess, I'm still here. I still don't know why they didn't. They were going to.

There were worse things. The tricks they play on me at night. You wouldn't believe them. I once got so I couldn't sleep at all, just waiting in the night. I had to sleep in the daytime. It's better now. I get more sleep. I asked the other kids at playground; we talk. We make just a few words mean a lot. We know more words than we can use right, so what words we have have to work hard for us. Their parents have special books too.

I'm always afraid they'll do something to my penis. I break out in a sweat when I think about that. That's why I'm so damned afraid at night. One of the reasons.

I used to try to make friends with them, before I got so old. I tried to go get in bed with them, once. They'd fixed up this alarm system; or it came with the book or was part of this course the mailman brings, I think. Oh, it went off with all sorts of sounds and lights flashing and weird feelings. There I was, trapped, exposed alone on the floor, halfway to their bed, and I just peed all over the carpet.

"Oh, Christ! It's two o'clock in the morning!" That's what he said. Here I was, as scared as anything, standing there, blinking my eyes, and he makes a stupid statement like that.

"Make him feel guilty," she said. "That's what the book says."

"You're a filthy shit!" he screamed at me.

I guess I am. There must be some reason they want to cut my penis off. I heard them say, once, that all your real education takes place before you're four years old: by then your character is established. I think maybe I'll make it. It's still such a long ways off, so long, so long. But maybe I really will make it, even if I'm a nervous wreck.

So I don't feel so good about myself. It could be worse.

There is a place called India. You see it on the newscasts. I was afraid they'd send me there. I don't know why I thought that, but I did. It kept me awake too. I went hungry one day, wouldn't eat at all, just to see if I could take it. I couldn't. They can't either. They die. Several million are starving to death right now. I don't know exactly how many that is. It's more than ten.

But apparently they never intended to send me to India.

Or China.

Or a place called South America.

And people don't starve to death where I live. Except in the slums, and that's different. Whatever the slums are. So at least I'm spared that. It could be worse.

On the newscasts, you see big machines making big piles of people and pee-peeing on them and burning them up. "Why they burn those people, Momma?"

"Hush! It's too awful. They breed like flies and they can't *feed* themselves."

How do flies breed? What she mean by that? But I think they should let me watch: just to be sure they don't breed like flies do, however that is, so they can continue to feed themselves. I would feed them, though, if it really came to that. I wonder about the Indian children, sometimes. Nobody ever mentions them. Maybe there aren't any.

Flies all fits in, somehow, but it's not too clear to me. Last summer there was really this fly thing. Momma said it was because they couldn't burn people fast enough, and there was a world-wide plague, and I remember how scared they were that we couldn't keep it out. The time everybody had killing flies! It was all over the newscasts.

It went on until it got monotonous. In fact, most newscasts aren't very interesting after a while. They keep changing the places, but there's still this big machine pushing up piles of people and setting them on fire. I like the ones on our space program better. We have a colony on Mars.

We have to have.

For some reasons.

Most people go out every day, all the Poppas, and cheer for this program. I've never seen them do it, but I guess it's like a football game. It's called work. They pay him money for it that Momma writes checks on to pay for credit cards with. They must know what they're doing.

I'm coming along in figuring them out. Every once in a while I think I have it.

I think they have a machine somewhere that makes time, or maybe a press that prints it like a book. They never mention this. Maybe I have to learn how they make electricity, first. They say I'm going to start learning about things like that pretty soon.

And you really have to try to figure the big bastards out. Don't ask me why. You do. You can't do anything about them. They're still going to batter you around. Shaping the personality, it's called. But you have to keep trying, keep hoping. Every once in a great while you can get a conversation going with them. Usually about candy, unfortunately. You learn to like candy, though, and I guess that's something. Sometimes I think it's the most important thing in the whole world.

But if they'd just stop and think every once in a while. If they'd just slow down and talk to you, it might be better. But they don't stop to think. They're always rushing. I give an example. I start up some of the electronic equipment in the basement. We got this electronic dirt remover. I put my bedclothes in it. Sheets, blanket, pillow. Don't you think that wasn't a job! Down two windy flights of stairs with them.

Dropping them, picking them up, trying not to make any noise. House quiet. Real early. Everybody asleep.

Off she goes! Beautiful!

It don't stop, though. Like it does for Momma. I hear the bedclothes being torn up. Rip, rip-rip, rip. I better go tell them.

I go into their room. They are still asleep. I tiptoe toward Momma. She maybe won't take it as bad as Poppa.

Bam! I walk into this stupid new fly screen they have on and I forgot about. It shakes hell out of me, and I start to cry. Poppa sets up and screams, "You filthy shit!"

"What time is it?" asks Momma.

I don't understand about all this time thing, but I tell her about the bedclothes.

"My God!"

Stark naked, both of them, down the stairs. They get in each other's way.

I trail after. It's a lot of work, a little boy going down big stairs, trying to hurry. You have to be careful not to fall.

Poppa got it turned off. "That was close. It could have blown up half the house."

"You filthy shit!" Momma screams at me.

"Shut up, Hazel, this is serious. The kid could have killed himself."

I got a long lecture, right there, on how dangerous modern devices are. I wanted them to show me how to operate it right, so I wouldn't do it wrong again. But they were too dumb to do that. No, just leave it *alone*! How can I learn if they won't ever let me do anything? Why did they think I brought the bedclothes down in the first place?

Momma says, "First we got to give you a personality—we got to fix it so you can grow up to be the kind of man you want to be. *Then,* after that, you start going to school to learn things. When you get to be four years old, you start to school to learn things. You're only three and a half!"

Do you know how long you're three and a half? You're three and a half forever. There isn't any time at all. Some-

139

thing has gone wrong with their press, and they don't know it.

"What kind of man I want to be?"

"The country needs scientists," Poppa said. "We take a course from the government called: How to Make Scientists. How to shape personalities who want to understand how things work—who always have to figure things out, who aren't happy unless they're figuring things out. It's a good personality. Don't go on fiddling with this electronic gear any more or you'll get killed."

So that's what I'm going to be, a scientist. I don't know what the other choices were, but I guess it's too late anyhow. They might have been worse, at least I like to think that. Like going to India.

We kids at playground, we talk about the big bastards all the time. They used to be like us. Something happened to them that made them forget how to think.

I guess I will too. I get big, like them, I won't remember any of this, either. Lots of things I can't remember, already. There was a time, so long ago I just about can't remember, when Momma and Poppa loved me. That was in the beginning. But I guess maybe that's what it said in the book to do, too. It was nicer, then, but I forget so much. So all this I'll just forget. Because I'm not really me yet. They're still making me.

Right now, I think a lot about those people in India, I don't know why I should. I think it would be sensible to set them down to a table and feed them. I think that would be a good thing to do. But I guess when I get interested in learning how things work I won't think that way any more. And I guess I'll just forget all this.

I'm still standing here, crying, by the open drawer that's filled with this strange world of things. I've finally gotten to her. "What do you *want?*"

It's too late to find out whether there really is candy in there. It always was. She'd never spend all that time to search through there with me. It's too late to find out what this thing is for which there is no conceivable use. I've been

140

crying so long, I feel hurt by it and I can't stop crying.

"What do you *want*?"

I want to start forgetting. Like what they do to me, some-times, at night, to shape my personality. You wouldn't be-lieve how bad I want to forget that. And it's such a long time more, such a long, long, long time. I don't know if I can last, sometimes. I've got to hurry up and start forgetting. "I want to hurry up and be four years old!"

Afterword:

In "From the Government Printing Office", I have tried to project a future in which the education of children involves striking terror into their hearts in the hopes of producing more creative individuals. Perhaps this is not unlike what we have always done, with our frightening stories of witches and goblins and evil spirits and threats of hell. In my view, children are our most important product and should be bet-ter handled, but in any event one need only listen closely to the speech of children to hear the history of the future.

LAND OF THE GREAT HORSES

Introduction to

LAND OF THE GREAT HORSES:

Look out your window. What do you see? The gang fight on the corner, with the teenie-boppers using churchkeys on each other's faces; the scissors grinder with his multicolored cart and tinkling bells; a pudgy woman in a print dress too short for her fat legs, hoeing her lawn; a three-alarm fire with children trapped on the fifth story; a mad dog attached to the leg of a peddler of Seventh Day Adventist literature; an impending race riot with a representative of RAM on a sound truck. Any or all? It takes no special powers of observation to catalogue the unclassifiable. But now look again. What do you see? What you usually see? An empty street. *Now* catalogue:

Curbstones, without which cars would run up onto front lawns. Mailboxes, without which touch with the world would be diminished. Telephone poles and wires, without which communication would screech to a halt. Gutters, sewers and manholes, without which you would be flooded when it rains. Blacktop, without which the car you own wouldn't last a month on the crushed rock. The breeze, without which, well, a day is diminished. What are these things? They are the obvious. So obvious they become invisible. How many water hydrants and mailboxes did you pass today? None? Hardly. You passed dozens, but you did not see them. They are the incredibly valuable, absolutely necessary, totally ignored staples of a well-run community.

Speculative fiction is a small community. It has its obvious flashy residents. Knight, Sheckley, Sturgeon, Bradbury, Clarke, Vonnegut. We see them and take note of them, and know what they're about. But the community would not run one thousandth as well as it does without the quiet writers, the ones who turn out story after story, not hack work but really excellent stories, time after time. The kind you settle back and think about, after finishing them, saying, "That was a *good* story." And you promptly forget who wrote it. Perhaps later you recall the story. "Oh yeah, remember that one about . . ." and then you wrinkle down and say, "What the hell was the name of the guy who wrote it? He's done a bunch of things, you know, pretty fair writer. . . ."

The problem is a matter of cumulativeness. Each story is an excellence, standing alone. But somehow it never makes a totality, an image of a writer, a career in perspective. This is the sad but obvious thing about R. A. Lafferty's place in speculative fiction.

He is a man of substantiality, whose writing is top-flight. Not merely competent fiction, but genuinely exemplary fiction. He has been writing for—how many years? More than six, but less than fifteen? Something like that. Yet he is seldom mentioned when fans gather to discuss The Writers. Even though he has been anthologized many times, been included in Judith Merril's *Year's Best SF* on several occasions, and the Carr-Wollheim *World's Best* anthology twice, and appeared in almost all the science fiction magazines. He is the invisible man.

It will be rectified here. Raphael Aloysius Lafferty will emerge, will speak, will declare himself, and then you will read another extra-brilliant story by him. And dammit, this time *remember*!

Lafferty speaking: "I am, not necessarily in this order, fifty-one years old, a bachelor, an electrical engineer, a fat man.

"Born in Iowa, came to Oklahoma when I was four years old, and except for four years in the army have been here all my life. Also, one year on a little civil service job in Washington DC. The only college I've ever attended was a couple of years in the University of Tulsa's night school division long ago, mostly math and German. I've spent close to thirty years working for electrical jobbers, mostly as buyer and price-quotation man. During WWII I was stationed in

Texas, North Carolina, Florida, California, Australia, New Guinea, Morotai (Dutch East Indies, now Indonesia), and the Philippines. I was a *good* staff sergeant, and at one time I could talk pretty fair *pasar* Malay and Tagalog (of the Philippines).

"What does a man say about himself? Never the important things. I was a heavy drinker for a few years and gave it up about six years ago. This left a gap: when you give up the company of the more interesting drinkers, you give up something of the colorful and fantastic. So I substituted writing science fiction. Something I read in one of the writers' magazines gave me the silly idea that science fiction would be easy to write. It isn't, for me. I wasn't raised on the stuff like most of the writers in this form seem to have been.

"My hobby is language. Any language. I've got at least a thousand dollars in self-teach grammars and readers and dictionaries and Linguaphone and Cortinaphone courses. I've picked up a rough reading knowledge of all the languages of the Latin, German and Slavic families, as well as Irish and Greek; but actually Spanish, French and German are the only ones I read freely with respectable speed. I'm a Catholic of the out-of-season or conservative variety. As to politics, I am the only member of the American Centrist Party, whose tenets I will one day set out in an ironic-Utopia story. I'm a compulsive walker; turn me loose in a strange town and I'll explore every corner of it on foot inside a week. I don't think of myself as a very interesting fellow."

This is the editor again, for a final comment. Lafferty is about as uninteresting as his stories. Which is to say, not at all. As entered for the prosecution's case against RA's contention that he's a neb, the following story, one of my particular favorites in this book.

LAND OF THE GREAT HORSES

by R. A. Lafferty

"They came and took our country away from us," the people had always said. But nobody understood them.

Two Englishmen, Richard Rockwell and Seruno Smith, were rolling in a terrain buggy over the Thar Desert. It was bleak, red country, more rock than sand. It looked as though the top had been stripped off it and the naked underland left uncovered.

They heard thunder and it puzzled them. They looked at each other, the blond Rockwell and the dark Smith. It never thundered in the whole country between New Delhi and Bahawalpur. What would this rainless North India desert have to thunder with?

"Let's ride the ridges here," Rockwell told Smith, and he sent the vehicle into a climb. "It never rains here, but once before I was caught in a draw in a country where it never rained. I nearly drowned."

It thundered again, heavy and rolling, as though to tell them that they were hearing right.

"This draw is named Kuti Tavdavi—Little River," Smith said darkly. "I wonder why."

Then he jerked back as though startled at himself.

"Rockwell, why did I say that? I never saw this draw before. How did a name like that pop into my mind? But it's the low draw that would be a little river if it ever rained in this country. This land can't have significant rain. There's no high place to tip whatever moisture goes over."

"I wonder about that every time I come," said Rockwell, and raised his hand towards the shimmering heights—the Land of the Great Horses, the famous mirage. "If it were really there it would tip the moisture. It would make a lush savanna of all this."

They were mineral explorers doing ground minutiae on

148

promising portions of an aerial survey. The trouble with the Thar was that it had everything—lead, zinc, antimony, copper, tin, bauxite—in barely submarginal amounts. Nowhere would the Thar pay off, but everywhere it would almost pay.

Now it was lightning about the heights of the mirage, and they had never seen that before. It had clouded and lowered. It was thundering in rolling waves, and there is no mirage of sound.

"There is either a very large and very busy bird up there or this is rain," Rockwell said.

And it had begun to rain, softly but steadily. It was pleasant as they chukkered along in the vehicle through the afternoon. Rain in the desert is always like a bonus.

Smith broke into a happy song in one of the Northwest India tongues, a tune with a ribald swing to it, though Rockwell didn't understand the words. It was full of double rhymes and vowel-packed words such as a child might make up.

"How the devil do you know the tongues so well?" Rockwell asked. "I find them difficult, and I have a good linguistic background."

"I didn't have to learn them," Smith said, "I just had to remember them. They all cluster around the *boro jib* itself."

"Around the what? How many of the languages do you know?"

"All of them. The Seven Sisters, they're called: Punjabi, Kashmiri, Gujarati, Marathi, Sindhi, Hindi."

"Your Seven Sisters only number six," Rockwell jibed.

"There's a saying that the seventh sister ran off with a horse trader," Smith said. "But that seventh lass is still encountered here and there around the world."

Often they stopped to survey on foot. The very color of the new rivulets was significant to the mineral men, and this was the first time they had ever seen water flow in that country. They continued on fitfully and slowly, and ate up a few muddy miles.

Rockwell gasped once and nearly fell off the vehicle. He had seen a total stranger riding beside him, and it shook him.

Then he saw that it was Smith as he had always been, and he was dumbfounded by the illusion. And, soon, by something else.

"Something is very wrong here," Rockwell said.

"Something is very right here," Smith answered him, and then broke into another song in an India tongue.

"We're lost," Rockwell worried out loud. "We can't see any distance for the rain, but there shouldn't be rising ground here. It isn't mapped."

"Of course it is," Smith sang. "It's the Jalo Char."

"The what? Where did you get a name like that? The map's a blank here, and the country should be."

"Then the map is defective. Man, it's the sweetest valley in the world! It will lead us all the way up. How could the map forget it? How could we all forget it for so long?"

"Smith! What's wrong? You're pie-eyed."

"Everything's right, I tell you. I was reborn just a minute ago. It's a coming home."

"Smith! We're riding through green grass."

"I love it. I could crop it like a horse."

"That cliff, Smith! It shouldn't be that close! It's part of the mir—"

"Why, sir, that is Lolo Trusul."

"But it's not real! It's not on any topography map!"

"Map, sir? I'm a poor *kalo* man who wouldn't know about things like that."

"Smith! You're a qualified cartographer!"

"Does seem that I followed a trade with a name like that. But the cliff is real enough. I climbed it in my boyhood—in my other boyhood. And that yonder, sir, is Drapengoro Rez—the Grassy Mountain. And the high plateau ahead of us which we begin to climb is Diz Boro Grai—the Land of the Great Horses."

Rockwell stopped the terrain buggy and leaped off. Smith followed him in a happy daze.

"Smith, you're wide-eyed crazy!" Rockwell gasped. "And what am I? We're terribly lost somehow. Smith, look at the log chart and the bearings recorder!"

"Log chart, sir? I'm a poor *kalo* man who wouldn't know—"

"Damn you, Smith, you *made* these instruments. If they're correct we're seven hundred feet too high and have been climbing for ten miles into a highland that's supposed to be part of a mirage. These cliffs can't be here. We can't be here. Smith!"

But Seruno Smith had ambled off like a crazy man.

"Smith, where are you trotting off to? Can't you hear me?"

"You call to me, sir?" asked Smith. "And by such a name?"

"Are the two of us as crazy as the country?" Rockwell moaned. 'I've worked with you for three years. Isn't your name Smith?"

"Why, yes, sir, I guess it might be englished as Horse-Smith or Black-Smith. But my name is Pettalangro and I'm going home."

And the man who had been Smith started on foot up to the Land of the Great Horses.

"Smith, I'm getting on the buggy and I'm going back," Rockwell shouted. "I'm scared liverless of this country that changes. When a mirage turns solid it's time to quit. Come along now! We'll be back in Bikaner by tomorrow morning. There's a doctor there, and a whisky bar. We need one of them."

"Thank you, sir, but I must go up to my home," Smith sang out. "It was kind of you to give me a ride along the way."

'I'm leaving you, Smith. One crazy man is better than two."

"*Ashava, Sarishan,*" Smith called a parting.

"Smith, unriddle me one last thing," Rockwell called, trying to find a piece of sanity to hold to. "What is the name of the seventh sister?"

"Deep Romany," Smith sang, and he was gone up into the high plateau that had always been a mirage.

In an upper room on Olive Street in St. Louis, Missouri, a half-and-half couple were talking half-and-half.

"The *rez* has *riser'd*," the man said, "I can *sung* it like *brishindo*. Let's *jal*."

"All right," the wife said, "if you're *awa*."

"Hell, I bet I can *ricker* plenty *bano* on the *beda* we got here. I'll have *kakko* come *kinna* it *saro*."

"With a little *bachi* we can be *jal'd* by *areat*," said the wife.

"*Nashiva*, woman, *nashiva!*"

"All right," the wife said, and she began to pack their suitcases.

In Camargo in the Chihuahua State of Mexico, a shade-tree mechanic sold his business for a hundred pesos and told his wife to pack up—they were leaving.

"To leave now when business is so good?" she asked.

"I only got one car to fix and I can't fix that," the man said.

"But if you keep it long enough, he will pay you to put it together again even if it isn't fixed. That's what he did last time. And you've a horse to shoe."

"I'm afraid of that horse. It has come back, though. Let's go."

"Are you sure we will be able to find it?"

"Of course I'm not sure. We will go in our wagon and our sick horse will pull it."

"Why will we go in the wagon, when we have a car, of sorts?"

"I don't know why. But we will go in the wagon, and we will nail the old giant horseshoe up on the lintel board."

A carny in Nebraska lifted his head and smelled the air.

"It's come back," he said. "I always knew we'd know. Any other Romanies here?"

"I got a little *rart* in me," said one of his fellows. "This *narvelengero dives* is only a two-bit carnival anyhow. We'll tell the boss to shove it up his *chev* and we'll be gone."

In Tulsa, a used-car dealer named Gypsy Red announced the hottest sale on the row:

"Everything for nothing! I'm leaving. Pick up the papers and drive them off. Nine new heaps and thirty good ones. All free."

"You think we're crazy?" the people asked. "There's a catch."

Red put the papers for all the cars on the ground and put a brick on top of them. He got in the worst car on the lot and drove it off forever.

"All free," he sang out as he drove off. "Pick up the papers and drive the cars away."

They're still there. You think people are crazy to fall for something like that that probably has a catch to it?

In Galveston a barmaid named Margaret was asking merchant seamen how best to get passage to Karachi.

"Why Karachi?" one of them asked her.

"I thought it would be the nearest big port," she said. "It's come back, you know."

"I kind of felt this morning it had come back," he said. "I'm a *chal* myself. Sure, we'll find something that way."

In thousands of places fawney-men and dukkerin-women, kakki-baskros and hegedusies, clowns and commission men, Counts of Condom and Dukes of Little Egypt *parvel'd* in their chips and got ready to roll.

Men and families made sudden decisions in every country. *Athinganoi* gathered in the hills above Salonika in Greece and were joined by brothers from Serbia and Albania and the Rhodope Hills of Bulgaria. *Zingari* of North Italy gathered around Pavia and began to roll towards Genoa to take ship. *Boemios* of Portugal came down to Porto and Lisbon.

Gitanos of Andalusia and all southern Spain came to Sanlúcar and Málaga. *Ziguener* from Thuringia and Hanover thronged to Hamburg to find ocean passage. *Gioboga* and their mixed-blood *Shelta* cousins from every *cnoc* and *coill* of Ireland found boats at Dublin and Limerick and Bantry.

From deeper Europe, *Tsigani* began to travel overland eastward. The people were going from two hundred ports of every continent and over a thousand highroads—many of them long forgotten.

Balauros, Kalo, Manusch, Melelo, Tsigani, Moro, Romani, Flamenco, Sinto, Cicara, the many-named people was traveling in its thousands. The *Romani Rai* was moving.

Two million Gypsies of the world were going home.

At the Institute, Gregory Smirnov was talking to his friends and associates.

"You remember the thesis I presented several years ago," he said, "that, a little over a thousand years ago, Outer Visitors came down to Earth and took a sliver of our Earth away with them. All of you found the proposition comical, but I arrived at my conclusion by isostatic and eustatic analysis carried out minutely. There is no doubt that it happened."

"One of our slivers is missing," said Aloysius Shiplap. "You guessed the sliver taken at about ten thousand square miles area and no more than a mile thick at its greatest. You said you thought they wanted to run this sliver from our Earth through their laboratories as a sample. Do you have something new on our missing sliver?"

"I'm closing the inquiry," Gregory said. "They've brought it back."

It was simple really, *jekvasteskero*, Gypsy-simple. It is the *gadjo*, the non-Gypsies of the world, who give complicated answers to simple things.

"They came and took our country away from us," the Gypsies had always said, and that is what had happened.

The Outer Visitors had run a slip under it, rocked it

gently to rid it of nervous fauna, and then taken it away for study. For a marker, they left an immaterial simulacrum of that high country as we ourselves sometimes set name or picture tags to show where an object will be set later. This simulacrum was often seen by humans as a mirage.

The Outer Visitors also set simulacra in the minds of the superior fauna that fled from the moving land. This would be a homing instinct, inhibiting permanent settlement anywhere until the time should come for the resettlement; entwined with this instinct were certain premonitions, fortune-showings, and understandings.

Now the Visitors brought the slice of land back, and its old fauna homed in on it.

"What will the—ah—patronizing smile on my part—Outer Visitors do now, Gregory?" Aloysius Shiplap asked back at the Institute.

"Why, take another sliver of our Earth to study, I suppose, Aloysius," Gregory Smirnov said.

Low-intensity earthquakes rocked the Los Angeles area for three days. The entire area was evacuated of people. Then there was a great whistle blast from the sky as if to say, "All ashore that's going ashore."

Then the surface to some little depth and all its superstructure was taken away. It was gone. And then it was quickly forgotten.

From the TWENTY-SECOND-CENTURY COMPREHENSIVE ENCYCLOPEDIA, Vol 1, page 389—

ANGELENOS. (*See also* Automobile Gypsies and Prune Pickers.) A mixed ethnic group of unknown origin, much given to wandering in automobiles. It is predicted that they will be the last users of this vehicle, and several archaic chrome-burdened models are still produced for their market. These people are not beggars; many of them are of superior intelligence. They often set up in business, usually as real estate dealers, gamblers, confidence men, managers of mail-order diploma mills, and promoters of one sort or other. They seldom remain long in one location.

Their pastimes are curious. They drive for hours and days on old and seldom-used cloverleafs and freeways. It has been said that a majority of the Angelenos are narcotics users, but Harold Freelove (who lived for some months as an Angeleno) has proved this false. What they inhale at their frolics (smog-crocks) is a black smoke of carbon and petroleum waste laced with monoxide. Its purpose is not clear.

The religion of the Angelenos is a mixture of old cults with a very strong eschatological element. The Paradise Motif is represented by reference to a mystic "Sunset Boulevard". The language of the Angelenos is a colorful and racy argot. Their account of their origin is vague:

"They came and took our dizz away from us," they say.

Afterword:

We are all cousins. I don't believe in reincarnation, but the only system of reincarnation that satisfies justice is that every being should become successively (or sometimes simultaneously) every other being. This would take a few billion lifetimes; the writer with a feel for the Kindred tries to do it in one.

We are all Romanies, as in the parable here, and we have a built-in homing to and remembrance of a woollier and more excellent place, a reality that masquerades as a mirage. Whether the more excellent place is here or heretofore or hereafter, I don't know, or whether it will be our immediate world when it is sufficiently animated; but there is an intuition about it which sometimes passes through the whole community. There is, or there ought to be, these shimmering heights; and they belong to us. Controversy (or polarity) is between ourselves as individuals and as members of the incandescent species, confronted with the eschatological thing. I'd express it more intelligently if I knew how.

But I didn't write the story to point up this notion, but to drop a name. There *is* a Margaret the barmaid—not the one in the story, of course (for we have to abide by the disavowal "Any resemblance to actual persons living or dead is purely coincidental"), but another of the same name—and she is a Romany. "Put my name in a story, just Margaret the barmaid," she told me. "I don't care what, even name a dog that." "But you won't know it," I said, "you don't read anything, and none of the people you run around with do." "I will know it exactly," she said, "when someone else reads it someday, when they come to the name Margaret the barmaid. I know things like that."

Not from me, but from someone who reads it here, Margaret will receive the intuition, and both parties will know it. "Hey, the old bat did it," Margaret will say. I don't know what the reader-sender caught in the middle will say or think.

I am pleased to be a member of this august though sometimes raffish company playing here in this production. It has an air of excellence, and some of it will rub off on me. We are, all of us, Counts of Con-dom and Dukes of Little Egypt.

THE RECOGNITION

Introduction to

THE RECOGNITION:

I have this theory. In point of fact I have a barnhouse full of
theories, but I've got this *particular* theory about the men
who wind up as leaders of movements. It would not surprise
me to find out (through the discovery of some new Dead Sea
Scrolls perhaps) that allofasudden Jesus turned around (so to
speak) on the cross and looked down and said, "How the hell
did I get into this?" Did he really think he was going to
become the head of a big-deal Movement? Did Gandhi? Did
Hitler? Yeah, well, maybe him, but what can you expect
from a short ugly plasterer? Did Stokeley Carmichael? Did
J. G. Ballard? Oh! *There* we are!

Jim Ballard, who seems to me to write peculiarly Ballardian stories—tales difficult to pin down as to one style or
one theme or one approach but all very personally trade-
marked Ballard—is the acknowledged leader of the "British
school of science fiction." I'm sure if you said this to Ballard
(who chooses to pronounce it Buh-*lard*), he would stare at
you as if you were daft. He certainly doesn't write like the
leader of a movement, for a movement generally involves
easily cited examples, jingoism, obviousness and a strong
dose of predictability. None of these is present in the work of
J. G. Ballard.

Among his highly celebrated books are *The Drowned
World*, *The Wind from Nowhere*, *Terminal Beach*, *The
Voices of Time*, *The Burning World*, *Billenium* and *The
Crystal World*. None of these contains ideas so revolutionary
or arresting that they should comprise a rationale for being a
"new movement". Yet *in totality* they present a kind of en-
riched literacy, a darker yet somehow clearer—perhaps the
word is "poignant"—approach to the materials of speculative writing. There is a flavor of surrealism to Ballard's

writing. No, it's not that, either It is, in some ways, *serene*, as oriental philosophy is serene. Resigned yet vital. There appears to be a superimposed reality that covers the underlying pure fantasy of Ballardian conception. Frankly, Ballard's work defies categorization or careful analysis. It is like four-color lithography. The most exquisite Wyeth landscape, when examined more and more minutely, begins to resemble pointillism, and finally nothing but a series of disconnected colored dots. So do Ballard's stories, when subjected to the unfeeling scrutiny of cold analysis, break down into disconnected parts. When read, when assimilated as they stand, they become something greater than the sum of the parts.

One such story is the one you are about to read. It is a prime example of Ballard at his most mysterious, his most compelling. The story says all that need be said about Ballard the writer. As for Ballard the man, the information is as sparse as the stories: he was born in Shanghai, China, in 1930, of English parents; during WWII he was interned in a Japanese prison camp and in 1946 was repatriated to England; he later studied medicine at Cambridge University.

As stated elsewhere in this book about another story, I have no idea whether this is science fiction, or fantasy, or allegory, or cautionary tale. All I know for certain is that it is immensely entertaining, thought-provoking and fits perfectly something Saul Bellow said about the excuse for a story's existence. He said it in 1963:

". . . a story should be interesting, highly interesting, as interesting as possible—inexplicably absorbing. There can be no other justification for any piece of fiction."

THE RECOGNITION

by J. G. Ballard

On Midsummer's Eve a small circus visited the town in the West Country where I was spending my holiday. Three days earlier the large travelling fair which always came to the town in the summer, equipped with a ferris wheel, merry-go-rounds and dozens of booths and shooting galleries, had taken up its usual site on the open common in the centre of the town, and this second arrival was forced to pitch its camp on the waste ground beyond the warehouses along the river.

At dusk, when I strolled through the town, the ferris wheel was revolving above the coloured lights, and people were riding the carousels and walking arm in arm along the cobbled roads that surrounded the common. Away from this hubbub of noise the streets down to the river were almost deserted, and I was glad to walk alone through the shadows past the boarded shopfronts. Midsummer's Eve seemed to me a time for reflection as much as for celebration, for a careful watch on the shifting movements of nature. When I crossed the river, whose dark water flowed through the town like a gilded snake, and entered the woods that stretched to one side of the road, I had the unmistakable sensation that the forest was preparing itself, and that within its covens even the roots of the trees were sliding through the soil and testing their sinews.

It was on the way back from this walk, as I crossed the bridge, that I saw the small itinerant circus arrive at the town. The procession, which approached the bridge by a side road, consisted of no more than half a dozen wagons, each carrying a high barred cage and drawn by a pair of careworn horses. At its head a young woman with a pallid face and bare arms rode on a grey stallion. I leaned on the balustrade in the centre of the bridge and watched the procession reach the embankment. The young woman hesitated, pulling on the heavy leather bridle, and looked over her shoulder as the wagons closed together. They began to ascend the bridge. Although the gradient was slight, the horses seemed barely able to reach the crest, tottering on their weak legs, and I had ample time to make a first scrutiny of this strange caravan that was later to preoccupy me.

163

Urging on her tired stallion, the young woman passed me—at least, it seemed to me then that she was young, but her age was so much a matter of her own moods and mine. I was to see her on several occasions—sometimes she would seem little more than a child of twelve, with an unformed chin and staring eyes above the bony cheeks. Later she would appear to be almost middle-aged, the grey hair and skin revealing the angular skull beneath them.

At first, as I watched from the bridge, I guessed her to be about twenty years old, presumably the daughter of the proprietor of this threadbare circus. As she jogged along with one hand on the reins the lights from the distant fairground shone intermittently in her face, disclosing a high-bridged nose and firm mouth. Although by no means beautiful, she had that curious quality of attractiveness that I had often noticed in the women who worked at fairgrounds, an elusive sexuality despite their shabby clothes and surroundings. As she passed she looked down at me, her quiet eyes on some unfelt point within my face.

The six wagons followed her, the horses heaving the heavy cages across the camber. Behind the bars I caught a glimpse of worn straw and a small hutch in the corner, but there was no sign of the animals. I assumed them to be too undernourished to do more than sleep. As the last wagon passed I saw the only other member of the troupe, a dwarf in a leather jacket driving the wooden caravan at the rear.

I walked after them across the bridge, wondering if they were late arrivals at the fair already in progress. But from the way they hesitated at the foot of the bridge, the young woman looking to left and right while the dwarf sat hunched in the shadow of the cage in front of him, it was plain they had no connection whatever with the brilliant ferris wheel and the amusements taking place on the common. Even the horses, standing uncertainly with their heads lowered to avoid the coloured lights, seemed aware of this exclusion.

After a pause they moved off along the narrow road that followed the bank, the wagons rolling from side to side as the wooden wheels slipped on the grass-covered verge. A short distance away was a patch of waste ground that separated the warehouses near the wharves from the terraced cottages below the bridge. A single street lamp on the north side cast a dim light over the cinder surface. By now dusk had settled over the town and seemed to isolate this dingy patch of ground, no longer enlivened in any way by the movement of the river.

The procession headed towards this dark enclosure. The young woman turned her horse off the road and led the wagons across the cinders to the high wall of the first warehouse. Here they stopped, the wagons still in line ahead, the horses obviously glad to be concealed by the darkness. The dwarf jumped down from his perch and trotted round to where the woman was dismounting from the stallion.

At this time I was strolling along the bank a short distance behind them. Something about this odd little troupe intrigued me, though in retrospect it may be that the calm eyes of the young woman as she looked down at me had acted as more of a spur than seemed at the time. Nonetheless, I was puzzled by what seemed the very pointlessness of their existence. Few things are as drab as a down-at-heel circus, but this one was so travel-worn and dejected as to deny them the chance of making any profit whatever. Who were this strange pale-haired woman and her dwarf? Did they imagine that anyone would actually come to this dismal patch of ground by the warehouses to look at their secretive animals? Perhaps they were simply delivering a group of aged creatures to an abbatoir specializing in circus animals, and pausing here for the night before moving on.

Yet, as I suspected, the young woman and the dwarf were already moving the wagons into the unmistakable pattern of a circus. The woman dragged at the bridles while the dwarf darted between her feet, switching at the horses' ankles with his leather hat. The docile brutes heaved at their wagons, and within five minutes the cages were arranged in a rough circle. The horses were unshackled from their shafts, and the dwarf, helped by the young woman, led them towards the river where they began cropping quietly at the dark grass.

Within the cages there was a stir of movement, and one or two pale forms shuffled about in the straw. The dwarf scurried up the steps of the caravan and lit a lamp over a stove which I could see in the doorway. He came down with a metal bucket and moved along the cages. He poured a little water into each of the pails and pushed them towards the hutches with a broom.

The woman followed him, but seemed as uninterested as the dwarf in the animals inside the cages. When he put away the bucket she held a ladder for him and he climbed onto the roof of the caravan. He lowered down a bundle of clapboard signs fastened together by a strip of canvas. After untying them the dwarf carried the signs over to the cages. He climbed up the ladder again and began to secure the signs over the bars.

In the dim light from the street lamp I could make out only the faded designs painted years earlier in the traditional style of fairground marquees, the floral patterns and cartouches overlaid with lettering of some kind. Moving nearer the cages, I reached the edge of the clearing. The young woman turned and saw me. The dwarf was fixing the last of the signs, and she stood by the ladder, one hand on the shaft, regarding me with an unmoving gaze. Perhaps it was her protective stance as the diminutive figure moved about above her, but she seemed far older than when she had first appeared with her menagerie at the outskirts of the town. In the faint light her hair had become almost grey, and her bare arms seemed lined and work-worn. As I drew closer, passing the first of the cages, she turned to follow me with her eyes, as if trying to take some interest in my arrival on the scene.

At the top of the ladder there was a flurry of movement. Slipping through the dwarf's fingers, the sign toppled from the roof and fell to the ground at the woman's feet. Whirling his short arms and legs, the dwarf leapt down from the ladder. He picked himself off the ground, wobbling about like a top as he regained his balance. He dusted his hat against his boots and put it back on his head, then started up the ladder again.

The woman held his arm. She moved the ladder further along the cage, trying to balance the shafts against the bars.

On an impulse, more or less out of sympathy, I stepped forward.

"Can I help you?" I said. "Perhaps I can reach the roof. If you hand me the sign . . ."

The dwarf hesitated, looking at me with his doleful eyes. He seemed prepared to let me help, but stood there with his hat in one hand as if prevented from saying anything to me by an unstated set of circumstances, some division of life as formal and impassable as those of the most rigid castes.

The woman, however, gestured me to the ladder, turning her face away as I settled the shafts against the bars. Through the dim light she watched the horses cropping the grass along the bank.

I climbed the ladder, and then took the sign lifted up to me by the dwarf. I settled it on the roof, weighing it down with two half bricks left there for the purpose, and read the legends painted across the warped panel. As I deciphered the words "marvels" and "spectacular" (obviously the signs bore no relation to the animals within the cages, and had been stolen from another fair or found on some refuse heap) I noticed a sudden movement from the cage below me. There was a burrowing through the straw, and a low, pale-skinned creature retreated into its burrow.

This disturbance of the straw—whether the animal had darted out from fear or in an attempt to warn me off I had no means of telling—had released a strong and obscurely familiar smell. It hung around me as I came down the ladder, muffled but vaguely offensive. I searched the hutch for a glimpse of the animal, but it had scuffled the straw into the door.

The dwarf and the woman nodded to me as I turned from the ladder. There was no hostility in their attitude—the dwarf, if anything, was in the point of thanking me, his mouth moving in a wordless rictus—but for some reason they seemed to feel unable to make any contact with me. The woman was standing with her back to the street lamp, and her face, softened by the darkness, now appeared small and barely formed, like that of an unkempt child.

"You're all ready," I said half jocularly. With something of an effort, I added: "It looks very nice."

I glanced at the cages when they made no comment. One or two of the animals sat at the backs of their hutches, their pale forms indistinct in the faint light. "When do you open?" I asked. "Tomorrow?"

"We're open now," the dwarf said.

"Now?" Not sure whether this was a joke, I started to point at the cages, but the statement had obviously been meant at its face value.

"I see . . . you're open this evening." Searching for something to say—they seemed prepared to stand there indefinitely with me—I went on: "When do you leave?"

"Tomorrow," the woman told me in a low voice. "We have to go in the morning."

As if taking their cue from this, the two of them moved across the small arena, clearing to one side the pieces of newspaper and other refuse. By the time I walked away, baffled by the entire purpose of this pitiful menagerie, they had already finished, and stood waiting between the cages for their first customers. I paused on the bank beside the cropping horses, whose quiet figures seemed as insubstantial as those of the dwarf and their mistress, and wondered what bizarre logic had brought them to the town, when a second fair, almost infinitely larger and gayer, was already in full swing.

At the thought of the animals I recalled the peculiar smell that hung about the cages, vaguely unpleasant but reminiscent of an odour I was certain I knew well. For some reason I was also convinced that this familiar smell was a clue to the strange nature of the circus. Beside me the horses gave off a pleasant scent of bran and sweat. Their downcast heads, lowered to the grass by the water's edge, seemed to hide from me some secret concealed within their luminous eyes.

I walked back towards the centre of the town, relieved to see the illuminated superstructure of the ferris wheel rotating above the rooftops. The roundabouts and amusement arcades, the shooting galleries and the tunnel of love were part of a familiar world. Even the witches and vampires painted over the house of horrors were nightmares from a predictable quarter of the evening sky. By contrast the young woman—or was she young?—and her dwarf were travellers from an unknown country, a vacant realm where nothing had any meaning. It was this absence of intelligible motive that I found so disturbing about them.

I wandered through the crowds below the marquees, and on an impulse decided to ride on the ferris wheel. As I waited my turn with the group of young men and women, the electrified gondolas of the wheel rose high into the evening air, so that all the music and light of the fair seemed to have been scooped from the star-filled sky.

I climbed into my gondola, sharing it with a young woman and her daughter, and a few moments later we were revolving through the brilliant air, the fairground spread below us. During the two or three minutes of the ride I was busy shouting to the young woman and her child as we pointed out to each other familiar landmarks in the town. However, when we stopped and sat at the top of the wheel as the passengers below disembarked, I noticed for the first time the bridge I had crossed earlier that evening. Following the course of the river, I saw the single street lamp that shone over the waste ground near the warehouses where the white-faced woman and the dwarf had set up their rival circus. As our gondola moved forward and began its descent the dim forms of two of the wagons were visible in an interval between the rooftops.

Half an hour later, when the fair began to close, I walked back to the river. Small groups of people were moving arm in arm through the streets, but by the time the warehouses came into sight I was almost alone on the cobbled pavements that wound between the terraced cottages. Then the street lamp appeared, and the circle of wagons beyond it.

To my surprise, a few people were actually visiting the menagerie. I stood in the road below the street lamp and watched the two couples and a third man who were wandering around the cages and trying to identify the animals. Now and then they would go up to the bars and peer through them, and there was a shout of laughter as one of the women pretended to flinch away in alarm. The man with her held a few shreds of straw in his hand and threw them at the door of the hutch, but the animal refused to appear. The group resumed their circuit of the cages, squinting in the dim light.

Meanwhile the dwarf and the woman remained silent to one side. The woman stood by the steps of the caravan, looking out at her patrons as if unconcerned whether they came or not. The dwarf, his bulky hat hiding his face, stood patiently on the other side of the arena, moving his ground as the party of visitors continued their tour. He was not carrying a collection bag or roll of tickets, and it seemed likely, even if only reasonable, that there was no charge for admission.

Something of the peculiar atmosphere, or perhaps their failure to bring the animals from their hutches, seemed to transmit itself to the party of visitors. After trying to read the signs, one of the men began to rattle a stick between the bars of the cages. Then, losing interest abruptly, they made off together without a backward glance at either the woman or the dwarf. As he passed me the man with the stick pulled a face and waved his hand in front of his nose.

I waited until they had gone and then approached the cages. The dwarf appeared to remember me—at least, he made no effort to scuttle away but watched me with his drifting eyes. The woman sat on the steps of the caravan, gazing across the cinders with the expression of a tired and unthinking child.

I glanced into one or two of the cages. There was no sign of the animals, but the smell that had driven off the previous party was certainly pronounced. The familiar pungent odour quickened my nostrils. I walked over to the young woman.

"You've had some visitors," I commented.

"Not many," she replied. "A few have come."

I was about to point out that she could hardly expect a huge attendance if none of the animals in the cages was prepared to make an appearance, but the girl's hangdog look restrained me. The top of her robe revealed a small childlike breast, and it seemed impossible that this pale young woman should have been put in sole charge of such a doomed enterprise. Searching for an excuse that might console her, I said: "It's rather late, there's the other fair . . ." I pointed to the cages. "That smell, too. Perhaps you're used to it, but it might put people off." I forced a smile. "I'm sorry, I don't mean to—"

"I understand," she said matter-of-factly. "It's why we have to leave so soon." She nodded at the dwarf. "We clean them every day."

I was about to ask what animals the cages held—the smell reminded me of the chimpanzee house at the zoo—when there was a commotion from the direction of the bank. A group of sailors, two or three girls among them, came swaying along the towpath. They greeted the sight of the menagerie with boisterous shouts. Linked arm in arm, they made a drunken swerve up the bank, then stamped across the cinders to the cages. The dwarf moved out of their way, and watched from the shadows between two of the wagons, hat in hand.

The sailors pushed over to one of the cages and pressed their faces to the bars, nudging each other in the ribs and whistling in an effort to bring the creature out of its hutch. They moved over to the next cage, pulling at each other in a struggling mêlée.

One of them shouted at the woman, who sat on the steps of the caravan. "Are you closed, or what? The perisher won't come out of his hole!"

There was a roar of laughter at this. Another of the sailors rattled one of the girls' handbags, and then dug into his pockets.

"Pennies out, lads. Who's got the tickets?"

171

He spotted the dwarf and tossed the penny towards him. A moment later a dozen coins showered through the air around the dwarf's head. He scuttled about, warding them off with his hat, but made no effort to pick up the coins.

The sailors moved on to the third cage. After a fruitless effort to draw the animal towards them they began to rock the wagon from side to side. Their good humour was beginning to fade. As I left the young woman and strolled past the cages several of the sailors had started to climb up onto the bars.

At this point one of the doors sprang open. As it clanged against the bars the noise fell away. Everyone stepped back, as if expecting some huge striped tiger to spring out at them from its hutch. Two of the sailors moved forward and gingerly reached for the door. As they closed it one of them peered into the cage. Suddenly he leapt up into the doorway. The others shouted at him, but the sailor kicked aside the straw and stepped across to the hutch.

"It's bloody empty!"

As he shouted this out there was a delighted roar. Slamming the door—curiously enough, the bolt was on the inside—the sailor began to prance around the cage, gibbering like a baboon through the bars. At first I thought he must be mistaken, and looked round at the young woman and the dwarf. Both were watching the sailors but gave no inkling that there was any danger from the animal within. Sure enough, as a second sailor was let into the cage and dragged the hutch over to the bars, I saw that it was unoccupied.

Involuntarily I found myself staring at the young woman. Was this, then, the point of this strange and pathetic menagerie—that there were no animals at all, at least in most of the cages, and that what was being exhibited was simply nothing, merely the cages themselves, the essence of imprisonment with all its ambiguities? Was this a zoo in the abstract, some kind of bizarre comment on the meaning of life? Yet neither the young woman nor the dwarf seemed subtle enough for this, and possibly there was a less farfetched explanation. Perhaps once there had been animals, but these had died out, and the girl and her companion had found that people would still come and gaze at the empty cages, with much the same fascination of visitors to disused cemeteries. After a while they no longer charged any admission, but drifted aimlessly from town to town. . . .

Before I could pursue this train of thought there was a shout behind me. A sailor ran past, brushing my shoulder. The discovery of the empty cage had removed any feelings of restraint, and the sailors were chasing the dwarf among the wagons. At this first hint of violence the woman stood up and disappeared into the caravan, and the poor dwarf was left to fend for himself. One of the sailors tripped him up and snatched the hat off his head as the little figure lay in the dust with his legs in the air.

The sailor in front of me caught the hat and was about to toss it up onto one of the wagon roofs. Stepping forward, I held his arm, but he wrenched himself away. The dwarf had vanished from sight, and another group of sailors were trying to turn one of the wagons and push it towards the river. Two of them had got among the horses and were lifting the women onto their backs. The grey stallion which had led the procession across the bridge suddenly bolted along the bank. Running after it through the confusion, I heard a warning shout behind me. There was the thud of hooves on the wet turf, and a woman's cry as a horse swerved above me. I was struck on the head and shoulder and knocked heavily to the ground.

It must have been some two hours later that I awoke, lying on a bench beside the bank. Under the night sky the town was silent, and I could hear the faints sounds of a water vole moving along the river and the distant splash of water around the bridge. I sat up and brushed away the dew that had formed on my clothes. Further along the bank the circus wagons stood in the clearing darkness, the dim forms of the horses motionless by the water.

Collecting myself, I decided that after being knocked down by the horse I had been carried to the bench by the sailors and left there to recover when and as soon as I could. Nursing my head and shoulders, I looked around for any sign of the party, but the bank was deserted. Standing up, I slowly walked back towards the circus, in the vague hope that the dwarf might help me home.

Twenty yards away, I saw something move in one of the cages, its white form passing in front of the bars. There was no sign of the dwarf or the young woman, but the wagons had been pushed back into place.

Standing in the centre of the cages, I peered about uncertainly, aware that their occupants had at last emerged from the hutches. The angular grey bodies were indistinct in the darkness, but as familiar as the pungent smell that came from the cages.

A voice shouted behind me, a single obscene word. I turned to find its source, and saw one of the occupants watching me with cold eyes. As I stared he raised his hand and moved the fingers in a perverted gesture.

A second voice called out, followed by a chorus of abusive catcalls. With an effort, I managed to clear my head, then began a careful walk around the cages, satisfying myself for the last time as to the identity of their tenants. Except for the one at the end, which was empty, the others were occupied. The thin figures stood openly in front of the bars that protected them from me, their pallid faces shining in the dim light. At last I recognized the smell that came from the cages.

As I walked away their derisive voices called after me, and the young woman roused from her bed in the caravan watched quietly from the steps.

Afterword:

"The Recognition" expresses a cordial distaste for the human race—not inappropriately. The temper of the times seems to be one of self-love, if of a strange sort—Caliban asleep across a mirror stained with vomit. But perhaps the story also illustrates the paradox that the only real freedom is to be found

in a prison. Sometimes it is difficult to tell on which side of
the bars we are—the real gaps between the bars are the su-
tures of one's own skull. Originally I toyed with the notion
of the narrator entering a cage and joining the circus, but
this would have destroyed an important point. The story is
not in fact a piece of hard-won misanthropy but a comment
on some of the more unusual perspectives that separate us.
The most important characters, whose motives are a key to
the story, are the young woman and her dwarf. Why do they
take this dismal circus on its endless tour?

JUDAS

Introduction to

JUDAS:

Seated at the right hand of God, I was asked, "Give the operable word for John Brunner, the well-known English science fiction novelist." I thought a moment and suggested "urbane". God smiled benignly, but was obviously not satisfied with the initial response. " 'Suave?' " I ventured. God made a tiny *moue* of vexation. " 'Chivalrous? Refined? Cultured? Gracious?' " God gave me one of *those* looks. " 'Charming?' " I said, in a small voice. God broke into a helluva smile. He clapped me on the back with camaraderie. "Excellent, Harlan, excellent!" he said in his mellow voice.

"Thank you, Mr. Brunner," I replied.

The first time I heard of John Brunner was in 1952. He had one half the magazine known as *Two Complete Science-Adventure Novels* (I *think* *t*hat was the title. It's been quite a few years. But I do recall the story on the other half of the magazine was a Poul Anderson epic). I don't recall the name of the novelette (which they invariably called a "complete novel") but it was published by Fiction House, so it must have been something like "Sex Kings of the Plutonian Pleasure Domes". It was written by Killian Huston Brunner. Ha-*ha*, Brunner, now we gotcha! [And this comment from John Brunner: "Your memory anent the issue of *TCSAB* in which you first saw my name is a trifle astray. It wasn't 1952 but 1953. The other half was Brian Berry's 'Mission to Marakee', not a Poul Anderson story. The name was—and is—(John) Kilian Houston Brunner (not Killian Huston). And for what it's worth the story was titled 'The Wanton of Argus'."]

John Brunner was born in 1934, in Oxfordshire, England. He has written the Hugo nominee *The Whole Man*, which was brilliant. In 1940 he found a copy of Wells's *War of the Worlds* in his nursery and was hooked. He has written *The Long Result*, which was almost a total success. In 1943 he started (but did not finish) writing his first s-f story, because he couldn't find enough of the stuff to read. He has written "The Squares of the City", which is a small masterpiece of technique. In 1947 he collected his first rejection slip, and in 1951 sold his first paperback in the United Kingdom. He has written "The Dreaming Earth", which fell apart badly in the last section but was fascinating up to that point. In 1952 he made his first sales to American magazines, and from 1953 to 1955 he was a (drafted without enthusiasm) pilot officer in the RAF. He has written *Wear the Butchers' Medal*, which is a stunning suspense-adventure novel. In 1956 he was a technical abstractor on a magazine edited by "John Christopher" and from 1956 to 1958 was a publishers' editor under Jonathan Burke. He has written *The Space-Time Juggler* and *Astronauts Must Not Land* and *Castaways' World* and *Listen! The Stars!* and ten others all for one publisher who slapped the insipid names just listed on books that may not be classics in the field of speculative fiction but are, each and every one, well written, entertaining and worth reading, which makes it a shame they are albatrossed by such hideous titles. But since 1958, when John Brunner got married and turned free lance, he has published over forty books, so he takes the bitter with the sweet.

He has written mainly speculative fiction but his output also includes thrillers and straight novels. He has contributed to almost every magazine in sight, written a great many topical "folk" songs including one recorded by Pete Seeger, and he has managed to visit about fourteen different countries thus far. ("I have the impression that I'm losing ground, though," he writes. "Every time I notch up a new one, another declares its independence and leaves me with just as many still unvisited.")

He lives in Hampstead, London, his favorite place, drives a Daimler V-8 convertible, and enjoys his work so much it seems to be almost a hobby for him. Brunner's current ambition: to build a villa in Greece and get away from the English winter, which is almost always wet.

The story you are about to read was the third Brunner submission for DANGEROUS VISIONS. Not that either of the first two wouldn't have done marvelously, but there were some minor entanglements. On the first one, called "The Vitanuls", I had the temerity to disagree with John on the manner of presentation of an absolutely brilliant and original concept. I sent him about five single-spaced pages of perceptive, intelligent, pithy comment, outlining rewrite, and with his usual good grace, and with almost a surfeit of *panache*, he wrote me back and told me to get stuffed.

So that took care of *that* one. The stupid bastard doesn't know a new Maxwell Perkins when he sees one. But, great in my magnanimity, I accepted a second submission from Brunner's agent, a wildly hilarious black comedy called "Nobody Axed You," and was ready to send out the check when I was informed, rather sheepishly, by the agent, that there was, uh, one small, er, minor, really insig*nif*icant, uh, problem with my publishing the story as a brand-new, never-before-in-print original. It had been published in England. But that didn't matter, the agent hastily assured me. After all, it had only been in a British magazine so none of the readers of my anthology could *poss*ibly have seen it. So that took care of *that* one.

A month later Brunner, shamefaced, and having received a cable from the sanitarium where I was under heavy sedation, sent me a story on his own. That story, "Judas", begins on the next page.

You'd love Brunner. He's quiet, but deadly. Like a curare-tipped blow dart in the back of the neck.

JUDAS

by John Brunner

The Friday evening service was drawing to its close. The rays of the declining spring sun slanted through the polychrome plastic of the windows and lay along the floor of the central aisle like a pool of oil spilt on a wet road. On the polished steel of the altar a silver wheel spun continually, glinting between two ever burning mercury vapour lamps; above it, silhouetted against the darkling eastern sky, there stood a statue of God. The surpliced choir was singing an anthem—"The Word Made Steel"—and the minister sat listening with his hand cupped under his chin, wondering if God had approved of the sermon he had just preached on the Second Coming.

Most of the large congregation was enraptured by the music. Only one man present, at the end of the rearmost row of bare steel pews, fidgeted impatiently, flexing the rubber pad from the forehead rest before him in nervous fingers. He had to keep his hands occupied, or else they kept straying to the bulge in the inside pocket of his plain brown jacket. His watery blue eyes wandered restlessly along the climatic, sweeping lines of the metal temple and shifted away every time they came to the wheel motif which the architect—probably God himself—had incorporated wherever possible.

The anthem closed on a thrilling dissonance and the congregation knelt, their heads against the rubber rests, while the minister pronounced the blessing of the Wheel. The man in brown wasn't really listening, but he caught a few phrases: "May he guide you in your appointed courses ... serve you as your eternal pivot ... bring you at last to the peace of the true eternal round ..."

Then he stood with the rest of them while the choir marched out to the strains of the electronic organ. Directly the minister had disappeared through the vestry door, the worshippers began to shuffle towards the main exits. He alone remained sitting in his pew.

He was not the sort of person one would look at twice. He had sandy hair and a worn, tired face; his teeth were stained and irregular, his clothes fitted badly, and his eyes were a fraction out of focus, as though he needed glasses. Plainly the service had not brought him peace of mind.

Eventually, when everybody else had gone, he stood up and replaced the rubber pad with scrupulous exactitude. For a moment his eyes closed and his lips moved soundlessly; as if this act had endowed him with the courage for a decision, he seemed to draw himself up like a diver poising on a high board. Abruptly he left the pew and walked—soundless on the rubber carpet of the nave—towards the small steel door that bore the single word VESTRY.

Beside it there was a bell. He rang.

Shortly the door was opened by a junior acolyte, a youth in a grey robe woven of metallic links that jingled as he moved, hands in grey shiny gloves, scalp hidden under a smooth steel cap. In a voice made impersonal by careful practice, the acolyte said, "You wish counsel?"

The man in brown nodded, shifting a trifle nervously from foot to foot. Through the doorway were visible many devotional pictures and statues; he dropped his gaze before them.

"What is your name?" the acolyte inquired.

"Karimov," said the man in brown. "Julius Karimov."

He tensed fractionally as he spoke, his eyes fleeting over the acolyte's face in search of any reaction. None showed, and he relaxed on the youth's curt order to wait while he informed the minister.

The moment he was alone, Karimov crossed the vestry and examined a painting on the far wall: Anson's "Immaculate Manufacture", depicting the legendary origin of God—a bolt of lightning from heaven smiting an ingot of pure steel. It was excellently done, of course; the artist's use of electroluminescent paint for the lightning, in particular, was masterly. But from Karimov it provoked an expression of

183

physical nausea, and after only seconds he had to turn away.

At length the minister entered in the officiating robe which identified him as one of the Eleven closest to God, his headpiece—which during the service had concealed his shaven scalp—discarded, his white, slender hands playing with a jewelled emblem of the Wheel that hung around his neck on a platinum chain. Karimov turned slowly to confront him, right hand slightly raised in a stillborn gesture. It had been a calculated risk to give his real name; he thought that was probably still a secret. But his real face . . .

No, no hint of recognition. The minister merely said in his professionally resonant voice, "What may I do for you, my son?"

The man in brown squared his shoulders and said simply, "I want to talk to God."

With the resigned air of one well used to dealing with requests of that sort, the minister sighed. "God is extremely busy, my son," he murmured. "He has the spiritual welfare of the entire human race to look after. Cannot I help you? Is there a particular problem on which you need advice, or do you seek generalized divine guidance in programming your life?"

Karimov looked at him diffidently and thought: *This man really believes! His faith isn't just pretence for profit, but deep-seated honest trust, and it is more terrifying than everything else that even those who were with me at the beginning should believe!*

He said after a little, "You are kind, Father, but I need more than mere advice. I have"—he seemed to stumble at the word—"prayed much, and sought help from several ministers, and still I have not attained to the peace of the true round. Once, long ago, I had the privilege of seeing God in the steel; I wish to do so again, that's all. I have no doubt, of course, that He will remember me."

There was a long silence, during which the minister's dark eyes remained fixed on Karimov. Finally he said, "Remember you? Oh yes, he will certainly remember you! But *I* remember you too—now!"

His voice shook with uncontrollable fury, and he reached for a bell on the wall.

Strength born of desperation poured through Karimov's scrawny frame. He hurled himself at the minister, striking aside the outstretched arm inches from its goal, bowling the tall man over, seizing the tough chain around his neck, and pulling with every ounce of force he could muster.

The chain bit deep into pale flesh; as if possessed, Karimov tugged and tugged at it, twisted, took a fresh grip and tugged again. The minister's eyes bulged, mouth uttered loathsome formless grunts, fists beat at his attacker's arms—and grew weaker, and ceased.

Karimov drew back, shaking at what he had done, and compelled himself unsteadily to his feet. To the former colleague who now had gone beyond all hope of hearing he muttered his sick apology, then calmed himself with deep breaths and approached the door by which he had not entered the room.

On his throne beneath its wheel-shaped canopy of steel, God sat. His polished limbs gleamed under the muted lights, his head was beautifully designed to suggest a human face without possessing a single human feature—even eyes.

Blind insensate thing, thought Karimov as he shut the door behind him. Unconsciously his hand touched what he had in his pocket.

The voice too was more than humanly perfect, a deep pure tone as if an organ spoke. It said, "My son—"

And stopped.

Karimov gave an audible sigh of relief and his nervousness dropped from him like a cloak. He stepped forward casually and sat down in the central one of the eleven chairs arranged in a horseshoe before the throne, while the blank shiny gaze of the robot rested on him and the whole metal frame locked in astonishment.

"Well?" Karimov challenged. "How do you like meeting somebody who doesn't believe in you for a change?"

The robot moved in human fashion, relaxing. Steel fingers

linked under his chin while he reconsidered the intruder with interest instead of amazement. The voice rang out afresh.

"So it's you, Black!"

Karimov nodded with a faint smile. "That's what they used to call me in the old days. I used to think it was a silly affectation—assigning the scientists who worked on top-secret projects false names. But it's turned out to have advantages, for me at any rate. I gave my own name of Karimov to your—ah—late apostle outside, and it meant nothing to him. Speaking of real names, by the way: how long is it since anyone addressed you as A-46?"

The robot jerked. "It is sacrilege to apply that term to me!"

"Sacrilege be—bothered. I'll go further and remind you what the A stands for in A-46. Android! An imitation of a man! A sexless insensate assembly of metal parts which I helped to design, and it calls itself God!" Scathing contempt rode the lashing words. "You and your fantasies of Immaculate Manufacture! Blasted by a bolt of heavenly lightning from a chunk of untooled steel! Talk about making men in God's own image—you're the 'God' who was made in man's!"

They had even incorporated the facility of shrugging in their design, Karimov recalled with a start as the robot made use of it.

"Leaving sacrilege on one side for a moment, then," the machine said, "is there any real reason why you should deny that I am God? Why should not the second Incarnation be an Inferration—in imperishable steel? As for your benighted and deluded belief that you created the metal part of me—which is anyway supremely unimportant since the spirit alone is eternal—it's long been said that a prophet is without honour in his own country, and since the Inferration took place near your experimental station ... Well!"

Karimov laughed. He said, "Well I'm damned! I think you believe it yourself!"

"You are beyond question damned. For a moment I

hoped, seeing you enter my throne room, that you'd learned the error of your ways and come to acknowledge my divinity at last. Of my infinite compassion I will give you one final chance to do so before I call my ministers to take you away. Now or never, Black or Karimov or whatever you choose to call yourself: do you repent and believe?"

Karimov wasn't listening. He was staring past the shining machine into nowhere, while his hand caressed the bulge in his pocket. He said in a low voice, "I've plotted years for this moment—twenty years, ever since the day we turned you on and I began to suspect we'd gone wrong. Not till now was there anything I could have done. And in the meantime, while I sweated and hunted for a way to stop you, I've seen the ultimate humiliation of mankind.

"We've been slaves to our tools since the first caveman made the first knife to help him get his supper. After that there was no going back, and we built till our machines were ten million times more powerful than ourselves. We gave ourselves cars when we might have learned to run; we made airplanes when we might have grown wings; and then the inevitable. We made a machine our God."

"And why not?" the robot boomed. "Can you name any single way in which I am not your superior? I am stronger, more intelligent and more durable than a man. I have mental and physical powers that shame comparison. I feel no pain. I am immortal and invulnerable and yet you say I am not God. Why? From perverseness!"

"No," said Karimov with terrible directness. "Because you are mad.

"You were the climax of a decade's work by our team: the dozen most brilliant living cyberneticists. Our dream was to create a mechanical analogue of a human being which could be programmed directly with intelligence drawn from the patterns in our own brains. In that we succeeded—far too well!

"I've had time enough in the past twenty years to work out where we went astray. If was my fault, God help me—the real God, if He exists, not you, you mechanical

187

fraud! Always somewhere at the back of my mind while we were working on you there lurked the thought that to build the machine we had envisaged would be to become as God: to make a creative intelligence, that none save He had yet achieved! That was megalomania, and I'm ashamed, but it *was* in my mind, and from mine it was transferred to yours. No one knew of it; even I was afraid to admit it to myself, for shame is a saving human grace. But you! What could you know of shame, of self-restraint, of empathy and love? Once implanted in your complex of artificial neurones, that mania grew till it knew no bounds, and ... here you are. Insane with the lust for divine glory! Why else the doctrine of the Word Made Steel, and the image of the Wheel, the mechanical form that does not occur in nature? Why else the trouble you go to to make parallels in your godless existence with that of the greatest Man who ever lived?"

Karimov was still speaking in the same low tones, but his eyes were ablaze with hatred.

"You have no soul and you accuse me of sacrilege. You're a collection of wires and transistors and you call yourself God. Blasphemy! Only a man could be God!"

The robot shifted with a clang of metal limbs and said, "All this is not merely nonsense but a waste of my valuable time. Is that all you came for—to rave at me?"

"No," said Karimov. "I came to kill you."

At long last his hand dipped into the bulging pocket and produced the object there concealed: a curious little weapon, less than six inches long. A short metal tube extended forward from it; backward from the handgrip a flex disappeared inside his coat; under his thumb there was a small red stud.

He said, "It took me twenty years to design and build this. We chose steel for your body that only an atomic bomb could destroy; how, though, could one man walk into your presence with a nuclear weapon on his back? I had to wait until I had a means of cutting your steel as easily as a knife cuts a man's weak flesh. Here it is—and now I can undo the wrong I did to my own species!"

He pressed the stud.

The robot, motionless till that moment as if incapable of believing that anyone could really wish to harm him, jolted upright, turned half around, and stood paralysed as a tiny hole appeared in the metal of his side. Steel began to form little drops around the hole; the surrounding area glowed red, and the drops flowed like water—or blood.

Karimov held the weapon steady, though it scorched his fingers. Sweat stood out on his forehead. Another half minute, and the damage would be irreparable.

Behind him a door slammed open. He cursed, for his weapon would not work on a man. To the last moment he kept it aimed; then he was seized from behind and pinioned, and the weapon torn from its flex and hurled to the floor and stamped into ruin.

The robot did not move.

The tension of twenty hate-filled years broke and his relief boiled up into hysterical laughter which he fought to quell. When he finally succeeded, he saw that the man who held him was the junior acolyte who had admitted him to the vestry, and that there were other men around, strangers, gazing in utter silence at their God.

"Look at him, look at him!" Karimov crowed. "Your idol was nothing but a robot, and what men make they can destroy. He said he was divine, but he wasn't even invulnerable! I've freed you! Don't you understand? *I've set you free!*"

But the acolyte wasn't paying him any attention. He stared fixedly at the monstrous metal doll, licking his lips, until at last he said in a voice that was neither relieved nor horrified, but only awed, "The Hole in the Side!"

A dream began to die in Karimov's mind. Numb, he watched the other men walk over to the robot and peer into the hole, heard one of them say, "How long to repair the damage?" and the other reply offhandedly, "Oh, three days, I guess!" And it was clear to him what he had done.

Wasn't this a Friday, and in spring? Hadn't he himself known that the robot made careful parallels between his own career and that of the man he parodied? Now it had reached the climax: there had been a death, and there would be a resurrection—on the third day . . .

And the grip of the Word Made Steel would never be broken.

In turn the men made the sign of the Wheel and departed, until one only remained. Stern, he came down from the throne to confront Karimov and address the acolyte who held him in a rigid grasp.

"Who is he, anyway?" the man demanded.

The acolyte gazed at the limp figure slumped on the chair with the weight of all the ages crushing him, and his mouth rounded in an O of comprehension. He said, "*Now* I understand! He calls himself Karimov.

"But his real name must be Iscariot."

Afterword:

I don't really know how "Judas" came about, but I suspect it has its roots in the tendency I've noticed in myself as well as in other people to anthropomorphize machinery. I once had a Morgan sports car, a honey of a vehicle with a distinct and rather cranky personality which was about eight years old before I took it over. I swear it hated traffic in the rush hour, and complained bitterly when it was parked unless I'd consoled it for all that overheating and inching along in bottom gear by taking a detour down a stretch of fast road where I could let it out to about fifty or so.

I hope our growing habit of handing over not merely our drudgery but our capacity for making up our minds to our shiny new gadgetry doesn't culminate in literal machine-worship, but just in case it does—there's the story.

TEST TO DESTRUCTION

Introduction to

TEST TO DESTRUCTION

I have done so many riffs on who and what Keith Laumer is (not the least of which is a verbose and sententious introduction to his Doubleday collection, *Nine by Laumer*) that, frankly, I don't know what to say that I haven't already said. But . . .

Laumer is a tall, rugged, rather good-looking man, if you admire that kind of cruel mouth and beady little eyes like a marmoset. He has written several volumes of stories about a professional diplomat in the galactic future, a fellow named Retief. It is no mere coincidence that Laumer has been a diplomat, in the U.S. Foreign Service. But the Retief stories are lighthearted, and many readers have failed to take notice (as I pointed out at dreary length in my introduction to his collection) of Laumer's serious work. His many allegories of the world in which we live—stories that take a hard, betimes distressed look at what we do to each other. His dynachrome stories with their inherent warnings about the age of the computers. His chase-adventures through the Structured Society where the man alone is doomed from the start, yet makes his play because he *is* a man. *These* stories are the real Laumer, and it is a shame he can sell the Retief stuff so easily, because it allows him to coast, allows him to tell extended jokes when he should be grappling with more complex themes, such as the one he offers in the story you are about to read.

Laumer is a singular man. He is a mass of contradictions, a driven talent, a pillar of strength, a man who values and understands ethics and morality on almost a cellular level. It shows up in his work. He is a writer who refuses to ignore reality, even when writing interstellar fantasies. There are basics in the Universe that are immutable to Laumer. I cannot find it in my heart to disagree with him. Love and courage and determination are good; war and laziness and hypocrisy are bad. If I could name a man I have met who seemed to me incorruptible, it would have to be Laumer. (I am cautious about making these value judgments, however. Too often I've raised mere mortals to the pedestal, only to find out they are as strong-and-weak as all other mere mortals, including myself. Laumer may well be an exception.)

Keith's biographical notes are rather interesting. I include them here just as they were submitted, for I think they reflect the truth of what I've just said about him.

"I was born in New York State, lived there until age twelve, then to Florida. Thus, I can see the Civil War from both sides. Perhaps this is at the bottom of my inability to become a true believer in any of the popular causes. (I find that humans can be divided only into two meaningful categories: Decent Humans and Sonsofbitches; both types appear to be evenly distributed among all shapes, colors, sizes and nationalities.)

"In 1943, at age eighteen, I went into the army. Saw Texas, Georgia, Germany, France, Belgium, Holland, Luxembourg, and other strange places. They all seemed to be populated by the same kind of grubby, greedy, lovable/hateable people I had known back home. In 1946, I found myself on the University of Illinois campus, studying architecture. Five years later I had a wife, two tots, and two degrees. Meantime, I had put the final conclusions to my theories about people by having met bastards both black and white, Good Christians and Good Jews. None of them seemed to have a corner on virtue or villainy.

"In 1953, I fooled the authorities by going into the air force as a first lieutenant before they could draft me for WWIII, then imminent. They fooled me instead, by finking out on the war. I spent a year in solitary on a rock in Labrador. In '56, I left the air force to enter the foreign service. Discovered a teeny-weeny preponderance of Sonsofbitches there. I did two years in Burma standing on my ear, and discovered (surprise!) I was a writer. I went back into the air force in 1960, did a tour in London, quit my job in 1965 to become a full-time writer, and I never intend to change jobs again."

He neglects to mention such books as *Embassy*, *Catastrophe Planet*, *Envoy to New Worlds*, *Worlds of the Imperium*, *Retief's War* and *Earthblood* (written with Rosel G. Brown). He also neglects to mention he is one of the very few major new talents to emerge in the field of speculative fiction in the past five years. But we can attribute that to Keith's incredible modesty.

Earlier I commented on the serious nature of the best of Laumer's work. What follows, the story "Test to Destruction", is indicative of this seriousness. But Laumer is no mere Edgar Guest of science fiction—a mouther of platitudes—life is real, life is earnest—for he offers us a dangerous vision about the basic nature of man. And it is a comment on his drive to become the compleat storyteller that this tale of morality is couched in the time-honored form of the chase-action-adventure.

TEST TO DESTRUCTION

by Keith Laumer

ONE

The late October wind drove icy rain against Mallory's face above his turned-up collar where he stood concealed in the shadows at the mouth of the narrow alley.

"It's ironic, Johnny," the small, grim-faced man beside him muttered. "You—the man who should have been World Premier tonight—skulking in the back streets while Koslo and his bully boys drink champagne in the Executive Palace."

"That's all right, Paul," Mallory said. "Maybe he'll be too busy with his victory celebration to concern himself with me."

"And maybe he won't," the small man said. "He won't rest easy as long as he knows you're alive to oppose him."

"It will only be a few more hours, Paul. By breakfast time Kolso will know his rigged election didn't take."

"But if he takes you first, that's the end, Johnny. Without you the *coup* will collapse like a soap bubble."

"I'm not leaving the city," Mallory said flatly. "Yes, there's a certain risk involved; but you don't bring down a dictator without taking a few chances."

"You didn't have to take this one, meeting Crandall yourself."

"It will help if he sees me, knows I'm in this all the way."

In silence, the two men awaited the arrival of their fellow conspirator.

TWO

Aboard the interstellar dreadnought cruising half a parsec from Earth, the Compound Ree mind surveyed the distant Solar System.

Radiation on many wave lengths from the third body, the Perceptor cells directed the impulse to the 6934 units comprising the segmented brain which guided the ship. *Modulations over the forty-ninth through the ninety-first spectra of mentation.*

A portion of the pattern is characteristic of exocosmic manipulatory intelligence, the Analyzers extrapolated from the data. *Other indications range in complexity from levels one through twenty-six.*

This is an anomalous situation, the Recollectors mused. *It is the essential nature of a Prime Intelligence to destroy all lesser competing mind-forms, just as I/we have systematically annihilated those I/we have encountered on my/our exploration of the Galactic Arm.*

Before action is taken, clarification of the phenomenon is essential, the Interpreters pointed out. *Closure to a range exceeding one radiation/second will be required for extraction and analysis of a representative mind-unit.*

In this event, the risk level rises to Category Ultimate, the Analyzers announced dispassionately.

RISK LEVELS NO LONGER APPLY, the powerful thought-impulse of the Egon put an end to the discussion. NOW OUR SHIPS RANGE INTO NEW SPACE, SEEKING EXPANSION ROOM FOR THE GREAT RACE. THE UNALTERABLE COMMAND OF THAT WHICH-IS-SUPREME REQUIRES THAT MY/OUR PROBE BE PROSECUTED TO THE LIMIT OF REE CAPABILITY, TESTING MY/YOUR ABILITY FOR SURVIVAL AND DOMINANCE. THERE CAN BE NO TIMIDITY, NO EXCUSE FOR FAILURE. LET ME/US NOW ASSUME A CLOSE SURVEILLANCE ORBIT!

In utter silence, and at a velocity a fraction of a kilometer below that of light, the Ree dreadnought flashed toward Earth.

THREE

Mallory tensed as a dark figure appeared a block away under the harsh radiance of a polyarc.

"There's Crandall now," the small man hissed. "I'm glad—" he broke off as the roar of a powerful turbine engine sounded suddenly along the empty avenue. A police car exploded from a side street, rounded the corner amid a shriek of overstressed gyros. The man under the light turned to run—and the vivid blue glare of a SURF-gun winked and stuttered from the car. The burst of slugs caught the runner, slammed him against the brick wall, kicked him from his feet, rolled him, before the crash of the guns reached Mallory's ears.

"My God! They've killed Tony!" the small man blurted. "We've got to get out . . ."

Mallory took half a dozen steps back into the alley, froze as lights sprang up at the far end. He heard booted feet hit pavement, a hoarse voice that barked a command.

"We're cut off,' he snapped. There was a rough wooden

door six feet away. He jumped to it, threw his weight against it. It held. He stepped back, kicked it in, shoved his companion ahead of him into a dark room smelling of moldy burlap and rat droppings. Stumbling, groping in the dark, Mallory led the way across a stretch of littered floor, felt along the wall, found a door that hung by one hinge. He pushed past it, was in a passage floored with curled linoleum, visible in the feeble gleam filtered through a fanlight above a massive, barred door. He turned the other way, ran for the smaller door at the far end of the passage. He was ten feet from it when the center panel burst inward in a hail of wood splinters that grazed him, ripped at his coat like raking talons. Behind him, the small man made a choking noise; Mallory whirled in time to see him fall back against the wall and go down, his chest and stomach torn away by the full impact of a thousand rounds from the police SURF-gun.

An arm came through the broached door, groping for the latch. Mallory took a step, seized the wrist, wrenched backward with all his weight, felt the elbow joint shatter. The scream of the injured policeman was drowned in a second burst from the rapid-fire weapon—but Mallory had already leaped, caught the railing of the stair, pulled himself up and over. He took the steps five at a time, passed a landing littered with broken glass and empty bottles, kept going, emerged in a corridor of sagging doors and cobwebs. Feet crashed below, furious voices yelled. Mallory stepped inside the nearest door, stood with his back to the wall beside it. Heavy feet banged on the stairs, paused, came his way . . .

Mallory tensed, and as the policeman passed the door, he stepped out, brought his hand over and down in a side-handed blow to the base of the neck that had every ounce of power in his shoulders behind it. The man seemed to dive forward, and Mallory leaped, caught the gun before it struck the floor. He took three steps, poured a full magazine into the stair well. As he turned to sprint for the far end of the passage, return fire boomed from below.

A club, swung by a giant, struck him in the side, knocked the breath from his lungs, sent him spinning against the wall. He recovered, ran on; his hand, exploring, found a deep gouge that bled freely. The bullet had barely grazed him.

He reached the door to the service stair, recoiled violently as a dirty gray shape sprang at him with a yowl from the darkness—in the instant before a gun flashed and racketed in the narrow space, shattering plaster dust from the wall above his head. A thickset man in the dark uniform of the Security Police, advancing up the stair at a run, checked momentarily as he saw the gun in Mallory's hands—and before he recovered himself, Mallory had swung the empty weapon, knocked him spinning back down onto the landing. The cat that had saved his life—an immense, battle-scarred Tom—lay on the floor, half its head blown away by the blast it had intercepted. Its lone yellow eye was fixed on him; its claws raked the floor, as, even in death, it advanced to the attack. Mallory jumped over the stricken beast, went up the stairs.

Three flights higher, the stair ended in a loft stacked with bundled newspapers and rotting cartons from which mice scuttled as he approached. There was a single window, opaque with grime. Mallory tossed aside the useless gun, scanned the ceiling for evidence of an escape hatch, saw nothing. His side ached abominably.

Relentless feet sounded beyond the door. Mallory backed to a corner of the room—and again, the deafening shriek of the SURF-gun sounded, and the flimsy door bucked, disintegrated. For a moment there was total silence. Then:

"Walk out with your hands up, Mallory!" a brassy voice snarled. In the gloom, pale flames were licking over the bundled papers, set afire by the torrent of steel-jacketed slugs. Smoke rose, thickened.

"Come out before you fry," the voice called.

"Let's get out of here," another man bawled. "This dump will go up like tinder!"

"Last chance, Mallory!" the first man shouted, and now the flames, feeding on the dry paper, were reaching for the ceiling, roaring as they grew. Mallory went along the wall to the window, ripped aside the torn roller shade, tugged at the sash. It didn't move. He kicked out the glass, threw a leg over the sill, and stepped out onto a rusted fire escape. Five stories down, light puddled on grimy concrete, the white dots of upturned faces—and half a dozen police cars blocking the rain-wet street. He put his back to the railing, looked up. The fire escape extended three, perhaps four stories higher. He threw his arm across his face to shield it from the billowing flames, forced his aching legs to carry him up the iron treads three at a time.

The topmost landing was six feet below an overhanging cornice. Mallory stepped up on the rail, caught the edge of the carved stone trim with both hands, swung himself out. For a moment he dangled, ninety feet above the street; then he pulled himself up, got a knee over the coping, and rolled onto the roof.

Lying flat, he scanned the darkness around him. The level was broken only by a ventilator stack and a shack housing a stair or elevator head.

He reconnoitered, found that the hotel occupied a corner, with a parking lot behind it. On the alley side, the adjoining roof was at a level ten feet lower, separated by a sixteen-foot gap. As Mallory stared across at it, a heavy rumbling shook the deck under his feet: one of the floors of the ancient building, collapsing as the fire ate through its supports.

Smoke was rising all around him now. On the parking lot side, dusky flames soared up thirty feet above him, trailing an inverted cascade of sparks into the wet night sky. He went to the stairhead, found the metal door locked. A rusty ladder was clamped to the side of the structure. He wrenched it free, carried it to the alley side. It took all his strength to force the corroded catches free, pull the ladder out to its full extension. Twenty feet, he estimated. Enough—maybe.

He shoved the end of the ladder out, wrestled it across to rest on the roof below. The flimsy bridge sagged under his weight as he crawled up on it. He moved carefully out, ignoring the swaying of the fragile support. He was six feet from the far roof when he felt the rotten metal crumple under him, with a frantic lunge he threw himself forward. Only the fact that the roof was at a lower level saved him. He clawed his way over the sheet-metal gutter, hearing shouts ring out below as the ladder crashed to the bricks of the alley.

A bad break, he thought. *Now they know where I am. . . .*

There was a heavy trap door set in the roof. He lifted it, descended an iron ladder into darkness, found his way to a corridor, along it to a stair. Faint sounds rose from below. He went down.

At the fourth floor, lights showed below, voices sounded, the clump of feet. He left the stair at the third floor, prowled along a hall, entered an abandoned office. Searchlights in the street below threw oblique shadows across the discolored walls.

He went on, through a connecting door into a room on the alley side. A cold draft, reeking of smoke, blew in through a glassless window. Below, the narrow way appeared to be deserted. Paul's body was gone. The broken ladder lay where it had fallen. It was, he estimated, a twenty-feet drop to the bricks; even if he let himself down to arm's length and dropped, a leg-breaker . . .

Something moved below him. A uniformed policeman was standing at a spot directly beneath the window, his back against the wall. A wolf smile drew Mallory's face tight. In a single motion, he slid his body out over the sill, chest down, held on for an instant, seeing the startled face below turn upward, the mouth open for a yell—

He dropped; his feet struck the man's back, breaking his fall. He rolled clear, sat up, half dazed. The policeman sprawled on his face, his spine twisted at an awkward angle.

Mallory got to his feet—and almost fell at the stab of pain from his right ankle. Sprained, or broken. His teeth set against the pain, he moved along the wall. Icy rain water, sluicing from the downspout ahead, swirled about his ankles. He slipped, almost went down on the slimy bricks. The lesser darkness of the parking lot behind the building showed ahead. If he could reach it, cross it—then he might still have a chance. He had to succeed—for Monica, for the child, for the future of a world.

Another step, and another. It was as though there were a steel spike through his ankle. The bullet wound in his side was a vast ache that caught at him with every breath. His blood-soaked shirt and pants leg hung against him, icy cold. Ten feet more, and he would make his run for it—

Two men in the black uniforms of the State Security Police stepped out into his path, stood with blast-guns leveled· at his chest. Mallory pushed away from the wall, braced himself for the burst of slugs that would end his life. Instead, a beam of light speared out through the misty rain, dazzling his eyes.

"You'll come with us, Mr. Mallory."

FOUR

Still no contact, the Perceptors reported. *The prime-level minds below lack cohesion; they flicker and dart away even as I/we touch them.*

The Initiators made a proposal: *By the use of appropriate harmonics a resonance field can be set up which will reinforce any native mind functioning in an analogous rhythm.*

I/we find that a pattern of the following character will be most suitable. . . . A complex symbolism was displayed.

PERSEVERE IN THE FASHION DESCRIBED, the Egon commanded. ALL EXTRANEOUS FUNCTIONS WILL BE DISCONTINUED UNTIL SUCCESS IS ACHIEVED.

With total singleness of purpose, the Ree sensors probed across space from the dark and silent ship, searching for a receptive human mind.

FIVE

The Interrogation Room was a totally bare cube of white enamel. At its geometric center, under a blinding white glare panel, sat a massive chair constructed of polished steel, casting an ink-black shadow.

A silent minute ticked past; then heels clicked in the corridor. A tall man in a plain, dark military tunic came through the open door, halted, studying his prisoner. His wide, sagging face was as gray and bleak as a tombstone.

"I warned you, Mallory," he said in a deep, growling tone.

"You're making a mistake, Koslo," Mallory said.

"Openly arresting the people's hero, eh?" Koslo curved his wide, gray lips in a death's-head smile. "Don't delude yourself. The malcontents will do nothing without their leader."

"Are you sure you're ready to put your regime to the test so soon?"

"It's that or wait, while your party gains strength. I chose the quicker course. I was never as good at waiting as you, Mallory."

"Well—you'll know by morning."

"That close, eh?" Koslo's heavy-lidded eyes pinched down on glints of light. He grunted. "I'll know many things by morning. You realize that your personal position is hopeless?" His eyes went to the chair.

"In other words, I should sell out to you now in return for—what? Another of your promises?"

"The alternative is the chair," Koslo said flatly.

"You have great confidence in machinery, Koslo—more than in men. That's your great weakness."

Koslo's hand went out, caressing the rectilinear metal of the chair. "This is a scientific apparatus designed to accomplish a specific task with the least possible difficulty to me. It creates conditions within the subject's neural system conducive to total recall, and at the same time amplifies the subvocalizations that accompany all highly cerebral activity. The subject is also rendered amenable to verbal cuing." He paused. "If you resist, it will destroy your mind—but not before you've told me everything: names, locations, dates, organization, operational plans—everything. It will be simpler for us both if you acknowledge the inevitable and tell me freely what I require to know."

"And after you've got the information?"

"You know my regime can't tolerate opposition. The more complete my information, the less bloodshed will be necessary."

Mallory shook his head. "No," he said bluntly.

"Don't be a fool, Mallory! This isn't a test of your manhood!"

"Perhaps it is, Koslo: man against machine."

Koslo's eyes probed at him. He made a quick gesture with one hand.

"Strap him in."

Seated in the chair, Mallory felt the cold metal suck the heat from his body. Bands restrained his arms, legs, torso. A wide ring of woven wire and plastic clamped his skull firmly to the formed headrest. Across the room, Fey Koslo watched.

"Ready, Excellency," a technician said.

"Proceed."

Mallory tensed. An unwholesome excitement churned his stomach. He'd heard of the chair, of its power to scour a man's mind clean and leave him a gibbering hulk.

Only a free society, he thought, *can produce the technology that makes tyranny possible . . .*

He watched as a white-smocked technician approached, reached for the control panel. There was only one hope left: if he could fight the power of the machine, drag out the interrogation, delay Koslo until dawn . . .

A needle-studded vise clamped down against Mallory's temples. Instantly his mind was filled with whirling fever images. He felt his throat tighten in an aborted scream. Fingers of pure force struck into his brain, dislodging old memories, ripping open the healed wounds of time. From somewhere, he was aware of a voice, questioning. Words trembled in his throat, yearning to be shouted aloud.

I've got to resist! The thought flashed through his mind

and was gone, borne away on a tide of probing impulses that swept through his brain like a millrace. *I've got to hold out ... long enough ... to give the others a chance....*

SIX

Aboard the Ree ship, dim lights glowed and winked on the panel that encircled the control center

I/we sense a new mind—a transmitter of great power, the Perceptors announced suddenly. *But the images are confused. I/we sense struggle, resistance....*

IMPOSE CLOSE CONTROL, the Egon ordered. NARROW FOCUS AND EXTRACT A REPRESENTATIVE PERSONALITY FRACTION!

It is difficult; I/we sense powerful neural currents, at odds with the basic brain rhythms.

COMBAT THEM!

Again the Ree mind reached out, insinuated itself into the complex field-matrix that was Mallory's mind, and began, painstakingly, to trace out and reinforce its native symmetries, permitting the natural egomosaic to emerge, free from distracting counterimpulses.

SEVEN

The technician's face went chalk-white as Mallory's body went rigid against the restraining bands.

"You fool!' Koslo's voice cut at him like a whipping rod. "If he dies before he talks—"

"He ... he fights strongly, Excellency." The man's eyes scanned instrument faces. "Alpha through delta rhythms normal, though exaggerated," he muttered. "Metabolic index .99 ..."

Mallory's body jerked. His eyes opened, shut. His mouth worked.

"Why doesn't he speak?" Koslo barked.

"It may require a few moments, Excellency, to adjust the power flows to ten-point resonance—"

"Then get on with it, man! I risked too much in arresting this man to lose him now!"

EIGHT

White-hot fingers of pure force landed from the chair along the neural pathways within Mallory's brain—and met the adamantine resistance of the Ree probe. In the resultant confrontation, Mallory's battered self-awareness was tossed like a leaf in a gale.

Fight! The remaining wisp of his conscious intellect gathered itself—

—and was grasped, encapsulated, swept up and away. He was aware of spinning through a whirling fog of white light shot through with flashes and streamers of red, blue, violet. There was a sensation of great forces that pressed at him, flung him to and fro, drew his mind out like a ductile wire until it spanned the Galaxy. The filament grew broad, expanded into a diaphragm that bisected the universe. The plane assumed thickness, swelled out to encompass all space/time. Faint and far away, he sensed the tumultuous coursing of the energies that ravened just beyond the impenetrable membrane of force—

The imprisoning sphere shrank, pressed in, forcing his awareness into needle-sharp focus. He knew, without knowing how he knew, that he was locked in a sealed and airless chamber, constricting, claustrophobic, all sound and sensation cut off. He drew breath to scream—

No breath came. Only a weak pulse of terror, quickly fading, as if damped by an inhibiting hand. Alone in the dark, Mallory waited, every sense tuned, monitoring the surrounding blankness. . . .

NINE

I/we have him! The Perceptors pulsed, and fell away. At the center of the chamber, the mind trap pulsed with the flow-

ing energies that confined and controlled the captive brain pattern.

TESTING WILL COMMENCE AT ONCE. The Egon brushed aside the interrogatory impulses from the mind-segments concerned with speculation. INITIAL STIMULI WILL BE APPLIED AND RESULTS NOTED. NOW!

TEN

... and was aware of a faint glimmer of light across the room: the outline of a window. He blinked, raised himself on one elbow. Bedsprings creaked under him. He sniffed. An acrid odor of smoke hung in the stifling air. He seemed to be in a cheap hotel room. He had no memory of how he came to be there. He threw back the coarse blanket and felt warped floor boards under his bare feet—

The boards were hot.

He jumped up, went to the door, grasped the knob—and jerked his hand back. The metal had blistered his palm.

He ran to the window, ripped aside the dirt-stiff gauze curtains, snapped open the latch, tugged at the sash. It didn't budge. He stepped back, kicked out the glass. Instantly a coil of smoke whipped in through the broken pane. Using the curtain to protect his hand, he knocked out the shards, swung a leg over the sill, stumbled onto the fire escape. The rusted metal cut at his bare feet. Groping, he made his way down half a dozen steps—and fell back as a sheet of red flame billowed from below.

Over the rail he saw the street, lights puddled on grimy concrete ten stories down, white faces, like pale dots, upturned. A hundred feet away, an extension ladder swayed, approaching another wing of the flaming building, not concerned with him. He was lost, abandoned. Nothing could save him. For forty feet below, the iron ladder was an inferno.

It would be easier, quicker, to go over the rail, escape the pain, die cleanly, the thought came into his mind with dreadful clarity.

There was a tinkling crash and a window above blew out. Scalding embers rained down on his back. The iron was hot underfoot. He drew a breath, shielded his face with one arm, and plunged downward through the whipping flames. . . .

He was crawling, falling down the cruel metal treads and risers. The pain across his face, his back, his shoulder, his arm, was like a red-hot iron, applied and forgotten. He caught a glimpse of his arm, flayed, oozing, black-edged. . . .

His hands and feet were no longer his own. He used his knees and elbows, tumbled himself over yet another edge, sliding down to the next landing. The faces were closer now; hands were reaching up. He groped, got to his feet, felt the last section swing down as his weight went on it. His vision was a blur of red. He sensed the blistered skin sloughing from his thighs. A woman screamed.

". . . my God, burned alive and still walking!" a thin voice cawed.

". . . poor devil . . ."

". . . his hands . . . no fingers . . ."

Something rose, smashed at him, a ghostly blow as blackness closed in . . .

ELEVEN

The response of the entity was anamalous, the Analyzers reported. *Its life tenacity is enormous! Confronted with apparent imminent physical destruction, it chose agony and mutilation merely to extend survival for a brief period.*

The possibility exists that such a response represents a mere instinctive mechanism of unusual form, the Analyzers pointed out.

If so, it might prove dangerous. More data on the point is required.

I/WE WILL RESTIMULATE THE SUBJECT, the Egon ordered. THE PARAMETERS OF THE SURVIVAL DRIVE MUST BE ESTABLISHED WITH PRECISION. RESUME TESTING!

TWELVE

In the chair, Mallory writhed, went limp.

"Is he . . . ?"

"He's alive, Excellency! But something's wrong! I can't get through to a vocalization level! He's fighting me with some sort of fantasy complex of his own!"

"Bring him out of it!"

"Excellency, I tried. I can't reach him! It's as though he'd tapped the chair's energy sources and were using them to reinforce his own defense mechanism!"

"Override him!"

"I'll try—but his power is fantastic!"

"Then we'll use more power!"

"It's . . . dangerous, Excellency."

"Not more dangerous than failure!"

Grim-faced, the technician reset the panel to step up the energy flows through Mallory's brain.

THIRTEEN

The subject stirs! the Perceptors burst out. *Massive new energies flow in the mind-field! My/our grip loosens . . .*

HOLD THE SUBJECT! RESTIMULATE AT ONCE, WITH MAXIMUM EMERGENCY FORCE!

While the captive surged and fought against the restraint, the segmented mind of the alien concentrated its forces, hurled a new stimulus into the roiling captive mind-field.

FOURTEEN

. . . Hot sun beat down on his back. A light wind ruffled the tall grass growing up the slope where the wounded lion had taken cover. Telltale drops of dark purple blood clinging to the tall stems marked the big cat's route. It would be up there, flattened to the earth under the clump of thorn trees, its yellow eyes narrowed against the agony of the .375 bullet in his chest, waiting, hoping for its tormentor to come to it. . . .

His heart was thudding under the damp khaki shirt. The heavy rifle felt like a toy in his hands—a useless plaything against the primitive fury of the beast. He took a step; his mouth twisted in an ironic grimace. What was he proving? There was no one here to know if he chose to walk back and sit under a tree and take a leisurely swig from his flask, let an hour or two crawl by—while the cat bled to death—and then go in to find the body. He took another step. And now he was walking steadily forward. The breeze was cool on his forehead. His legs felt light, strong. He drew a deep breath, smelled the sweetness of the spring air. Life had never seemed more precious—

There was a deep, asthmatic cough, and the great beast broke from the shadows, yellow fangs bared, muscles pumping under the dun hide, dark blood shining black along the flank—

He planted his feet, brought the gun up, socketed it against his shoulder as the lion charged down the slope. *By the book*, he thought sardonically. *Take him just above the sternum, hold on him until you're sure.* . . . At a hundred feet he fired—just as the animal veered left. The bullet smacked home far back along the ribs. The cat broke stride, recovered. The gun bucked and roared again, and the snarling face exploded in a mask of red—and still the dying carnivore came on. He blinked sweat from his eyes, centered the sights on the point of the shoulder—

The trigger jammed hard. A glance showed him the spent cartridge lodged in the action. He raked at it vainly, standing his ground. At the last instant he stepped aside, and the hurtling monster skidded past him, dead in the dust. And the thought that struck him then was that if Monica had been watching from the car at the foot of the hill she would not have laughed at him this time. . . .

FIFTEEN

Again the reaction syndrome is inharmonious with any concept of rationality in my/our experience, the Recollector cells expressed the paradox with which the captive mind had presented the Ree intelligence. *Here is an entity which clings to personality survival with a ferocity unparalleled—yet faces Category Ultimate risks needlessly, in response to an abstract code of behavioral symmetry.*

I/we postulate that the personality segment selected does not represent the true-Egon-analog of the subject, the Speculators offered. *It is obviously incomplete, non-viable.*

Let me/us attempt a selective withdrawal of control over peripheral regions of the mind-field, the Initiators proposed, *thus permitting greater concentration of stimulus to the central matrix.*

By matching energies with the captive mind, it will be possible to monitor its rhythms and deduce the key to its total control, the Calculators determined quickly.

This course offers the risk of rupturing the matrix and the destruction of the specimen.

THE RISK MUST BE TAKEN.

With infinite precision, the Ree mind narrowed the scope of its probe, fitting its shape to the contours of Mallory's embattled brain, matching itself in a one-to-one correspondence to the massive energy flows from the Interrogation chair.

Equilibrium, the Perceptors reported at last. *However, the balance is precarious.*

The next test must be designed to expose new aspects of the subject's survival syndrome, the Analyzers pointed out.

A stimulus pattern was proposed and accepted. Aboard the ship in its sublinar orbit, the Ree mind-beam again lanced out to touch Mallory's receptive brain. . . .

. . . Blackness gave way to misty light. A deep rumbling shook the rocks under his feet. Through the whirling spray he saw the raft, the small figure that clung to it: a child, a little girl perhaps nine years old, crouched on hands and knees, looking toward him.

"Daddy!" A high, thin cry of pure terror. The raft bucked and tossed in the wild current. He took a step, slipped, almost went down on the slimy rocks. The icy water swirled about his knees. A hundred feet downstream, the river curved in a gray metal sheen, over and down, veiled by the mists of its own thunderous descent. He turned, scrambled back up, ran along the bank. There, ahead, a point of rock jutted. Perhaps . . .

The raft bobbed, whirled, fifty feet away. Too far. He saw the pale, small face, the pleading eyes. Fear welled in him, greasy and sickening. Visions of death rose up, of his broken body bobbing below the falls, lying wax-white on a slab, sleeping, powdered and false in a satin-lined box, corrupting in the close darkness under the indifferent sod. . . .

He took a trembling step back.

For an instant a curious sensation of unreality swept over him. He remembered darkness, a sense of utter claustrophobia—and a white room, a face that leaned close. . . .

He blinked—and through the spray of the rapids his eyes met those of the doomed child. Compassion struck him like a club. He grunted, felt the clean white flame of anger at himself, of disgust at his fear. He closed his eyes and leaped far out, struck the water and went under, came up gasping. His strokes took him toward the raft. He felt a heavy blow as the current tossed him against a rock, choked as chopping spray whipped in his face. The thought came that broken ribs didn't matter now, nor air for breathing. Only to reach the raft before it reached the edge, that the small, frightened soul might not go down alone into the great darkness. . . .

His hands clawed the rough wood. He pulled himself up, caught the small body to him as the world dropped away and the thunder rose deafeningly to meet him . . .

"Excellency! I need help!" The technician appealed to the grim-faced dictator. "I'm pouring enough power through his brain to kill two ordinary men—and he still fights back! For a second there, a moment ago, I'd swear he opened his eyes and looked right through me! I can't take the responsibility—"

"Then cut the power, you blundering idiot!"

"I don't dare! the backlash will kill him!"

"He ... must ... talk!" Koslo grated. "Hold him! Break him! Or I promise you a slow and terrible death!"

Trembling, the technician adjusted his controls. In the chair, Mallory sat tense, no longer fighting the straps. He looked like a man lost in thought. Perspiration broke from his hairline, trickled down his face.

SIXTEEN

Again new currents stir in the captive! the Perceptors announced in alarm. *The resources of this mind are staggering!*

MATCH IT! the Egon directed.

My/our resources are already overextended! the Calculators interjected.

WITHDRAW ENERGIES FROM ALL PERIPHERAL FUNCTIONS! LOWER ALL SHIELDING! THE MOMENT OF THE ULTIMATE TEST IS UPON ME/US!

Swiftly the Ree mind complied.

The captive is held, the Calculators announced. *But I/we point out that this linkage now presents a channel of vulnerability to assault.*

THE RISK MUST BE TAKEN.

Even now the mind stirs against my/our control!

HOLD IT FAST!

Grimly, the Ree mind fought to retain its control of Mallory's brain.

SEVENTEEN

In one instant, he was not. Then, abruptly, he existed. *Mallory,* he thought. *That symbol represents I/we....*

The alien though faded. He caught at it, held the symbol. *Mallory.* He remembered the shape of his body, the feel of his skull enclosing his brain, the sensations of light, sound, heat—but here there was no sound, no light. Only the enclosing blackness, impenetrable, eternal, changeless. . . .

But where was here?

He remembered the white room, the harsh voice of Koslo, the steel chair—

And the might roar of the waters rushing up at him—

And the reaching talons of a giant cat—

And the searing agony of flames that licked around his body. . . .

But there was no pain now, no discomfort—no sensation of any kind. Was this death, then? At once he rejected the idea as nonsense.

Cogito ergo sum. I am a prisoner—where?

His senses stirred, questing against emptiness, sensationlessness. He strained outward—and heard sound; voices, pleading, demanding. They grew louder, echoing in the vastness:

". . . talk, damn you! Who are your chief accomplices? What support do you expect from the armed forces? Which of the generals are with you? Armaments . . . ? Organization . . .? Initial attack points . . .?"

Blinding static sleeted across the words, filled the universe, grew dim. For an instant Mallory was aware of straps cutting into the tensed muscles of his forearms, the pain of the band clamped around his head, the ache of cramping muscles. . . .

. . . was aware of floating, gravityless, in a sea of winking, flashing energies. Vertigo rose up; frantically he fought for stability in a world of chaos. Through spinning darkness he reached, found a matrix of pure direction, intangible, but, against the background of shifting energy flows, providing an orienting grid. He seized on it, held. . . .

EIGHTEEN

Full emergency disengage! The Receptors blasted the command through all the 6934 units of the Ree mind—and recoiled in shock. *The captive mind clings to the contact! We cannot break free!*

Pulsating with the enormous shock of the prisoner's sudden outlashing, the alien rested for the fractional nanosecond required to restablish intersegmental balance.

The power of the enemy, though unprecedentedly great, is not sufficient to broach the integrity of my/our entityfield, the Analyzers stated, tensely. *But I/we must retreat at once!*

NO! I/WE LACK SUFFICIENT DATA TO JUSTIFY WITHDRAWAL OF PHASE ONE, the Egon countermanded. HERE IS A MIND RULED BY CONFLICTING DRIVES OF GREAT POWER. WHICH IS PARAMOUNT? THEREIN LIES THE KEY TO ITS DEFEAT.

Precious microseconds passed while the compound mind hastily scanned Mallory's mind for symbols from which to reassemble the necessary gestalt-form.

Ready, the Integrators announced. *But it must be pointed out that no mind can long survive intact the direct confrontation of antagonistic imperatives. Is the stimulus to be carried to the point of non-retrieval?*

AFFIRMATIVE, the Egon's tone was one of utter finality. TEST TO DESTRUCTION.

NINETEEN

Illusions, Mallory told himself. *I'm being bombarded by illusions. . . .* He sensed the approach of a massive new wave front, descending on him like a breaking Pacific comber. Grimly he clung to his tenuous orientation—But the smashing impact whirled him into darkness.

Far away, a masked inquisitor faced him.

"Pain has availed nothing against you," the muffled voice

said. "The threat of death does not move you. And yet there is a way. ...." A curtain fell aside, and Monica stood there, tall, slim, vibrantly alive, as beautiful as a roe deer. And, beside her, the child.

He said "No!" and started forward, but the chains held him. He watched, helpless, while brutal hands seized the woman, moved casually, intimately, over her body. Other hands gripped the child. He saw the terror on the small face, the fear in her eyes—

Fear that he had seen before. ....

But of course he had seen her before. The child was his daughter, the precious offspring of himself and the slender female—

Monica, he corrected himself.

—had seen those eyes, through swirling mist, poised above a cataract—

No. That was a dream. A dream in which he had died, violently. And there had been another dream, of facing a wounded lion as it charged down on him—

"You will not be harmed." The Inquisitor's voice seemed to come from a remote distance. "But you will carry with you forever the memory of their living dismemberment. ...."

With a jerk, his attention returned to the woman and the child. He saw them strip Monica's slender, tawny body. Naked, she stood before them, refusing to cower. But of what use was courage now? The manacles at her wrists were linked to a hook set in the damp stone wall. The glowing iron moved closer to her white flesh. He saw the skin darken and blister. The iron plunged home. She stiffened, screamed. ....

A woman screamed.

"My God, burned alive," a thin voice cawed. *"And still walking!"*

He looked down. There was no wound, no scar. The skin was unbroken. But a fleeting almost-recollection came of crackling flames that seared with a white agony as he drew them into his lungs. ....

216

"A dream," he said aloud. "I'm dreaming. I have to wake up!" He closed his eyes and shook his head. . . .

TWENTY

"He shook his head!" the technician choked. "Excellency, it's impossible—but I swear the man is throwing off the machine's control!"

Koslo brushed the other roughly aside. He seized the control lever, pushed it forward. In the chair, Mallory stiffened. His breathing became hoarse, ragged.

"Excellency, the man will die . . ."

"Let him die! No one defies me with impunity!"

TWENTY-ONE

Narrow focus! the Perceptors flashed the command to the sixty-nine hundred and thirty-four energy-producing segments of the Ree mind. *The contest cannot continue long! Almost we lost the captive then . . . !*

The probe beam narrowed, knifing into the living heart of Mallory's brain, imposing its chosen patterns. . . .

TWENTY-TWO

. . . the child whimpered as the foot-long blade approached her fragile breast. The gnarled fist holding the knife stroked it almost lovingly across the blue-veined skin. Crimson blood washed down from the shallow wound.

"If you reveal the secrets of the Brotherhood to me, truly your comrades in arms will die," the Inquisitor's faceless voice droned. "But if you stubbornly refuse, your woman and your infant will suffer all that my ingenuity can devise."

He strained against his chains. "I can't tell you," he croaked. "Don't you understand, nothing is worth this horror! Nothing . . ."

Nothing he could have done would have saved her. She crouched on the raft, doomed. But he could join her—

But not this time. This time chains of steel kept him from her. He hurled himself against them, and tears blinded his eyes. . . .

Smoke blinded his eyes. He looked down, saw the faces upturned below. Surely, easy death was preferable to living immolation. But he covered his face with his arms and started down. . . .

Never betray your trust! the woman's voice rang clear as a trumpet across the narrow dungeon.

Daddy! the child screamed.

We can die only once! the woman called.

The raft plunged downward into boiling chaos. . . .

"Speak, damn you!" The Inquisitor's voice had taken on a new note. "I want the names, the places! Who are your accomplices? What are your plans? When will the rising begin? What signal are they waiting for? Where . . . ? When . . . ?"

Mallory opened his eyes. Blinding white light, a twisted face that loomed before him goggling.

"Excellency! He's awake. He's broken through. . . ."

"Pour full power to him! Force, man! Force him to speak!"

"I—I'm afraid, Excellency! We're tampering with the mightiest instrument in the universe: a human brain! Who knows what we may be creating—"

Koslo struck the man aside, threw the control lever full against the stop.

TWENTY-THREE

. . . the darkness burst into a coruscating brilliance that became the outlines of a room. A transparent man whom he recognized as Koslo stood before him. He watched as the dictator turned to him, his face contorted.

"Now talk, damn you!"

His voice had a curious, ghostly quality, as though it represented only one level of reality.

"Yes," Mallory said distinctly. "I'll talk."

"And if you lie—" Koslo jerked an ugly automatic pistol from the pocket of his plain tunic. "I'll put a bullet in your brain myself!"

"My chief associates in the plot," Mallory began, "are . . ." As he spoke, he gently *disengaged* himself—that was the word that came to his mind—from the scene around him. He was aware at one level of his voice speaking on, reeling off the facts for which the other man hungered so nakedly. And he reached out, channeling the power pouring into him from the chair . . . spanning across vast distances compressed now to a dimensionless plane. Delicately, he quested farther, entered a curious, flickering net of living energies. He pressed, found points of weakness, poured in more power.

A circular room leaped into eerie visibility. Ranged around it were lights that winked and glowed. From ranked thousands of cells, white wormforms poked blunt, eyeless heads. . . .

HE IS HERE! the Egon shrieked the warning, and hurled a bolt of pure mind-force along the channel of contact—and met a counterbolt of energy that seared through him, blackened and charred the intricate organic circuitry of his cerebrum, left a smoking pocket in the rank of cells. For a moment Mallory rested, sensing the shock and bewilderment sweeping through the leaderless Ree mind segments. He felt the automatic death urge that gripped them as the realization reached them that the guiding overpower of the Egon was gone. As he watched, a unit crumpled inward and expired. And another—

"Stop!" Mallory commanded. "I assume control of the mind-complex! Let the segments link in with me!"

Obediently, the will-less fragments of the Ree mind obeyed.

"Change course," Mallory ordered. He gave the necessary instructions, then withdrew along the channel of contact.

TWENTY-FOUR

"So . . . the great Mallory broke." Koslo rocked on his heels before the captive body of his enemy. He laughed. "You were slow to start, but once begun you sang like a turtledove. I'll give my orders now, and by dawn your futile revolt will be a heap of charred corpses stacked in the plaza as an example to others!" He raised the gun.

"I'm not through yet," Mallory said. "The plot runs deeper than you think, Koslo."

The dictator ran a hand over his gray face. His eyes showed the terrible strain of the last hours.

"Talk then," he growled. "Talk fast!"

—as he spoke on, Mallory again shifted his primary awareness, settled into resonance with the subjugated Ree intelligence. Through the ship's sensors he saw the white planet swelling ahead. He slowed the vessel, brought it in on a long parabolic course which skimmed the stratosphere. Seventy miles above the Atlantic, he entered a high haze layer, slowed again as he sensed the heating of the hull.

Below the clouds, he sent the ship hurtling across the coast. He dropped to treetop level, scanned the scene through sensitive hullplates—

For a long moment he studied the landscape below. Then suddenly he understood. . . .

TWENTY-FIVE

"Why do you smile, Mallory?" Koslo's voice was harsh; the gun pointed at the other's head. "Tell me the joke that makes a man laugh in the condemned seat reserved for traitors."

"You'll know in just a moment—" He broke off as a crashing sound came from beyond the room. The floor shook and trembled, rocking Koslo on his feet. A dull *boom!* echoed. The door burst wide.

"Excellency! The capital is under attack!" the man fell

forward, exposing a great wound on his back. Koslo whirled on Mallory—

With a thunderous crash, one side of the room bulged and fell inward. Through the broached wall a glittering torpedo shape appeared, a polished intricacy of burnished metal floating lightly on pencils of blue-white light. The gun in the hand of the dictator came up, crashed deafeningly in the enclosed space. From the prow of the invader, pink light winked. Koslo spun, fell heavily on his face.

The twenty-eight-inch Ree dreadnought came to rest before Mallory. A beam speared out, burned through the chair control panel. The shackles fell away.

I/we await your/our next command, the Ree mind spoke soundlessly in the awesome silence.

TWENTY-SIX

Three months had passed since the referendum which swept John Mallory into office as Premier of the First Planetary Republic. He stood in a room of his spacious apartment in the Executive Palace, frowning at the slender black-haired woman as she spoke earnestly to him:

"John—I'm afraid of that—that infernal machine, eternally hovering, waiting for your orders."

"But why, Monica? That infernal machine, as you call it, was the thing that made a free election possible—and even now it's all that holds Koslo's old organization in check."

"John—" Her hand gripped his arm. "With that—thing—always at your beck and call, you can control anyone, anything on Earth! No opposition can stand before you!"

She looked directly at him. "It isn't right for anyone to have such power, John. Not even you. No human being should be put to such a test!"

His face tightened. "Have I misused it?"

"Not yet. That's why . . ."

"You imply that I will?"

"You're a man, with the failings of a man."

"I propose only what's good for the people of Earth," he said sharply. "Would you have me voluntarily throw away the one weapon that can protect your hard-won freedom?"

"But, John—who are you to be the sole arbiter of what's good for the people of Earth?"

"I'm Chairman of the Republic—"

"You're still human. Stop—while you're still human!"

He studied her face. "You resent my success, don't you? What would you have me do? Resign?"

"I want you to send the machine away—back to wherever it came from."

He laughed shortly. "Are you out of your mind? I haven't begun to extract the technological secrets the Ree ship represents."

"We're not ready for those secrets, John. The race isn't ready. It's already changed you. In the end it can only destroy you as a man."

"Nonsense. I control it utterly. It's like an extension of my own mind—"

"John—please. If not for my sake or your own, for Dian's."

"What's the child got to do with this?"

"She's your daughter. She hardly sees you once a week."

"That's the price she has to pay for being the heir to the greatest man—I mean—damn it, Monica, my responsibilities don't permit me to indulge in all the suburban customs."

"John—" Her voice was a whisper, painful in its intensity. "Send it away."

"No. I won't send it away."

Her face was pale. "Very well, John. As you wish."

"Yes. As I wish."

After she left the rooom, Mallory stood for a long time staring out through the high window at the tiny craft, hovering in the blue air fifty feet away, silent, ready.

Then: *Ree mind*, he sent out the call. *Probe the apart-*

ments of the woman, Monica. I have reason to suspect she plots treason against the state. . . .

Afterword:

The process of writing a story is often as enlightening for me as, hopefully, for the reader.

I began this one with the concept of submitting a human being to an ultimate trial in the same way that an engineer will load a beam until it collapses, testing it to destruction. It is in emotional situations that we meet our severest tests: fear, love, anger drive us to our highest efforts. Thus the framework of the story suggested itself.

As the tale evolved, it became apparent that any power setting out to put mankind to the test—as did Koslo and the Ree—places its own fate in the balance.

In the end, Mallory revealed the true strength of man by using the power of his enemies against them. He won not only his freedom and sanity—but also immense new powers over other men.

Not until then did the danger in such total victory become apparent. The ultimate test of man in his ability to master himself.

It is a test which we have so far failed.

CARCINOMA ANGELS

Introduction to

CARCINOMA ANGELS:

This is the last introduction to be written, though not the
last in the book. Last, because I have put it off time after
time. And not because there is a dearth of material to be
written about Norman Spinrad, but because there is so much.
A leading editor for a hardcover house contends Norman is
the hottest young talent to emerge from the field of speculative fiction in years. Another editor, of a magazine, says Norman is an abominable writer (though he buys his work . . . go
figure *that*). I think he writes like a lunatic. When he is bad,
he is unreadable, which is infrequently. When he is good, he
tackles themes and styles only a nut would attempt (knowing
in advance the task was impossible) and has the audacity to
bring them off in spectacular fashion.

Take for instance his contribution here. It is a funny story
about cancer. Now tell me that isn't fresh ground, unbroken
by Leacock, Benchley or Thurber.

Spinrad is a product of the Bronx. He's a street kid, with
the classic hunger for achievement, status and worldly goods
that drives the have-nots to the top. He truly feels there is
nothing he can't do, nothing he can't write. He isn't writing
this novel, or *this* story, he is writing a career, and it pulses
out of him in volume after volume. At twenty-six he bids fair
to being the first writer of the genre to break out into the
big-time mainstream since Bradbury and Clarke. His drives
are worn like a suit of clothes, and they manifest themselves
in obvious ways. Let his bank balance sink below a thousand
dollars, and he gets twitchy, actually changes disposition like
a Jekyll-Hyde, becomes unbearable, driven. Let an idea of
purest gold come to him and he paces back and forth, rolls
his eyes, scratches his head, stands poised in the center of the
room with legs twined around each other like some great

redheaded bird ready to go up. He is a creature of emotion, stated in broadest terms. Love will send him driving across a continent. Friendship will plunge him into an emotional maelstrom rather than let someone down. Hate will push him to excesses of language and a killing urge to run other cars off the road. His inquisitiveness sends him where neither angels *nor* fools would tread. His critical faculties are so sharp I have seen him correctly postulate a theory for social behavior that was indicated by only the most casual occurrence. He is gullible. He is cynical. He knows where it's at in terms of his times, and he hasn't the faintest idea when he is being put on. He is truly a wise man, and he is the sheerest buffoon. People do not take him in, yet there have been times when I have seen Norman shucked thoroughly by inept practitioners of the art form. His first novel (*The Solarians*, 1966) is so bad it cannot be read. His third novel (*The Men in the Jungle*) is so brilliant it burns like the surface of the sun.

He was born in New York in 1940, graduating after the usual number of years from the Bronx High School of Science, a "highly overrated think-factory for the production of mad scientists, neurotic adolescent geniuses, bomb-hurling anarchists, and Stokeley Carmichael, who finished a year behind me." He graduated from CCNY in 1961 with the only Bachelor of Science degree in Esoterica ever granted by that institution. (His major consisted of courses such as Japanese Civilization, Asian Literature, Short Story Writing and Geology.)

While in his final term at CCNY, Norman's professor in short-story writing pleaded for stories that *really* pulled out all the stops, much like my request for this book. Norman handed the unsuspecting pedant a story so dirty it *still* hasn't been published. However, the professor was impressed and suggested Norman submit it to *Playboy*. The Bunny-Lovers' Gazette turned it down (though they have since rectified their shortsightedness in matters Spinradian; see "Deathwatch," *Playboy*, November 1965) but it only took once to get Spinrad into the habit of submitting things he had written to magazines. It seemed so much more advisable than shoving them into the cracks in the walls for insulation. (A simple jump of logic. If the magazine buys the stories, you take the *money* and jam it into the walls for insulation.)

After graduation he went to Mexico where he contracted various nameless diseases and aggravated an old one with a name. In some inexplicable manner this convinced him to become a writer. He returned to New York, wound up living and working in Greenwich Village and put in a stint in the hospital where he *contracted* something called toxic hepatitis, ran temperatures of 106° for five days straight, hallucinating all the while, and held off interns with a bedpan while calling the Pentagon (collect, naturally, he wasn't *that* nuts) and waking a general at 2 A.M., thus getting the idea for his story in this anthology—the interaction between external and internal mythical-subjective universes. Whatever the hell *that* means.

He sold his first story, "The Last of the Romany," in 1962 to *Analog* (thus inciting the rumor that he is a "Campbell writer," which Spinrad denies vehemently everywhere save in the presence of John W. Campbell, editor of *Analog*, at which time all he does is grin fatuously and say, "Yes, John." This is no slur. I know of *no* writer who is a Campbell writer, or even a writer who writes for Campbell [two different things, I assure you], who is not a YesJohn. I have never been a YesJohn. I have also never sold to *Analog*) and aside from a stint in a literary agency and a month as a welfare investigator (having stolen so much from them, he felt it behooved him to make amends by intimidating other poor boys and their tubercular children), he has been a full-time writer ever since. (There are those who say Norman is only a *part*-time writer, being a full-time *noodje*!)

He has had a second paperback novel published—aside from *The Solarians*, which was mentioned deprecatingly already—and *The Men in the Jungle*, both this year. The latter is a truly original experience, a Doubleday book that grew out of a projected short story for this collection and a deep concern with the morality and tactics of Vietnam-style so-called "Wars of National Liberation."

In the works, at this writing, is a new novel titled *Bug Jack Barron*, which Spinrad calls "a synthesis-novel written to satisfying the differing—though not necessarily conflicting—demands of serious mainstream avant-garde yessir boy writing, and science fiction; a coherent 'Nova Express', in a way." Spinrad gets carried away with his own talent. I have read parts of *Bug Jack Barron*. It is not a synthesis-novel about whachimacallit or avant garde or mainstream or none of that jazz. What *Bug Jack Barron* is, chiefly, is *awful dirty*. It will sell like crazy.

But until your minds can be properly tainted by the full effulgence of Spinrad's foulness, I suggest you pervert yourselves only slightly with "Carcinoma Angels", a funny story.

CARCINOMA ANGELS

by Norman Spinrad

At the age of nine Harrison Wintergreen first discovered that the world was his oyster when he looked at it side-wise. That was the year when baseball cards were *in*. The kid with the biggest collection of baseball cards was *it*. Harry Wintergreen decided to become *it*.

Harry saved up a dollar and bought one hundred random baseball cards. He was in luck—one of them was the very rare Yogi Berra. In three separate transactions, he traded his other ninety-nine cards for the only other three Yogi Berras in the neighborhood. Harry had reduced his holdings to four cards, but he had cornered the market in Yogi Berra. He forced the price of Yogi Berra up to an exorbitant eighty cards. With the slush fund thus accumulated, he successively cornered the market in Mickey Mantle, Willy Mays and Pee Wee Reese and became the J. P. Morgan of baseball cards.

Harry breezed through high school by the simple expedient of mastering only one subject—the art of taking tests. By his senior year, he could outthink any test writer with his gypsheet tied behind his back and won seven scholarships with foolish ease.

In college Harry discovered girls. Being reasonably good-looking and reasonably facile, he no doubt would've garnered his fair share of conquests in the normal course of events. But this was not the way the mind of Harrison Wintergreen worked.

Harry carefully cultivated a stutter, which he could turn on or off at will. Few girls could resist the lure of a good-looking, well-adjusted guy with a slick line who nevertheless carried with him some secret inner hurt that made him stutter. Many were the girls who tried to delve Harry's secret, while Harry delved *them*.

In his sophomore year Harry grew bored with college and reasoned that the thing to do was to become Filthy Rich. He assiduously studied sex novels for one month, wrote three of them in the next two which he immediately sold at $1,000 a throw.

With the $3,000 thus garnered, he bought a shiny new convertible. He drove the new car to the Mexican border and across into a notorious border town. He immediately contacted a disreputable shoeshine boy and bought a pound of marijuana. The shoeshine boy of course tipped off the border guards, and when Harry attempted to walk across the bridge to the States they stripped him naked. They found nothing and Harry crossed the border. He had smuggled nothing out of Mexico, and in fact had thrown the marijuana away as soon as he bought it.

However, he had taken advantage of the Mexican embargo on American cars and illegally sold the convertible in Mexico for $15,000.

Harry took his $15,000 to Las Vegas and spent the next six weeks buying people drinks, lending broke gamblers money, acting in general like a fuzzy-cheeked Santa Claus, gaining the confidence of the right drunks and blowing $5,000.

At the end of six weeks he had three hot market tips which turned his remaining $10,000 into $40,000 in the next two months.

Harry bought four hundred crated government surplus jeeps in four hundred-jeep lots of $10,000 a lot and immediately sold them to a highly disreputable Central American government for $100,000.

He took the $100,000 and bought a tiny island in the Pacific, so worthless that no government had ever bothered to claim it. He set himself up as an independent government with no taxes and sold twenty one-acre plots to twenty millionaires seeking a tax haven at $100,000 a plot. He unloaded the last plot three weeks before the United States, with U.N. backing, claimed the island and brought it under the sway of the Internal Revenue Department.

Harry invested a small part of his $2,000,000 and rented a large computer for twelve hours. The computer constructed a betting scheme by which Harry parlayed his $2,000,000 into $20,000,000 by taking various British soccer pools to the tune of $18,000,000.

For $5,000,000 he bought a monstrous chunk of useless desert from an impoverished Arabian sultanate. With another $2,000,000 he created a huge rumor campaign to the effect that this patch of desert was literally floating on oil. With another $3,000,000 he set up a dummy corporation which made like a big oil company and publicly offered to buy his desert for $75,000,000. After some spirited bargaining, a large American oil company was allowed to outbid the dummy and bought a thousand square miles of sand for $100,000,000.

Harrison Wintergreen was, at the age of twenty-five, Filthy Rich by his own standards. He lost his interest in money.

He now decided that he wanted to Do Good. He Did Good. He toppled seven unpleasant Latin American governments and replaced them with six Social Democracies and a Benevolent Dictatorship. He converted a tribe of Borneo headhunters to Roscrucianism. He set up twelve rest homes for overage whores and organized a birth control program which sterilized twelve million fecund Indian women. He contrived to make another $100,000,000 on the above enterprises.

At the age of thirty Harrison Wintergreen had had it with Do-Gooding. He decided to Leave His Footprints in the Sands of Time. He Left His Footprints in the Sands of Time. He wrote an internationally acclaimed novel about King Farouk. He invented the Wintergreen Filter, a membrane through which fresh water passed freely, but which barred salts. Once set up, a Wintergreen Desalinization Plant could desalinate an unlimited supply of water at a per-gallon cost approaching absolute zero. He painted one painting and was instantly offered $200,000 for it. He donated it to the Museum of Modern Art, gratis. He developed a mutated virus which destroyed syphilis bacteria. Like syphilis, it spread by sexual contact. It was a mild aphrodisiac. Syphilis was wiped out in eighteen months. He bought an island off the coast of California, a five-hundred-foot crag jutting out of the Pacific. He caused it to be carved into a five-hundred-foot statue of Harrison Wintergreen.

At the age of thirty-eight Harrison Wintergreen had Left sufficient Footprints in the Sands of Time. He was bored. He looked around greedily for new worlds to conquer.

This, then, was the man who, at the age of forty, was informed that he had an advanced, well-spread and incurable case of cancer and that he had one year to live.

Wintergreen spent the first month of his last year searching for an existing cure for terminal cancer. He visited laboratories, medical schools, hospitals, clinics, Great Doctors, quacks, people who had miraculously recovered from cancer, faith healers and Little Old Ladies in Tennis Shoes. There was no known cure for terminal cancer, reputable or otherwise. It was as he suspected, as he more or less even hoped. He would have to do it himself.

He proceeded to spend the next month setting things up to do it himself. He caused to be erected in the middle of the

Arizona desert an air-conditioned walled villa. The villa had a completely automatic kitchen and enough food for a year. It had a $5,000,000 biological and biochemical laboratory. It had a $3,000,000 microfilmed library which contained every word ever written on the subject of cancer. It had the pharmacy to end all pharmacies: a literal supply of quite literally every drug that existed—poisons, painkillers, hallucinogens, dandricides, antiseptics, antibiotics, viricides, headache remedies, heroin, quinine, curare, snake oil—everything. The pharmacy cost $20,000,000.

The villa also contained a one-way radiotelephone, a large stock of basic chemicals, incuding radioactives, copies of the *Koran*, the Bible, the *Torah*, the *Book of the Dead, Science and Health with Key to the Scriptures, the I Ching* and the complete works of Wilhelm Reich and Aldous Huxley. It also contained a very large and ultra-expensive computer. By the time the villa was ready, Wintergreen's petty cash fund was nearly exhausted.

With ten months to do that which the medical world considered impossible, Harrison Wintergreen entered his citadel.

During the first two months he devoured the library, sleeping three hours out of each twenty-four and dosing himself regularly with Benzedrine. The library offered nothing but data. He digested the data and went on to the pharmacy.

During the next month he tried aureomycin, bacitracin, stannous fluoride, hexylresorcinol, cortisone, penicillin, hexachlorophene, shark-liver extract and 7312 assorted other miracles of modern medical science, all to no avail. He began to feel pain, which he immediately blotted out and continued to blot out with morphine. Morphine addiction was merely an annoyance.

He tried chemicals, radioactives, viricides, Christian Science, yoga, prayer, enemas, patent medicines, herb tea, witchcraft and yogurt diets. This consumed another month, during which Wintergreen continued to waste away, sleeping less and less and taking more and more Benzedrine and morphine. Nothing worked. He had six months left.

He was on the verge of becoming desperate. He tried a different tack. He sat in a comfortable chair and contemplated his navel for forty-eight consecutive hours.

His meditations produced a severe case of eyestrain and two significant words: "spontaneous remission".

In his two months of research, Wintergreen had come upon numbers of cases where a terminal cancer abruptly reversed itself and the patient, for whom all hope had been abandoned, had been cured. No one ever knew how or why. It could not be predicted, it could not be artificially produced, but it happened nevertheless. For want of an explanation, they called it spontaneous remission. "Remission", meaning cure. "Spontaneous", meaning no one knew what caused it.

Which was not to say that it did not have a cause.

Wintergreen was buoyed; he was even ebullient. He knew that some terminal cancer patients had been cured. Therefore terminal cancer could be cured. Therefore the problem was removed from the realm of the impossible and was now merely the domain of the highly improbable.

And doing the highly improbable was Wintergreen's specialty.

With six months of estimated life left, Wintergreen set jubilantly to work. From his complete cancer library he culled every known case of spontaneous remission. He coded every one of them into the computer—data on the medical histories of the patients, on the treatments employed, on their ages, sexes, religions, races, creeds, colors, national origins, temperaments, marital status, Dun and Bradstreet ratings, neuroses, psychoses and favorite beers. Complete profiles of every human being ever known to have survived terminal cancer were fed into Harrison Wintergreen's computer.

Wintergreen programed the computer to run a complete series of correlations between ten thousand separate and distinct factors and spontaneous remission. If even one factor—age, credit rating, favorite food—*anything* correlated with spontaneous remission, the spontaneity factor would be removed.

Wintergreen had shelled out $100,000,000 for the computer. It was the best damn computer in the world. In two minutes and 7.894 seconds it had performed its task. In one succinct word it gave Wintergreen his answer:

"Negative."

Spontaneous remission did not correlate with *any* external factor. It was still spontaneous; the cause was unknown.

A lesser man would've been crushed. A more conventional man would've been dumbfounded. Harrison Wintergreen was elated.

He had eliminated the entire external universe as a factor in spontaneous remission in one fell swoop. Therefore, in some mysterious way, the human body and/or psyche was capable of curing itself.

Wintergreen set out to explore and conquer his own internal universe. He repaired to the pharmacy and prepared a formidable potation. Into his largest syringe he decanted the following: Novocain; morphine; curare; *vlut*, a rare Central Asian poison which induced temporary blindness; olfactorcain, a top-secret smell-deadener used by skunk farmers; tympanoline, a drug which temporarily deadened the auditory nerves (used primarily by filibustering senators); a large dose of Benzedrine; lysergic acid; psilocybin; mescaline; peyote extract; seven other highly experimental and most illegal hallucinogens; eye of newt and toe of dog.

Wintergreen laid himself out on his most comfortable couch. He swabbed the vein in the pit of his left elbow with alcohol and injected himself with the witch's brew.

His heart pumped. His blood surged, carrying the arcane chemicals to every part of his body. The Novocain blanked out every sensory nerve in his body. The morphine eliminated all sensations of pain. The *vlut* blacked out his vision. The olfactorcain cut off all sense of smell. The tympanoline made him deaf as a traffic court judge. The curare paralyzed him.

Wintergreen was alone in his own body. No external stimuli reached him. He was in a state of total sensory deprivation. The urge to lapse into blessed unconsciousness was irresistible. Wintergreen, strong-willed though he was, could not have remained conscious unaided. But the massive dose of Benzedrine would not let him sleep.

He was awake, aware, alone in the universe of his own body with no external stimuli to occupy himself with.

Then, one and two, and then in combinations like the fists of a good fast heavyweight, the hallucinogens hit.

Wintergreen's sensory organs were blanked out, but the brain centers which received sensory data were still active. It was on these cerebral centers that the tremendous charge of assorted hallucinogens acted. He began to see phantom colors, shapes, things without name or form. He heard eldritch symphonies, ghost echoes, mad howling noises. A million impossible smells roiled through his brain. A thousand false pains and pressures tore at him, as if his whole body had been amputated. The sensory centers of Wintergreen's brain were like a mighty radio receiver tuned to an empty band—filled with meaningless visual, auditory, olfactory and sensual static.

The drugs kept his sense blank. The Benzedrine kept him conscious. Forty years of being Harrison Wintergreen kept him cold and sane.

For an indeterminate period of time he rolled with the punches, groping for the feel of this strange new non-environment. Then gradually, hesitantly at first but with ever growing confidence, Wintergreen reached for control. His mind constructed untrue but useful analogies for actions that were not actions, states of being that were not states of being, sensory data unlike any sensory data received by the human brain. The analogies, constructed in a kind of calculated madness by his subconscious for the brute task of making the incomprehensible palpable, also enabled him to deal with his non-environment as if it were an environment, translating mental changes into analogs of action.

He reached out an analogical hand and tuned a figurative

237

radio, inward, away from the blank wave band of the outside side universe and towards the as yet unused wave band of his own body, the internal universe that was his mind's only possible escape from chaos.

He turned, adjusted, forced, struggled, felt his mind pressing against an atom-thin interface. He battered against the interface, an analogical translucent membrane between his mind and his internal universe, a membrane that stretched, flexed, bulged inward, thinned . . . and finally broke. Like Alice through the Looking Glass, his analogical body stepped through and stood on the other side.

Harrison Wintergreen was inside his own body.

It was a world of wonder and loathsomeness, of the majestic and the ludicrous. Wintergreen's point of view, which his mind analogized as a body within his true body, was inside a vast network of pulsing arteries, like some monstrous freeway system. The analogy crystallized. It *was* a freeway, and Wintergreen was driving down it. Bloated sacs dumped things into the teeming traffic: hormones, wastes, nutrients. White blood cells careened by him like mad taxicabs. Red corpuscles drove steadily along like stolid burghers. The traffic ebbed and congested like a crosstown rush hour. Wintergreen drove on, searching, searching.

He made a left, cut across three lanes and made a right down towards a lymph node. And then he saw it—a pile of white cells like a twelve-car collision, and speeding towards him a leering motorcyclist.

Black the cycle. Black the riding leathers. Black, dull pure light in his hand. Savage black dragons with blood-red eyes. And emblazoned across the front and back of the black motorcycle jacket in shining scarlet studs the legend: "Carcinoma Angels".

With a savage whoop, Wintergreen gunned his analogical car down the hypothetical freeway straight for the imaginary cyclist, the cancer cell.

Splat! Pop! Cuush! Wintergreen's car smashed the cycle and the rider exploded in a cloud of fine black dust.

Up and down the freeways of his circulatory system

Wintergreen ranged, barreling along arteries, careening down veins, inching through narrow capillaries, seeking the blackclad cyclists, the Carcinoma Angels, grinding them to dust beneath his wheels. . . .

And he found himself in the dark moist wood of his lungs, riding a snow-white analogical horse, an imaginary lance of pure light in his hand. Savage black dragons with blood-red eyes and flickering red tongues slithered from behind the gnarled bolls of great air-sac trees. St. Wintergreen spurred his horse, lowered his lance and impaled monster after hissing monster till at last the holy lungwood was free of dragons. . . .

He was flying in some vast moist cavern, above him the vague bulks of gigantic organs, below a limitless expanse of shining slimy peritoneal plain.

From behind the cover of his huge beating heart a formation of black fighter planes, bearing the insignia of a scarlet "C" on their wings and fusilages, roared down at him.

Wintergreen gunned his engine and rose to the fray, flying up and over the bandits, blasting them with his machine guns, and one by one and then in bunches they crashed in flames to the peritoneum below. . . .

In a thousand shapes and guises, the black and red things attacked. Black, the color of oblivion, red, the color of blood. Dragons, cyclists, planes, sea things, soldiers, tanks and tigers in blood vessels and lungs and spleen and thorax and bladder—Carcinoma Angels, all.

And Wintergreen fought his analogical battles in an equal number of incarnations, as driver, knight, pilot, diver, soldier, mahout, with a grim and savage glee, littering the battlefields of his body with the black dust of the fallen Carcinoma Angels.

Fought and fought and killed and killed and finally . . .

Finally found himself knee-deep in the sea of his digestive juices lapping against the walls of the dank, moist cave that was his stomach. And scuttling towards him on chitinous legs, a monstrous black crab with blood-red eyes, gross, squat, primeval.

Clicking, chittering, the crab scurried across his stomach towards him. Wintergreen paused, grinned wolfishly, and leaped high in the air, landing with both feet squarely on the hard black carapace.

Like a sun-dried gourd, brittle, dry, hollow, the crab crunched beneath his weight and splintered into a million dusty fragments.

And Wintergreen was alone, at last alone and victorious, the first and last of the Carcinoma Angels now banished and gone and finally defeated.

Harrison Wintergreen, alone in his own body, victorious and once again looking for new worlds to conquer, waiting for the drugs to wear off, waiting to return to the world that always was his oyster.

Waiting and waiting and waiting . . .

Go to the finest sanitarium in the world, and there you will find Harrison Wintergreen, who made himself Filthy Rich, Harrison Wintergreen, who Did Good, Harrison Wintergreen, who Left His Footprints in the Sands of Time, Harrison Wintergreen, catatonic vegetable.

Harrison Wintergreen, who stepped inside his own body to do battle with Carcinoma's Angels, and won.

And can't get out.

Afterword:

Cancer. Cancer has become a whisper-word, a myth word, a magic word, a dirty word; cancer, you should pardon the expression, is the 20th Century Pox. Prominent Public Personalities, alone, escape from its ravages, as any newspaper obituary column will tell you: "dying after a long, lingering illness", or "passing away from natural causes". Cancer the Crab has even lost his billing in some of the more sensitive Astrological Columns, his piece of the zodiacal pie being preempted by "Moon Children"—the powers that be having decided that reminding one-twelfth of the readership that they were born under the sign of cellular madness is bad for the circulation, not to mention the alimentary canal.

So what's with cancer anyway? (You have now read the word "cancer" six times. Found any suspicious-looking moles yet?) The Gallup Poll shows that seven out of ten Americans prefer tertiary syphilis to cancer. Such unpopularity must be deserved, but why? Just because cancer is your own body devouring itself like a wounded hyena? Simply because cancer is psychosis on a cellular level? Merely because cancer is inexplicable and incurable on the level of objective reality?

Ah, but what about on the level of mythical reality? How else do you expect to fight a myth anyway? Gotta fight Black Magic with White Magic. Couldn't cancer be psychosomatic (a magic word if ever there was one), the physical manifestation of some psychic vampirism? Cancer, after all, is the Ultimate Cannibalism—your body eating itself, cell by cell.

Wouldn't you rather forget about this morbid, unpleasant subject and think about something nicer, like gas ovens or thalidomide or Limited Pre-Emptive Thermonuclear War?

After all, as Henry Miller says in his preface to *The Subterraneans*, "*Cancer! Schmanser!* What's the difference, so long as you're healthy!"

AUTO-DA-FE

Introduction to

AUTO-DA-FE

It is refreshing to test oneself periodically and find out just how stern is the stuff of which one is composed. Such a test is concluded with this book. The temptation to begin the anthology with A-for-Asimov and end it with Z-for-Zelazny was almost enough to make me twitch with delight. But I have saved the closing spot for "Chip" Delany, for reasons which will be explained in *his* introduction, and moved Roger Zelazny into next-to-closing. The deciding factor was recognition. Delany needs the exposure. Zelazny has ascended to godhood already, and needs no helping hands.

Roger Zelazny is an emaciated, ascetic-looking man of Polish-Irish-Pennsylvania-Dutch origins with a reserved and gentle manner cloaking a sense of humor that might well have been envied by Torquemada. He was born, like the editor of this anthology, in Ohio. In point of fact, very near: Roger comes from Euclid, Ohio. It is a dismal town where once existed an ice cream shop that gave three dips for nine cents, but that was a long time ago. Zelazny's comment on his career prior to becoming a writer goes like this: "Rapidly rose to obscurity in government circles as a claims policy specialist in the Social Security Administration." He attended Western Reserve University and Columbia. God only knows if he won any degrees, and it doesn't matter much. The only writer extant with a more singular approach to the English language is Nabokov. He presently resides in Baltimore with an exceptionally pretty wife named Judy who is far too good for him.

Zelazny, author of such award-winning stories as "He Who Shapes", "A Rose for Ecclesiastes", "And Call Me Conrad" and "The Doors of His Face, the Lamps of His Mouth", has the bad taste to be a glutton for prizes. His novel, *Lord of Light*, will be published soon by Doubleday. At the age of twenty-nine, he has already copped a Hugo and two Nebulas, thus humiliating older, grayer, wiser heads in the field who have worked three times as long, five times as hard, and write one twentieth as well. It is unseemly for one so young.

Which is a strange thing, actually. For there is nothing young about Zelazny's work. His stories are sunk to the knees in maturity and wisdom, in bravura writing that breaks rules most writers only suspect exist. His concepts are fresh, his attacks bold, his resolutions generally trenchant. Thus leading us inexorably to the conclusion that Roger Zelazny is the reincarnation of Geoffrey Chaucer.

Seldom is a writer recognized and lauded so completely in his growth stages (particularly in the sillyass fickle field of science fiction) as Zelazny has been. It is a tribute to his tenacity, his talent and his personal visions of the world that, in any list of the current top writers of speculative fiction, Roger Zelazny's name appears prominently. We can delight in the prospect of many years of fine stories from his typewriter, and as the latest installment, consider the wry comment that follows, a penetrating extrapolation of our "mobile culture".

AUTO-DA-FE

by Roger Zelazny

Still do I remember the hot sun upon the sands of the Plaza de Autos, the cries of the soft-drink hawkers, the tiers of humanity stacked across from me on the sunny side of the arena, sunglasses like cavities in their gleaming faces.

Still do I remember the smells and the colors: the reds and the blues and the yellows, the ever present tang of petroleum fumes upon the air.

Still do I remember that day, that day with its sun in the

middle of the sky and the sign of Aries, burning in the blooming of the year. I recall the mincing steps of the pumpers, heads thrown back, arms waving, the white dazzles of their teeth framed with smiling lips, cloths like colorful tails protruding from the rear pockets of their coveralls; and the horns—I remember the blare of a thousand horns over the loudspeakers, on and off, off and on, over and over, and again, and then one shimmering, final note, sustained, to break the ear and the heart with its infinite power, its pathos.

Then there was silence.

I see it now as I did on that day so long ago . . .

He entered the arena, and the cry that went up shook blue heaven upon its pillars of white marble.

"Viva! El mechador! Viva! El mechador!"

I remember his face, dark and sad and wise.

Long of jaw and nose was he, and his laughter was as the roaring of the wind, and his movements were as the music of the theramin and the drum. His coveralls were blue and silk and tight and stitched with thread of gold and broidered all about with black braid. His jacket was beaded and there were flashing scales upon his breast, his shoulders, his back.

His lips curled into the smile of a man who has known much glory and has hold upon the power that will bring him into more.

He moved, turning in a circle, not shielding his eyes against the sun.

He was above the sun. He was Manolo Stillete Dos Muertos, the mightiest *mechador* the world has ever seen, black boots upon his feet, pistons in his thighs, fingers with the discretion of micrometers, halo of dark locks about his head and the angel of death in his right arm, there, in the center of the grease-stained circle of truth.

He waved, and a cry went up once more.

"Manolo! Manolo! Dos Muertos! Dos Muertos!"

After two years' absence from the ring, he had chosen this, the anniversary of his death and retirement to return—for

247

there was gasoline and methyl in his blood and his heart was a burnished pump ringed 'bout with desire and courage. He had died twice within the ring, and twice had the medics restored him. After his second death, he had retired, and some said that it was because he had known fear. This could not be true.

He waved his hand and his name rolled back upon him.

The horns sounded once more: three long blasts.

Then again there was silence, and a pumper wearing red and yellow brought him the cape, removed his jacket.

The tinfoil backing of the cape flashed in the sun as Dos Muertos swirled it.

Then there came the final, beeping notes.

The big door rolled upward and back into the wall.

He draped his cape over his arm and faced the gateway.

The light above was red and from within the darkness there came the sound of an engine.

The light turned yellow, then green, and there was the sound of cautiously engaged gears.

The car moved slowly into the ring, paused, crept forward, paused again.

It was a red Pontiac, its hood stripped away, its engine like a nest of snakes, coiling and engendering behind the circular shimmer of its invisible fan. The wings of its aerial spun round and round, then fixed upon Manolo and his cape.

He had chosen a heavy one for his first, slow on turning, to give him a chance to limber up.

The drums of its brain, which had never before recorded a man, were spinning.

Then the consciousness of its kind swept over it, and it moved forward.

Manolo swirled his cape and kicked its fender as it roared past.

The door of the great garage closed.

When it reached the opposite side of the ring the car stopped, parked.

Cries of disgust, booing and hissing arose from the crowd.

248

Still the Pontiac remained parked.

Two pumpers, bearing buckets, emerged from behind the fence and threw mud upon its windshield.

It roared then and pursued the nearest, banging into the fence. Then it turned suddenly, sighted Dos Muertos and charged.

His *veronica* transformed him into a statue with a skirt of silver. The enthusiasm of the crowd was mighty.

It turned and charged once more, and I wondered at Manolo's skill, for it would seem that his buttons had scraped cherry paint from the side panels.

Then it paused, spun its wheels, ran in a circle about the ring.

The crowd roared as it moved past him and recircled.

Then it stopped again, perhaps fifty feet away.

Manolo turned his back upon it and waved to the crowd.

—Again, the cheering and the calling of his name.

He gestured to someone behind the fence.

A pumper emerged and bore to him, upon a velvet cushion, his chrome-plated monkey wrench.

He turned then again to the Pontiac and strode toward it.

It stood there shivering and he knocked off its radiator cap.

A jet of steaming water shot into the air and the crowd bellowed. Then he struck the front of the radiator and banged upon each fender.

He turned his back upon it again and stood there.

When he heard the engagement of the gears he turned once more, and with one clean pass it was by him, but not before he had banged twice upon the trunk with his wrench.

It moved to the other end of the ring and parked.

Manolo raised his hand to the pumper behind the fence.

The man with the cushion emerged and bore to him the long-handled screwdriver and the short cape. He took the monkey wrench away with him, as well as the long cape.

Another silence came over the Plaza del Autos.

The Pontiac, as if sensing all this, turned once more and blew its horn twice. Then it charged.

There were dark spots upon the sand from where its radiator had leaked water. Its exhaust arose like a ghost behind it. It bore down upon him at a terrible speed.

Dos Muertos raised the cape before him and rested the blade of the screwdriver upon his left forearm.

When it seemed he would surely be run down, his hand shot forward, so fast the eye could barely follow it, and he stepped to the side as the engine began to cough.

Still the Pontiac continued on with a deadly momentum, turned sharply without braking, rolled over, slid into the fence, and began to burn. Its engine coughed and died.

The Plaza shook with the cheering. They awarded Dos Muertos both headlights and the tailpipe. He held them high and moved in slow promenade about the perimeter of the ring. The horns sounded. A lady threw him a plastic flower and he sent for a pumper to bear her the tailpipe and ask her to dine with him. The crowd cheered more loudly, for he was known to be a great layer of women, and it was not such an unusual thing in the days of my youth as it is now.

The next was the blue Chevrolet, and he played with it as a child plays with a kitten, tormenting it into striking, then stopping it forever. He received both headlights. The sky had clouded over by then and there was a tentative mumbling of thunder.

The third was a black Jaguar XKE, which calls for the highest skill possible and makes for a very brief moment of truth. There was blood as well as gasoline upon the sand before he dispatched it, for its side mirror extended further than one would think, and there was a red furrow across his rib cage before he had done with it. But he tore out its ignition system with such grace and artistry that the crowd boiled over into the ring, and the guards were called forth to

250

beat them with clubs and herd them with cattle prods back into their seats.

Surely, after all of this, none could say that Dos Muertos had ever known fear.

A cool breeze arose and I bought a soft drink and waited for the last.

His final car sped forth while the light was still yellow. It was a mustard-colored Ford convertible. As it went past him the first time, it blew its horn and turned on its windshield wipers. Everyone cheered, for they could see it had spirit.

Then it came to a dead halt, shifted into reverse, and backed toward him at about forty miles an hour.

He got out of the way, sacrificing grace to expediency, and it braked sharply, shifted into low gear, and sped forward again.

He waved the cape and it was torn from his hands. If he had not thrown himself over backward, he would have been struck.

Then someone cried: "It's out of alignment!"

But he got to his feet, recovered his cape and faced it once more.

They still tell of those five passes that followed. Never has there been such a flirting with bumper and grill! Never in all of the Earth has there been such an encounter between *mechador* and machine! The convertible roared like ten centuries of streamlined death, and the spirit of St. Detroit sat in its driver's seat, grinning, while Dos Muertos faced it with his tinfoil cape, cowed it and called for his wrench. It nursed its overheated engine and rolled its windows up and down, up and down, clearing its muffler the while with lavatory noises and much black smoke.

By then it was raining, softly, gently, and the thunder still came about us. I finished my soft drink.

Dos Muertos had never used his monkey wrench on the engine before, only upon the body. But this time he threw it. Some experts say he was aiming at the distributor; others say he was trying to break its fuel pump.

The crowd booed him.

251

Something gooey was dripping from the Ford onto the sand. The red streak brightened on Manolo's stomach. The rain came down.

He did not look at the crowd. He did not take his eyes from the car. He held out his right hand, palm upward, and waited.

A panting pumper placed the screwdriver in his hand and ran back toward the fence.

Manolo moved to the side and waited.

It leaped at him and he struck.

There was more booing.

He had missed the kill.

No one left, though. The Ford swept around him in a tight circle, smoke now emerging from its engine. Manolo rubbed his arm and picked up the screwdriver and cape he had dropped. There was more booing as he did so.

By the time the car was upon him, flames were leaping forth from its engine.

Now some say that he struck and missed again, going off balance. Others say that he began to strike, grew afraid and drew back. Still others say that, perhaps for an instant, he knew a fatal pity for his spirited adversary, and that this had stayed his hand. I say that the smoke was too thick for any of them to say for certain what had happened.

But it swerved and he fell forward, and he was borne upon that engine, blazing like a god's catafalque, to meet with his third death as they crashed into the fence together and went up in flames.

There was much dispute over the final *corrida*, but what remained of the tailpipe and both headlights were buried with what remained of him, beneath the sands of the Plaza, and there was much weeping among the women he had known. I say that he could not have been afraid or known pity, for his strength was as a river of rockets, his thighs were pistons and the fingers of his hands had the discretion of micrometers; his hair was a black halo and the angel of death rode on his right arm. Such a man, a man who has known truth, is mightier than any machine. Such a man is above anything but the holding of power and the wearing of glory.

Now he is dead though, this one, for the third and final time. He is as dead as all the dead who have ever died before the bumper, under the grill, beneath the wheels. It is well that he cannot rise again, for I say that his final car was his apotheosis, and anything else would be anticlimactic. Once I saw a blade of grass growing up between the metal sheets of the world in a place where they had become loose, and I destroyed it because I felt it must be lonesome. Often have I regretted doing this, for I took away the glory of its alone-ness. Thus does life the machine, I feel, consider man, sternly, then with regret, and the heavens do weep upon him through eyes that grief has opened in the sky.

All the way home I thought of this thing, and the hoofs of my mount clicked upon the floor of the city as I rode through the rain toward evening, that spring.

Afterword:

This is the first time I've had a chance to address the readers of one of my stories directly, rather than through the mimesis game we play. While I go along with the notion that a writer should hold a mirror up to reality, I don't necessarily feel that it should be the kind you look into when you shave or tweeze your eyebrows, or both as the case may be. If I'm going to carry a mirror around, holding it up to reality whenever I notice any, I might as well enjoy the burden as much as I can. My means of doing this is to tote around one of those mirrors you used to see in fun houses, back when they still had fun houses. Of course, not anything you reflect looks either as attractive or as grimly visaged as it may stand before the naked eyeball. Sometimes it looks more at-tractive, or more grimly visaged. You just don't really know, until you've tried the warping glass. And it's awfully hard to hold the slippery thing steady. Blink and—who knows?—you're two feet tall. Sneeze, and May the Good Lord Smile Upon You. I live in deathly fear of dropping the thing. I don't know what I'd do without it. Carouse more, probably. I love my cold and shiny burden, that's why. And I won't say anything about the preceding story, because if it didn't say everything it was supposed to say all by itself, then that's its own fault and I'm not going to dignify it with any more words. Any error is always attributable to the mirror—either to the way I'm holding it, or to the way you're looking into it—so don't blame me. I just work here. But . . . If anything *does* seem amiss with visions of this sort, keep on looking into the glass and take a couple quick steps backwards. Who knows? Maybe you'll turn into the powder room. . . .

AYE, AND GOMORRAH ...

Introduction to

AYE, AND GOMORRAH ...:

This is the last story in the book. For a very special reason
(and not merely because it is the last one to be set in type,
smart aleck). It is the end of an adventure and the beginning
of a journey. Finis for this anthology and the need to take one
last lunge at proving the point the book was intended to
prove (in the event, God forbid, all 239,000 words that have
gone before have not done the job *more* than adequately);
one last firecracker to light the scene. The end. The last one.
Maybe a kick in the ass, one to leave them gasping, a knock-
out.

The beginning of a journey; the career of a new writer.
You can be there as the boat sails, to offer the basket of fruit,
to throw the confetti, to wave good-by and we've got our eye
on you. The big trip into the big world. The trek. But why
this story, by *this* writer?

Toulouse-Lautrec once said, "One should never meet a
man whose work one admires. The man is always so much
less than the work." Painfully, almost always this is true.
The great novelist turns out to be a whiner. The penetrator
of the foibles of man picks his nose in public. The authority
on South Africa has never been beyond Levittown. The writer of swashbuckling adventures is a pathetic little homosexual who still lives with his invalid mother. Oh, Henri the
Mad, you were so right. But it is not so with the author of
the story I have chosen to close out this attempt at daring.

I have seldom been so impressed with a writer as I was
when I first met Samuel R. Delany. To be in the same room
with "Chip" Delany is to know you are in the presence of an
event about to happen. It isn't his wit, which is considerable,
or his intensity, which is like heat lightning, or his erudition,
which is whistle-provoking, or his sincerity, which is so real

it has shape and substance. It is an indefinable but none-theless commanding impression that this is a young man with great works in him. Thus far, he has written almost nothing but novels, and those for a paperback house praised for its giving newcomers a chance, but damned for the cheapjack look of their presentations. The titles are *The Jewels of Aptor, Captives of the Flame, The Towers of Toron, City of a Thousand Suns, The Ballad of Beta-2, Empire Star* and an incredible little volume called *Babel-17* which won the 1966 Nebula Award of the Science Fiction Writers of America. Ignore the titles. They are the flushed marketing delusions of editors on whose office walls are tacked reminders to COMPETE! But read the books. They demonstrate a lively, intricate, singular talent in its remarkable growth process. Chip Delany is destined to be one of the truly important writers produced by the field of speculative writing. A kind of writer who will move into other bags and become for the mainstream a Delany-shaped importance like Bradbury or Vonnegut or Sturgeon. The talent is *that* large.

Born April Fool's Day sometime during WWII, Delany grew up in New York's Harlem. Very private, very progressive elementary school education, thence to the Bronx High School of Science, sporadic attendance at City College with a term as poetry editor of the *Promethean*. He wrote his first science fiction novel at nineteen. He has worked, in the chinks between novels, as a bookstore clerk, laborer on shrimp boats off the Texas Gulf, folk singer in Greece, and has shuttled between New York City and Istanbul. He is married. He currently resides on the Lower East Side of NYC and is at work on a *huge* science fiction novel, *Nova* which will be published next year by Doubleday. Damned little to know about someone who writes as big as Delany does. But it's all he seems to want to say.

However, his fiction speaks more than eloquently. His novels approach timeworn and shopworn clichés of speculative fiction with a bold and compelling ingenuity. He brings freshness to a field that occasionally slumps into the line of least resistance. This freshness is eminently in evidence in the story you are about to read, in its way one of the best of the thirty-three winners here. It certainly classifies as a "dangerous" vision, and one which both Chip and I felt would have been difficult to market to the established periodicals. Though you may have seen a short story or novelette in print before you see the story that follows, be advised this was Chip Delany's *first* short story. He did nothing but novels before consenting to write a piece for this book. It ranks, for me, as one of the truly memorable solo flights in the history of the genre.

AYE, AND GOMORRAH ...

by Samuel R. Delany

And came down in Paris:

Where we raced along the Rue de Médicis with Bo and Lou and Muse inside the fence, Kelly and me outside, making faces through the bars, making noise, making the Luxembourg Gardens roar at two in the morning. Then climbed out, and down to the square in front of St. Sulpice where Bo tried to knock me into the fountain.

At which point Kelly noticed what was going on around us, got an ashcan cover, and ran into the pissoir, banging the walls. Five guys scooted out; even a big pissoir only holds four.

A very blond young man put his hand on my arm and smiled. "Don't you think, Spacer, that you ... people should leave?"

I looked at his hand on my blue uniform. *"Est-ce que tu es un frelk?"*

His eyebrows rose, then he shook his head. "Une *frelk*," he corrected. "No. I am not. Sadly for me. You look as though you may once have been a man. But now ..." He smiled. "You have nothing for me now. The police." He nodded

259

across the street where I noticed the gendarmerie for the first time. "They don't bother us. You are strangers, though ..."

But Muse was already yelling, "Hey, come on! Let's get out of here, huh?" And left. And went up again.

And came down in Houston:

"God damn!" Muse said. "Gemini Flight Control—you mean this is where it all started? Let's get *out* of here, *please*!"

So took a bus out through Pasadena, then the monoline to Galveston, and were going to take it down the Gulf, but Lou found a couple with a pickup truck—

"Glad to give you a ride, Spacers. You people up there on them planets and things, doing all that good work for the government."

—who were going south, them and the baby, so we rode in the back for two hundred and fifty miles of sun and wind.

"You think they're frelks?" Lou asked, elbowing me. "I bet they're frelks. They're just waiting for us give 'em the come-on."

"Cut it out. They're a nice, stupid pair of country kids."

"That don't mean they ain't frelks!"

"You don't trust anybody, do you?"

"No."

And finally a bus again that rattled us through Brownsville and across the border into Matamoros where we staggered down the steps into the dust and the scorched evening with a lot of Mexicans and chickens and Texas Gulf shrimp fishermen—who smelled worst—and *we* shouted the loudest. Forty-three whores—I counted—had turned out for the shrimp fishermen, and by the time we had broken two of the windows in the bus station they were all laughing. The shrimp fishermen said they wouldn't buy us no food but would get us drunk if we wanted, 'cause that was the custom with shrimp fishermen. But we yelled, broke another window; then, while I was lying on my back on the telegraph office steps, singing, a woman with dark lips bent over and put her hands on my cheeks. "You are very sweet." Her rough hair fell forward. "But the men, they are standing around and watching *you*. And that is taking up *time*. Sadly, their time is our money. Spacer, do you not think you ... people should leave?"

I grabbed her wrist. "*Usted!*" I whispered. "*Usted es una frelka.*"

"*Frelko in español.*" She smiled and patted the sunburst that hung from my belt buckle. "Sorry. But you have nothing that ... would be useful to me. It is too bad, for you look like you were once a woman, no? And I like women, too. ..."

I rolled off the porch.

"Is this a drag, or is this a drag!" Muse was shouting. "Come *on*! Let's *go*!"

We managed to get back to Houston before dawn, somehow. And went up.

And came down in Istanbul:

That morning it rained in Istanbul:

At the commissary we drank our tea from pear-shaped glasses, looking out across the Bosphorus. The Princes Islands lay like trash heaps before the prickly city.

"Who knows their way in this town?" Kelly asked.

"Aren't we going around together?" Muse demanded. "I thought we were going around together."

"They held up my check at the purser's office," Kelly explained. "I'm flat broke. I think the purser's got it in for me," and shrugged. "Don't want to, but I'm going to have to hunt up a rich frelk and come on friendly," went back to the tea; *then* noticed how heavy the silence had become. "Aw, come *on*, now! You gape at me like that and I'll bust every bone in that carefully-conditioned-from-puberty body of yours. Hey you!" meaning me "Don't give me that holier-than-thou gawk like you never went to no frelk!"

It was starting.

"I'm not gawking," I said and got quietly mad.

The longing, the old longing.

Bo laughed to break tensions. "Say, last time I was in Istanbul—about a year before I joined up with this platoon—I

261

remember we were coming out of Taksim Square down Istiqlal. Just past all the cheap movies we found a little passage lined with flowers. Ahead of us were two other spacers. It's a market in there, and farther down they got fish, and then a courtyard with oranges and candy and sea urchins and cabbage. But flowers in front. Anyway, we noticed something funny about the spacers. It wasn't their uniforms: they were perfect. The haircuts: fine. It wasn't till we heard them talking—They were a man and woman dressed up like spacers, trying *to pick up frelks*! Imagine, queer for frelks!"

"Yeah," Lou said. "I seen that before. There were a lot of them in Rio."

"We beat hell out of them two," Bo concluded. "We got them in a side street and went to *town*!"

Muse's tea glass clicked on the counter. "From Taksim down Istiqlal till you get to the flowers? Now why didn't you say that's where the frelks were, huh?" A smile on Kelly's face would have made that okay. There was no smile.

"Hell," Lou said, "nobody ever had to tell me where to look. I go out in the street and frelks smell me coming. I can spot 'em halfway along Piccadilly. Don't they have nothing but tea in this place? Where can you get a drink?"

Bo grinned. "Moslem country, remember? But down at the end of the Flower Passage there're a lot of little bars with green doors and marble counters where you can get a liter of beer for about fifteen cents in lira. And there're all these stands selling deep-fat-fried bugs and pig's gut sandwiches—"

"You ever notice how frelks can put it away? I mean liquor, not . . . pig's guts."

And launched off into a lot of appeasing stories. We ended with the one about the frelk some spacer tried to roll who announced: "There are two things I go for. One is spacers; the other is a good fight. . . ."

But they only allay. They cure nothing. Even Muse knew we would spend the day apart, now.

The rain had stopped, so we took the ferry up the Golden Horn. Kelly straight off asked for Taksim Square and Istiqlal and was directed to a dolmush, which we discovered was a taxicab, only it just goes one place and picks up lots and lots of people on the way. And it's cheap.

Lou headed off over Ataturk Bridge to see the sights of New City. Bo decided to find out what the Dolma Boche really was; and when Muse discovered you could go to Asia for fifteen cents—one lira and fifty krush—well, Muse decided to go to Asia.

I turned through the confusion of traffic at the head of the bridge and up past the gray, dripping walls of Old City, beneath the trolley wires. There are times when yelling and helling won't fill the lack. There are times when you must walk by yourself because it hurts so much to be alone.

I walked up a lot of little streets with wet donkeys and wet camels and women in veils; and down a lot of big streets with buses and trash baskets and men in business suits.

Some people stare at spacers; some people don't. Some people stare or don't stare in a way a spacer gets to recognize within a week after coming out of training school at sixteen. I was walking in the park when I caught her watching. She saw me see and looked away.

I ambled down the wet asphalt. She was standing under the arch of a small, empty mosque shell. As I passed she walked out into the courtyard among the cannons.

"Excuse me."

I stopped.

"Do you know whether or not this is the shrine of St. Irene?" Her English was charmingly accented. "I've left my guidebook home."

"Sorry. I'm a tourist too."

"Oh." She smiled. "I am Greek. I thought you might be Turkish because you are so dark."

"American red Indian." I nodded. Her turn to curtsy.

"I see. I have just started at the university here in Istanbul. Your uniform, it tells me that you are"—and in the pause, all speculations resolved—"a spacer."

I was uncomfortable. "Yeah." I put my hands in my pockets, moved my feet around on the soles of my boots,

263

licked my third from the rear left molar—did all the things you do when you're uncomfortable. *You're so* exciting *when you look like that,* a frelk told me once. "Yeah, I am." I said it too sharply, too loudly, and she jumped a little.

So now she knew I knew she knew I knew, and I wondered how we would play the Proust bit.

"I'm Turkish," she said. "I'm not Greek. I'm not just starting. I'm a graduate in art history here at the university. These little lies one makes for strangers to protect one's ego . . . why? Sometimes I think my ego is very small."

That's one strategy.

"How far away do you live?" I asked. "And what's the going rate in Turkish lira?" That's another.

"I can't pay you." She pulled her raincoat around her hips. She was very pretty. "I would like to." She shrugged and smiled. "But I am . . . a poor student. Not a rich one. If you want to turn around and walk away, there will be no hard feelings. I shall be sad though."

I stayed on the path. I thought she'd suggest a price after a little while. She didn't.

And *that's* another.

I was asking myself, *What do you want the damn money for anyway?* when a breeze upset water from one of the park's great cypresses.

"I think the whole business is sad." She wiped drops from her face. There had been a break in her voice and for a moment I looked too closely at the water streaks. "I think it's sad that they have to alter you to make you a spacer. If they hadn't, then *we*. . . . If spacers had never been, then we could not be . . . the way we are. Did you start out male or female?"

Another shower. I was looking at the ground and droplets went down my collar.

"Male," I said. "It doesn't matter."

"How old are you? Twenty-three, twenty-four?"

"Twenty-three," I lied. It's reflex. I'm twenty-five, but the younger they think you are, the more they pay you. But I didn't *want* her *damn* money—

"I guessed right then." She nodded. "Most of us are experts on spacers. Do you find that? I suppose we have to be." She looked at me with wide black eyes. At the end of the stare, she blinked rapidly. "You would have been a fine man. But now you are a spacer, building water-conservation units on Mars, programing mining computers on Ganymede, servicing communication relay towers on the moon. The alteration ..." Frelks are the only people I've ever heard say "the alteration" with so much fascination and regret. "You'd think they'd have found some other solution. They could have found another way than neutering you, turning you into creatures not even androgynous; things that are—"

I put my hand on her shoulder, and she stopped like I'd hit her. She looked to see if anyone was near. Lightly, so lightly then, she raised her hand to mine.

I pulled my hand away. "That are what?"

"They could have found another way." Both hands in her pockets now.

"They could have. Yes. Up beyond the ionosphere, baby, there's too much radiation for those precious gonads to work right anywhere you might want to do something that would keep you there over twenty-four hours, like the moon, or Mars, or the satellites of Jupiter—"

"They could have made protective shields. They could have done more research into biological adjustment—"

"Population Explosion time," I said. "No, they were hunting for any excuse to cut down kids back then—especially deformed ones."

"Ah yes." She nodded. "We're still fighting our way up from the neo-puritan reaction to the sex freedom of the twentieth century."

"It was a fine solution." I grinned and grabbed my crotch. "I'm happy with it." I've never known why that's so much more obscene when a spacer does it.

"Stop it," she snapped, moving away.

"What's the matter?"

"Stop it," she repeated. "Don't do that! You're a child."

"But they choose us from children whose sexual responses are hopelessly retarded at puberty."

"And your childish, violent substitutes for love? I suppose that's one of the things that's attractive. Yes, I know you're a child."

"Yeah? What about frelks?"

She thought awhile. "I think they're the sexually retarded ones they miss. Perhaps it was the right solution. You really don't regret you have no sex?"

"We've got you," I said.

"Yes." She looked down. I glanced to see the expression she was hiding. It was a smile. "You have your glorious, soaring life, *and* you have us." Her face came up. She glowed. "You spin in the sky, the world spins under you, and you step from land to land, while we . . ." She turned her head right, left, and her black hair curled and uncurled on the shoulder of her coat. "We have our dull, circled lives, bound in gravity, *worshiping* you."

She looked back at me. "Perverted, yes? In love with a bunch of corpses in free fall!" She suddenly hunched her shoulders. "I don't like having a free-fall-sexual-displacement complex."

"That always sounded like too much to say."

She looked away. "I don't like being a frelk. Better?"

"I wouldn't like it either. Be something else."

"You don't choose your perversions. *You* have no perversions at all. *You're* free of the whole business. I love you for that, spacer. My love starts with the fear of love. Isn't that beautiful? A pervert substitutes something unattainable for 'normal' love: the homosexual, a mirror, the fetishist, a shoe or a watch or a girdle. Those with free-fall-sexual-dis—"

"Frelks."

"Frelks substitute"—she looked at me sharply again—"loose, swinging meat."

"That doesn't offend me."

"I wanted it to."

"Why?"

266

"You don't have desires. You wouldn't understand."

"Go on."

"I want you because you can't want me. That's the pleasure. If someone really had a sexual reaction to ... us, we'd be scared away. I wonder how many people there were before there were you, waiting for your creation. We're necrophiles. I'm sure grave robbing has fallen off since you started going up. But you don't understand. ..." She paused. "If you did, then I would't be scuffing leaves now and trying to think from whom I could borrow sixty lira." She stepped over the knuckles of a root that had cracked the pavement. "And that, incidentally, is the going rate in Istanbul."

I calculated. "Things still get cheaper as you go east."

"You know," and she let her raincoat fall open, "you're different from the others. You at least *want* to know—"

I said, "If I spat on you for every time you'd said that to a spacer, you'd drown."

"Go back to the moon, loose meat." She closed her eyes. "Swing up on to Mars. There are satellites around Jupiter where you might do some good. Go up and come down in some other city."

"Where do you live?"

"You want to come with me?"

"Give me something," I said. "Give me something—it doesn't have to be worth sixty lira. Give me something that you like, anything of yours that means something to you."

"No!"

"Why not?"

"Because I—"

"—don't want to give up part of that ego. None of you frelks do!"

"You really don't understand I just want to buy you?"

"You have nothing to buy me with."

"You are a child," she said. "I love you."

We reached the gate of the park. She stopped, and we stood time enough for a breeze to rise and die in the grass. "I ..." she offered tentatively pointing without taking her

267

hand from her coat pocket. "I live right down there."

"All right," I said. "Let's go."

A gas main had once exploded along this street, she explained to me, a gushing road of fire as far as the docks, overhot and overquick. It had been put out within minutes, no building had fallen, but the charred facias glittered. "This is sort of an artist and student quarter." We crossed the cobbles. "Yuri Pasha, number fourteen. In case you're ever in Istanbul again." Her door was covered with black scales, the gutter was thick with garbage.

"A lot of artists and professional people are frelks," I said, trying to be inane.

"So are lots of other people." She walked inside and held the door. "We're just more flamboyant about it."

On the landing there was a portrait of Ataturk. Her room was on the second floor. "Just a moment while I get my key—"

Marsscapes! Moonscapes! On her easel was a six-foot canvas showing the sunrise flaring on a crater's rim! There were copies of the original Observer pictures of the moon pinned to the wall, and pictures of every smooth-faced general in the International Spacer Corps.

On one corner of her desk was a pile of those photo magazines about spacers that you can find in most kiosks all over the world: I've seriously heard people say they were printed for adventurous-minded high school children. They've never seen the Danish ones. She had a few of those too. There was a shelf of art books, art history texts. Above them were six feet of cheap paper-covered space operas: *Sin on Space Station No. 12, Rocket Rake, Savage Orbit.*

"Arrack?" she asked. "Ouzo or pernod? You've got your choice. But I may pour them all from the same bottle." She set out glasses on the desk, then opened a waist-high cabinet that turned out to be an ice-box. She stood up with a tray of lovelies: fruit puddings, Turkish delight, braised meats.

"What's this?"

"Dolmades. Grape leaves filled with rice and pignolias."

"Say it again?"

"Dolmades. Comes from the same Turkish word as 'dolmush'. They both mean 'stuffed'." She put the tray beside the glasses. "Sit down."

I sat on the studio-couch-that-becomes-bed. Under the brocade I felt the deep, fluid resilience of a glycogel mattress. They've got the idea that it approximates the feeling of free fall. "Comfortable? Would you excuse me for a moment? I have some friends down the hall. I want to see them for a moment." She winked. "They like spacers."

"Are you going to take up a collection for me?" I asked. "Or do you want them to line up outside the door and wait their turn?"

She sucked a breath. "Actually I was going to suggest both." Suddenly she shook her head. "Oh, what do you want!"

"What will you give me? I want something," I said. "That's why I came. I'm lonely. Maybe I want to find out how far it goes. I don't know yet."

"It goes as far as you will. Me? I study, I read, paint, talk with my friends"—she came over to the bed, sat down on the floor—"go to the theater, look at spacers who pass me on the street, till one looks back; I am lonely too." She put her head on my knee. "I want something. But," and after a minute neither of us had moved, "you are not the one who will give it to me."

"You're not going to pay me for it," I countered. "You're not, are you?"

On my knee her head shook. After a while she said, all breath and no voice, "Don't you think you ... should leave?"

"Okay," I said, and stood up.

She sat back on the hem of her coat. She hadn't taken it off yet.

I went to the door.

"Incidentally." She folded her hands in her lap. "There is a place in New York City you might find what you're looking for, called the Flower Passage—"

I turned toward her, angry. "The frelk hangout? Look, I don't *need* money! I said *any*thing would do! I don't want—"

She had begun to shake her head, laughing quietly. Now she lay her cheek on the wrinkled place where I had sat. "Do you persist in misunderstanding? It is a spacer hangout. When you leave, I am going to visit my friends and talk about . . . ah, yes, the beautiful one that got away. I thought you might find . . . perhaps someone you know."

With anger, it ended.

"Oh," I said. "Oh, it's a spacer hangout. Yeah. Well, thanks."

And went out. And found the Flower Passage, and Kelly and Lou and Bo and Muse. Kelly was buying beer so we all got drunk, and ate fried fish and fried clams and fried sausage, and Kelly was waving the money around, saying, "You should have seen him! The changes I put that frelk through, you should have *seen* him! Eighty lira is the going rate here, and he gave me a hundred and fifty!" and drank more beer. And went up.

Afterword:

What goes into an s-f story—this s-f story?

One high old month in Paris, a summer of shrimp fishing on the Texas Gulf, another month spent broke in Istanbul. In still another city I overheard two women at a cocktail party discussing the latest astronaut:

". . . so antiseptic, so inhuman, almost asexual!"

"Oh no! He's perfectly gorgeous!"

Why put all this in an s-f story? I sincerely feel the medium is the best in which to integrate clearly the disparate and technical with the desperate and human.

Someone asked of this particular story, "But what can they *do* with one another?"

At the risk of pulling my punch, let me say that this is basically a horror story. There is nothing they can do. Except go up and down.